little
· IT'S ...

Dear Little Black Dress Reader,

Thanks for picking up this Little Black Dress book, one of the great new titles from our series of fun, page-turning romance novels. Lucky you – you're about to have a fantastic romantic read that we know you won't be able to put down!

Why don't you make your Little Black Dress experience even better by logging on to

www.littleblackdressbooks.com

where you can:

- Enter our **monthly competitions** to win **gorgeous** prizes
- Get **hot-off-the-press** news about our latest titles
- Read **exclusive** preview chapters both from your **favourite** authors and from brilliant new writing talent
- Buy **up-and-coming** books online
- Sign up for an essential slice of romance via our **fortnightly email** newsletter

We love nothing more than to curl up and indulge in an addictive romance, and so we're delighted to welcome you into the Little Black Dress club!

With love from,

The *little black dress* team

Five interesting things about Kate Lace:

1. When I left school I joined the army instead of going to university – there were 500 men to every woman when I joined up – yesss.

2. While I was there I discovered that there were more sports than hockey and lacrosse and learnt to glide, rock climb, pot hole, sail and ski. I also discovered that I wasn't much good at any of them but I had a lot of fun.

3. I met my husband in the army. We've been married for donkey's years. (I was a child bride.)

4. Since I got married I have moved house 17 times. We now live in our own house and have done for quite a while so we know what is growing in the garden. Also, our children can remember what their address is.

5. I captained the Romantic Novelists' Association team on University Challenge the Professionals in 2005. We got to the grand finals so I got to meet Jeremy Paxman three times.

Also by Kate Lace

The Movie Girl

The Chalet Girl

Kate Lace

little
black
dress

First published in 2007
by LITTLE BLACK DRESS
An imprint of HEADLINE PUBLISHING GROUP

First published in paperback in 2007
by LITTLE BLACK DRESS

A LITTLE BLACK DRESS paperback

1

Cataloguing in Publication Data is available from the British Library

ISBN 978 0 7553 3831 3

Typeset in Transit511BT by Avon DataSet Ltd,
Bidford-on-Avon, Warwickshire

Printed and bound in Great Britain by Clays Ltd, St Ives plc

Headline's policy is to use papers that are natural, renewable and recyclable
products and made from wood grown in sustainable forests. The logging and
manufacturing processes are expected to conform to the environmental
regulations of the country of origin.

HEADLINE PUBLISHING GROUP
An Hachette Livre UK Company
338 Euston Road
London NW1 3BH

www.littleblackdressbooks.co.uk
www.headline.co.uk

To Penny, Victoria and Tim – with love

If it hadn't been for the encouragement of a number of my good writing friends in the Romantic Novelists' Association, I probably wouldn't have written this book: in particular, Jenny Haddon for pointing me in the direction of Little Black Dress when she first heard the news about the launch of the imprint; Annie Ashurst for badgering me to do it, and Evelyn Ryle for taking the time to read my draft manuscript and making some very valuable suggestions. I also need to thank my children: Penny, Victoria and Tim, whose fantastic skiing and boarding abilities were the inspiration for Millie's talent, and my husband Ian for encouraging me to keep on writing when, if I had a proper job, he might be able to consider taking early retirement. Lastly, I'd like to thank Cat Cobain and Claire Baldwin at Little Black Dress for the wonderful editorial comments.

Millie propped the door of the chalet open with the doormat and waited for the motorised sled carrying the new guests' luggage to pull up outside. Her breath made big puffy clouds in front of her face in the freezing, still night air but she didn't feel cold as the air was so dry. Her months of experience at the resort told her that it was likely to snow tonight. Good, the pistes were getting a bit patchy and a top-up would be brilliant.

Jack, another 'Surf and Snow' rep, drove the sled up to the door, killed the engine and climbed off it.

'Give us a hand, Millie,' he said as he began to unclip the securing cables. 'The mob is hard on my heels, and I've got another luggage delivery to make before I'm finished for tonight.'

'What are this lot like?' she asked as she lugged a couple of big cases into the chalet.

'The usual. Some look as if they think they're auditioning for a part in a film about Scott of the Antarctic and some seem to want roles in *Baywatch*; all teeth, tits and high heels. The rest are all right.'

Millie returned for more bags. 'And what are the girls like?'

'Ha ha. You may mock but you'll see. The fact they've got

to walk to the chalet from the road isn't going down a storm.'

They had just finished getting the last of the luggage stacked in the spacious hall of the chalet when voices, laughter and some yelps of despair rang through the clear alpine air. Millie cocked an ear to listen. She detected the distinctive shrieks of young females picking their way through the snowdrifts and slippery stretches of road. It would be a couple of minutes before they rounded the last two hairpins of the steep road that led up to the chalet. Jack gave her a cheery wave and sped off to the next chalet to drop off yet more cases. Millie kicked the doormat free and shut the door to keep the heat in.

She nipped into the kitchen and lit the gas under the mulled wine to bring it back up to blood heat and gave the leek and potato soup a quick stir, then she flicked open the grill, saw the croutons were done to a crisp and switched it off. She didn't, however, then go and stand by the door ready to throw it open as soon as the party of holidaymakers arrived, as if their arrival was the most important thing in her life. Yes, it was her job to look after them all, yes, she liked cooking, and yes she wanted her guests to have a fun, enjoyable holiday, but she'd learned that it was essential for her own sanity to make sure the guests knew where they stood with her and what her house rules were from the start. None of her rules was unreasonable and most of them were just about being considerate, which helped her out and ensured a pleasant stay for everyone. Also it made sure that everyone got off on the right footing from the start; some of the people who came skiing got terribly embarrassed about asking her to do the least thing – like provide more loo roll – and some would have treated her like dirt given half a chance and expected her to pick up after them morning, noon and night. Now, after the best part of four months in this game, Millie had being a chalet host sussed out.

The knock came and Millie sauntered to the door and opened it, plastering a big, I'm-your-friendly-chalet-host smile across her face as per company regulations.

'Come in, come in,' she entreated, as per yet more company regulations. 'I'm Millie. And can I ask you to take your snowy shoes off. Sorry,' she smiled, not feeling the least bit apologetic, 'but it's company regulations.' That last bit wasn't quite true, but as she was the one who would have to mop up dirty, snowy water, she felt perfectly entitled to make up whatever regulations she liked to make life easier for herself.

Millie clocked most of them as they sorted out shoes and hand luggage and hauled off coats. There was a mousy couple who looked completely wet, a short, stout older man with a tall lanky female partner who seemed to be entwined round him for support like some sort of vine, two giggly blondes with improbable busts and unsuitable clothing (had to be first-timers), an athletic bloke with *all* the right clothing (which probably meant this was his first time too), a man in a blindingly bright orange ski jacket with his hood up and his back to her, and then there was the couple who obviously felt they were the group organisers and who were already trying to get the other guests to take their cases out of the hall.

So, thought Millie, a complete mixed bag.

For the past months most of the groups who had booked this chalet had consisted of just one or two families or groups of friends; either they had all known each other from the outset or it had been easy to get them to gel. But this lot were totally different. It must be the special 'end-of-season' two-week offer that had resulted in such a random selection . of separate couples pitching up. Millie mentally steeled herself. It was going to take extra work from her to make sure they all had a good time and no one felt left out. But it was what she was employed to do and besides, she would feel she'd failed if people who had paid good money for a holiday didn't have the best time possible.

'Blimey, this is cosy,' said one of the blondes. She gazed about her, her big blue eyes wide as she took in the kitsch décor of the chalet.

'Isn't it?' agreed Millie, who actually thought the whole place was like something out of a chocolate box factory – all gingham curtains and heart shapes cut out of the backs of the chairs and the cupboard doors and forming twee little peepholes in the shutters. 'Let me show you to your rooms – and, yes please,' she added, pre-empting the bossy woman who had her mouth open ready to speak, 'bring your luggage with you.'

She led the way upstairs and showed the couples to their rooms, explained about limitations to the hot water if everyone showered at once and suggested they all met back in the main room in ten minutes for vin chaud and introductions.

A few minutes later the new bunch began to straggle downstairs in dribs and drabs. Millie busied herself in the kitchen while the guests snooped around, checked out the view from the balcony and the windows to the side, flicked through the books on the bookshelf and generally familiarised themselves with their new surroundings.

When Millie judged the majority were present she began to ladle the warm wine into glasses. She carefully filled a tray with the brimming tumblers and turned back to the group ready to hand them out. And nearly dropped the whole lot.

He*llo*. There, in front of her, was the most gorgeous man she had ever clapped eyes on. He was simply knock-out. Her stomach did a backflip and she felt her heart pound in her chest. He was so sensationally, devastatingly good-looking that Millie felt quite faint. What a hunk, what an *incredible* hunk.

OK, she'd had a couple of good-looking and single men stay in her chalet a month or so earlier but she and Helen (another chalet girl she shared a room with) had spent most of the season moaning about the lack of fit guys for them to ogle. However, even the two reasonably nice-looking blokes hadn't held a candle to this guy; not even close. Wow! Well, this would be something to tell Helen about. Or maybe not. Did she really want Helen muscling in? Hmmm.

The incredible hunk leaned forward and stopped her tray from tipping any more perilously.

'Steady,' he said in a voice as dark brown as his hair and eyes. He smiled at her and Millie felt her legs tremble. She tried to take a deep breath to steady herself but embarrassingly her lungs didn't seem to be functioning properly.

Despite the helping hand, the glasses slid further down the tray and clinked in warning as they neared the edge. Millie came out of her near swoon and paid attention again to what she was doing.

'Oh, God, yes. Sorry. Thanks. I've got it. Really. I'm fine. Honest.' She realised she was burbling, but she felt relieved that at least she hadn't made a complete idiot of herself and dropped all the drinks. She hauled her mental state and the tray back onto an even keel and handed out the wine. Then she grabbed a glass for herself. She hoped no one else noticed that her hand was trembling.

'Right, well, this is a good time for us all to get to know each other,' she said with a smile which she hoped would make everyone feel welcome and included. 'Now, in case you didn't catch it earlier, my name is Millie.' She smiled again. The hunk smiled lazily back at her. Their eyes connected and she felt a bolt of electricity shock her body. Goosebumps erupted all over. She swallowed and tore her eyes off him. She knew what company policy was on the subject of any hint of liaison between chalet hosts and their guests and there was no way she was going to jeopardise her job or her season's bonus. Anyway, she definitely did *not* want to get involved with a man. The last time had taught her a lesson she was never going to forget; it had almost ruined her life. She wasn't going to make that sort of mistake a second time, she told herself firmly. 'Er, what are your names?' This was more for the benefit of the guests. It was important to get people introduced to each other early on the first day, it helped break the ice and get the holiday going.

The group introduced themselves. The mousy couple turned out to be called Cuthbert and Deirdre Millington, 'but my friends call me Deedee', Deirdre simpered. Cuthbert simpered too. 'We've never done anything as exciting as skiing before. Normally we like to go on walking and rambling holidays, don't we, Cuthbert?' Deedee smiled adoringly at Cuthbert.

That figures, thought Millie. Their names! And rambling?! Still, *chacun à son goût*, as the French would say. If it made them happy . . .

The giggly blondes announced they were called Chelsea and Venice and turned out to be cousins, which explained their similarity to each other. Their dads were business partners – they made tents. Their mums worked for the company too, as did the two girls. Millie couldn't think of two more unlikely girls to be associated with the camping industry than these two. What with the hair and nails, to say nothing of their skimpy outfits and astounding figures, she couldn't think of any pair less likely to have anything to do with it. Deedee and Cuthbert, yes, but these two?

'So is there a significance to your names?' she asked innocently. She had to suck her cheeks in when it turned out that they were named after their respective mums' favourite places.

'Venice was named second,' explained Chelsea. 'Her mum pinched the idea off of my mum but went for somewhere more glam.'

'Oh, I don't know,' said Millie kindly. 'Chelsea is terribly smart. If you were Italian you'd probably think Chelsea was the more glam name.'

Chelsea brightened up at that. 'I've never thought of it like that.' She giggled. 'Just as well her favourite place wasn't Kilburn or Plaistow. Can you imagine?' She nudged Venice who giggled too. Millie liked them both. Giggly, girly and high-maintenance but also nice. *Nice*, in Millie's book, was an all too rare quality amongst chalet guests.

The short older guy with his much younger and taller partner were named Mike and Bella and seemed completely wrapped up in each other – or, more accurately, wrapped round each other, thought Millie, wondering if Mike was Bella's sugar daddy. Not that it was any of her business but she couldn't help being curious. Mike was pretty old compared to Bella and no great shakes in the looks department while Bella was quite pretty so surely his attraction had to lie elsewhere. All Millie could think of was money. They stood rather apart from the rest of the group and didn't seem to want to be drawn in. Well, thought Millie, if they didn't want to join in she couldn't make them but it was probably their loss.

She turned her attention to the two guys. The one with all the right gear was called Archie Green and had a wicked twinkle in his eye. He looked like a lot of fun. The sex god, she discovered, was Luke Hastings.

Luke, she said to herself with a sigh. What an absolutely fabulous name. So romantic.

Finally she turned to the bossy, middle-aged couple. 'John and Pat Barkham-Lumley,' bellowed the woman as if they were on parade. Millie jumped and almost saluted. Pat's silent partner, John, looked tired and resigned as if he'd given up trying to exert any influence himself, or get a word in edgeways, and had decided that letting his appalling wife have her own way was the only route to a quiet life. Millie felt sorry for him and wondered what she might be able to do to cheer him up.

'Right, now we all know who we all are, I propose a toast for a happy holiday.'

The blondes giggled and nudged each other as they raised their glasses. Pat Barkham-Lumley looked at the two girls disapprovingly. Millie thought she would be the sort to disapprove of almost anything – including being called by her first name until she had given permission for that level of familiarity. It looked like keeping her happy was going to be hard work, not just for Millie but for the group as a whole.

Millie went round the room, checking she could remember all the names, which she easily could. After several months of this lark she'd got the knack of it – she got the details off the manifest the morning of changeover day and learnt them as she stripped the beds. Then it was just a question of matching people up with them. Invariably the guests thought it terribly impressive.

'And I'm here to make sure you all have a good time,' Millie said, wondering if she'd set herself an impossible task with Mrs B-L and trying not to look at Luke and failing. God, she'd like to give *him* a good time. No, it didn't bear thinking about, not after what had happened with her last disastrous relationship. Oh bugger, she felt her colour rise in her face and knew one of her phenomenal blushes was in progress. One could always be guaranteed to let her down hideously, especially if it was really inappropriate. Maybe the guests wouldn't realise the reason and think that her high colour was the result of her physical exertions in the kitchen. She took a slurp of mulled wine to cover up her discomfiture.

The introductions had done the trick and all the group were now chatting, laughing and discussing such issues as the quality of the snow so late in the season and the merits of various other resorts. Millie patted herself on the back. Job well done.

Before she returned to making the supper, she couldn't help herself from sliding another look at Luke. He and Archie were talking and joking with the blondes.

There's a surprise, she thought morosely. Two single blokes and two single blondes and all of them attractive. That was the trouble with being the hired help; you were invisible unless they wanted something. Sadly, she didn't seem to be the something Luke wanted. Millie sighed and went to check on the food at the kitchen end of the big open-plan room.

Of course, being invisible was exactly what she had craved when she'd first got the job as a chalet girl. The guests would arrive and ask her name and after that would take no further interest in her. All the guests cared about was that they had a good time, the food was plentiful and tasty and that the chalet was clean and tidy. The last thing on the guests' minds was anything about her background, which had suited her very well and she'd been almost grateful to be virtually ignored.

Wistfully she looked at Venice and Chelsea and wondered what it would be like to be so attractive to the opposite sex. She'd love to experience the full-on attention of a couple of great men like Luke and Archie. Well, it wasn't going to happen, she told herself sternly, so there was no point in dreaming.

She filled a big jug with more mulled wine and passed it to Mrs Barkham-Lumley as she was nearest, before checking on the lasagne bubbling away in the oven.

'Now don't have too much of this vin chaud,' said Pat to the assembled company in stentorian tones. 'We don't want anyone tipsy.'

Millie turned back just in time to see faces around the room fall at the prospect of the mulled wine being rationed. Millie wasn't having this. Just because Mrs B-L didn't want to enjoy herself with a drink or two didn't mean the others couldn't loosen up in the evenings.

'Oh, don't worry about that,' said Millie breezily, abandoning the lasagne and sloshing wine into a second jug. She returned to the group and began pouring it into any tumbler near to hand. 'There's a whole vat of it in the kitchen and it doesn't keep, so drink up. I'd hate to have to ditch it. Such a waste.' She glanced at Pat who didn't look overly impressed. She dragged poor John out of reach of the jug before he had a chance to refill his glass. Millie smiled at him and saw his rather rueful shrug. Poor man! She vowed to make sure he got the carafe of wine right by him at dinner.

She left the jug with Archie, telling him to 'come back for more when it's empty', and got going with making a salad while keeping half an ear out for the conversation in the sitting room.

It transpired that Chelsea and Venice had never skied before but 'thought it would be a bit of a laugh', and Cuthbert and Deedee had always wanted to learn and felt they must take this opportunity before Deedee started 'making babies'. *Making babies*. Millie couldn't believe it. She nearly choked and then clutched the edge of the work-top to stop her shoulders shaking with silent laughter. She pulled herself together, regained a modicum of self-control and returned to making the salad as the conversation behind her continued. Pat and John had skied all their lives, 'it was part of John's army training', so no surprise there, and Mike and Bella had 'done a bit'.

Millie took the bowl of salad from the kitchen to the table in time to hear Pat Bossyboots pontificate on the subject of skiing.

'Oh, those of you who haven't done any shouldn't worry. The trick is to take proper lessons. No point in getting into bad habits. And if you've done a bit you'll find that it will all come back to you. Just like riding a bike.'

'There's nothing like riding a bike,' mused Luke to himself, staring at Chelsea and Venice.

Millie giggled and noticed that the joke went over the heads of the rest of the group.

'We fancy having lessons, don't we, Chel?'

'I'll say,' said Chelsea. 'We've heard all about those hunky French ski instructors. We want to check out how much is true.' They both giggled. They giggled at everything, thought Millie.

Pat looked pained. 'You can't expect to learn properly if you don't take it seriously. John and I had years of lessons to perfect our technique.'

'Oh,' said Deedee, sounding worried. 'Years? Is it terribly difficult? I know I won't be any good if it's too hard.'

'You'll be fine,' said Luke. 'Honestly, anyone can learn. It really isn't so very difficult.' Millie spotted him shoot a look at Pat as if daring her to contradict him and knock Deedee's limited confidence. 'Did you ever roller skate as a kid?'

'Oh yes,' said Deedee, perking up a little.

'Well, if you have the coordination to do that I expect you'll be fine on skis.'

'Really?' Deedee sounded more hopeful. 'I was quite good on skates – and on ice skates too. I could even skate backwards and do a couple of simple jumps.'

'There you are,' said Luke. 'I'm sure you'll crack the basics of skiing in no time.'

How nice of him, thought Millie.

'I'm sure you'll be fine, sweetie,' said Cuthbert, not to be outdone by Luke's charm. 'And we can help each other between lessons, can't we?'

Deedee looked adoringly at him. 'Yes, that would be lovely.'

'What about you boys?' asked Bella, surprising Millie by joining in for the first time. She'd hardly spoken a word till now, all her attentions being reserved for Mike.

'Oh, Archie and I ski a bit, don't we?'

Archie swallowed a slurp of his mulled wine and said, 'I'll say.'

'Will you be taking lessons?' asked Pat.

'Probably not,' said Luke flatly.

'Then you can ski with John and me.'

Millie looked up from slicing a tomato just in time to see Luke's eyebrows twitch fractionally. 'Oh, er, that'd be nice. So you and John snowboard too?'

'Oh no.' Pat was horrified. 'Not boarding. We do *proper* skiing.'

'I prefer improper skiing. Sorry.' Luke's eyes seemed to glitter a little as he leant across Archie and refilled his tumbler. He caught Millie's eye and winked. She turned away because she thought she was going to burst out laughing and carried on slicing tomatoes assiduously, not daring to look up again. Delicious to look at, charming and funny; practically perfect, Millie thought. Perhaps these two weeks were going to be OK after all.

Millie finished the tomato salad. Apart from whipping the cream for the trifle, dinner was ready. She filled a couple of carafes with red wine which she placed on the table and then took a couple more from the cupboard and made her way through the room.

'Forgive me,' she apologised, 'but I keep the white wine on the balcony so it's nice and chilled. I'll be as quick as I can.' She opened the window and a blast of freezing air whistled into the room. Millie pulled the door shut behind her, noting that the threatened snow had arrived and tiny flakes, almost grains, were swirling earthwards. She filled the jugs as fast as she could from the industrial-sized wine boxes that they bought from the wholesaler for the guests.

Despite only being outside for a couple of minutes she was perished by the time she got back indoors.

'You should have got one of us to do that for you,' said Luke. 'You've been rushing round ever since we got in, doing things for everyone. Do you always work this hard?'

'Yes,' she stammered, surprised by the comment. God, that sounded as if she wanted a sympathy vote. 'But it's my job,' she added quickly and wishing she didn't sound such a moron. Having longed for a bit of attention from Luke, she was bowled over now she'd got it. Feeling hugely self-conscious she sped past and put the two jugs on the table. She didn't want him to see he had succeeded in making her blush again.

She served the soup into bowls in the kitchen, taking her time and hoping it would give her colour a chance to subside. With no mirror handy to check it she had to trust to luck when she carried the tray to the table. Swiftly and efficiently she doled out the bowls and then returned with a couple of plates piled high with crispy garlic croutons. The guests tucked in with gusto; even Pat Barkham-Lumley seemed happy with the food on offer. The conversation died as the ten guests concentrated on their first course.

'That was fab,' said Bella, scraping her bowl.

'Simply delicious,' said Mike. 'Bella, you must get the recipe.'

Judging by Bella's expression, she wasn't so enamoured by the soup as to consider cooking it for herself.

'More?' offered Millie.

'Best not. My salopettes are already a bit tight.'

'Can't have you putting on weight,' said Mike.

Ooh, like you can talk, thought Millie, eyeing his pot belly. For the second time in the space of a few minutes

Millie wondered what made Mike so attractive to Bella.

Bella ignored the personal comment. 'Anyway, I can smell something else delicious and I want to save some space.'

Millie gathered the plates and staggered back with an enormous dish of bubbling lasagne. She plonked it down in front of Bella.

'Will you serve it?' she asked. Pat, who was sitting at the head of the table, looked deeply affronted. Millie smiled inwardly. She returned with a big serving spoon and ten plates then took it upon herself to refill wine glasses. She got to John's first so as to give him a racing chance of getting another drink before Pat saw what was going on. With a feeling of triumph she achieved her aim a second before Pat cottoned on.

'No, John. Is that wise? We want clear heads in the morning, don't we?'

Millie didn't think a few glasses of wine were going to render John incapable of hitting the slopes twelve hours later and, judging by the look of pure gratitude John shot her, neither did he.

'Pat?' Millie proffered the carafe in her direction.

'Not for me, I think. Enough is enough.'

Prissy old killjoy, thought Millie as she carried on round the table. None of the others had any such inhibitions and lapped up the booze as if they had just spent a year in Saudi and had not just stepped off a charter flight with a perfectly well-stocked bar.

'You're the last guests here this year and we're sloshing in wine. What doesn't get drunk will only end up going down the drain.'

'That sounds like a challenge,' said Luke. 'Does that

mean if I don't get drunk I'll end up down the drain too? Usually I only wind up in the drain if I *am* drunk.'

Millie smiled and filled up his glass again. 'Possibly.' She wrenched her eyes away from him. She really must stop staring at him quite so much. At least she seemed to have stopped burbling whenever he spoke to her. That was something to be grateful for.

While the guests ate, Millie helped herself to a plate of food, ate it in record time and then cracked on with the washing up. While she was doing that she answered questions about the chalet, the resort, the skiing conditions, the projected weather forecast and good bars for après ski. It was the usual stuff that all the previous holidaymakers had asked and Millie tried not to sound as if she was on autopilot.

The first few times she'd done this sort of briefing she'd had to really struggle to name the various brasseries in the village and remember how to describe the route up the mountains which involved the shortest lift queues. Now, at the end of the season, she didn't even have to think. It didn't matter what the punters were after, noisy clubs, quiet bars, the best hot chocolate or tastiest lunchtime snacks, Millie had all the information at her fingertips. It surprised her to think how familiar she was with the place. She knew it even better than her home town. Not that that was difficult, when she considered how sheltered her life had been before she'd escaped to France. She'd almost never gone out, and if she had, the rule was that she was home by eleven, hardly a drop of alcohol had passed her lips and pop music was something she listened to surreptitiously when her father wasn't around. And now? Well, she was hardly ever in bed before midnight, was on first-name terms with most of the bar owners in the resort and was completely familiar with the music scene.

'So where do you go to wind down at the end of the day?' Archie was asking.

Millie returned her attention to her guests. 'Depends what mood I'm in really. Tomorrow night, if you're up for it, Jack will take you on a bar crawl.' Chelsea and Venice looked at each other and whispered and giggled. The idea appealed to them at least. 'That way,' continued Millie, 'you can find out what this place has to offer for yourselves.'

And with any luck, she thought, you'll not find the Husky for a while. The Husky was where she escaped from the guests. It was her refuge and her lifeline and it was where she was able to indulge in her passion for music. So she told the guests about the other bars and clubs in the resort, where to go for various forms of entertainment, but she kept quiet about the place she hung out on most evenings.

Tonight, however, for the first time in the entire season, it crossed her mind that if she wanted to see more of Luke then maybe she ought to tell them about the place. Perhaps if he saw her off duty he might pay her some attention instead of being mesmerised by Chelsea and Venice. She glanced towards him and saw he was still, apparently, riveted by the cousins. The sight made her feel quite deflated. Sod him, thought Millie, sadly. If that was the type he went for, she had no chance. And as types went, these girls were stunningly pretty – masses of blonde hair, very blue eyes and Hollywood smiles. Millie knew that red hair like hers wasn't to everyone's taste and her grey eyes were definitely run-of-the-mill. As far as the cousins were concerned, she was simply no competition at all.

Millie, however, hadn't noticed that Luke had paid the

girls exactly the same amount of attention as he had everyone else in the room, because he was polite and had the sort of easy charm that meant he could get on with pretty well anyone. Even the dreadful Pat.

As soon as the guests finished eating, Millie, having had months of practice, had the coffee on the table and the dishwasher stacked with the crockery. For the first few weeks she'd taken until nearly ten thirty to get cleared up for the night but not any more. She'd got the whole chalet routine off pat and could get all her chores, both morning and evening, squared away with impressive ergonomic efficiency. And it was in her interests to be quick. Once she had fed everyone and cleared up, she was free to go. She glanced at her watch; just after nine. Great, she had plenty of time to enjoy herself before bed. Millie left Pat sternly pouring coffee and trying to ration the wine and slipped on her coat.

'OK then, everybody,' she said, reappearing in the living room. 'I'm off now. I'll be here to do breakfast in the morning. I stop serving at eight thirty so if you want to eat you have to be up before then. After breakfast we'll get those of you who need stuff to the ski shop to get you sorted out with kit. Jack will bring your lift passes here first thing. He'll also bring a stack of piste maps and tell you about some of the things we've arranged for your evening entertainment if you want to join in.'

'I'll make sure everyone is roused and ready,' said Pat ominously.

Luke, behind her back, rolled his eyes. Millie hid her smile behind her scarf and, mumbling thanks, headed to the door.

She let herself out into the crisp, cold night, flicking the hood of her red 'Surf and Snow' company issue ski jacket over her head as she shut the door behind her. Snow was still falling gently, fine powder that, if it carried on all night, would provide fabulous conditions tomorrow. The glow from the streetlights looked like big luminous pom-poms as the lamps reflected off the tiny granules of snow suspended in the almost still air. Under her feet the fresh snow was covering the ruts and bumps of footprints and ski tracks and turning the village into a picture-book fairy land. Her breath hung in the air in front of her and her feet crunched on the fine snow. It was like walking on cornflour the way the new powder squeaked under her boots.

Millie pulled her coat tighter round her and adjusted her scarf so that only her eyes were exposed between it and the furry hood. She trudged along the snow-covered road to the path that was the short cut to the village proper. Ahead of her were the bright lights of the pubs, clubs and bars. Strains of music of all varieties drifted across the air to her: the thumping bass of heavy metal; the beat of reggae; the brainless lyrics of some sort of Eurovision song . . . It was all there; whatever your musical fancy, it was catered for. But none of that was Millie's taste. She strolled along the main street, avoiding laughing, smiling couples and parties, waving at the other reps and friends that she'd made in her time in the resort, shouting greetings to bar owners and waiters and feeling thoroughly at home. She would be sad to leave this place in a couple of weeks when the ski season was over. Since she'd left Westhampton she'd adopted this French alpine village as her home and it had, in its turn, adopted her.

She walked briskly along to the very end of the village, away from the bright lights of the bars and window displays,

2

Luke had watched Millie put on her coat and felt bizarrely cheated that she was leaving. He had rather hoped that the 'chalet girl' slept in. Millie was something else. Her hair was an extraordinary shade of auburn gathered into a thick ponytail at the back of her neck and, when he had first seen her, Luke had experienced an odd desire to release it and see what Millie looked like with it down. He thought it would probably make her cool, slightly slanting, grey eyes look even more cat-like. There was definitely a touch of Sophia Loren in the way she looked – all sultry and banked-down fires. And the kid had a sense of humour. He'd seen her sucking in her cheeks at the nauseating comments from Deedee *and* she'd caught his comment about bikes. He liked a girl who could see the funny side of life. Luke had had enough of women who took everything seriously. Boy, had he had enough. A year of living with Julie had made sure of that.

But there was something else he'd noticed about Millie; when she wasn't smiling, there was a hint of sadness about her. There had been a point, early in the evening, when the guests had been getting to know each other and Millie had been in the kitchen. He'd found himself watching her and when she thought no one was looking she'd looked so unhappy he'd almost thought she might burst into tears. And then one of the guests had asked her a question and it was if she'd flicked a switch and the smile had come back on again. Was the smile fake and the sadness real? Luke wondered. Or was he misreading her? If Julie was to be believed, he was hopeless at trying to understand women so he'd probably got it all wrong about Millie too. Well, whatever it was, it was none of his business. He brought himself back to the here and now and looked around at the other chalet guests.

Dear God, he thought, an evening with this lot. If he'd known exactly what the others were like when his best mate Archie had persuaded him to take advantage of the end-of-season offer he might not have been so tempted. It would have been fine if he was into devil worship because obviously he had discovered Hell on Earth. What with Patricia, Deedee, Bella and the inflatable dolls, Luke wondered what his chances were of escaping from a fortnight in their company with his sanity intact. Not that Venice and Chelsea were unpleasant, and neither was Deedee for that matter, but they just weren't his type. None of them could have been described as bright and although Venice and Chelsea were very easy on the eye, he thought their endless chatter about fashion and make-up would pall after – ooh – all of ten minutes. Bella seemed to be besotted with Mike although he couldn't for the life of him think why, and as for Pat . . . Terrifying old bat, or what?

He looked at his fellow male guests. They didn't seem much better either. Cuthbert needed wringing out, poor John ought to try standing up to his wife, and Mike was the sort of old-fashioned chauvinist he despised, the sort who really didn't see what was wrong with women being chained to the sink; if it wasn't for Archie's company, Luke thought he'd despair. At least Archie would provide some sanity and a laugh or two.

The trick was going to be to reduce the time spent in their company to a minimum. Luke slugged his wine and pushed his chair back.

'I think I'll stretch my legs before I turn in,' he said, in a tone that made it quite plain he didn't want company.

'Oh,' said Pat. 'I was just thinking of breaking the ice with a jolly card game.'

'Thanks, but no thanks,' said Luke, opening the door and resisting the temptation to say what he *really* thought of the offer. He grinned at Archie who seemed perfectly happy to stay, judging by the way he was making sheep's eyes at the cousins. Idle bugger, thought Luke, a walk would do him good. But then Archie always did have an eye for a pretty girl and there was no doubt that Chelsea and Venice were pretty. Archie would be perfectly happy just to exercise his eyeballs rather than his legs and he certainly wouldn't worry about the quality of the conversation if the view was attractive enough.

Luke shut the door behind him and grabbed his coat off the hook in the hall. He let himself out of the chalet and stood on the doorstep for a second as he wondered which way to go. Then he saw Millie's footprints in the fresh snow. Well, she'd know the way to the centre of the village and he took a chance that that was where she was headed. Shrugging his collar up round his face, Luke followed the footprints along the road until they turned and dived between two rows of buildings. As he emerged at the other end of the narrow path onto the main street he paused again and took stock of his surroundings.

The hub of the village was to his left, that was obvious; lots of bright lights, neon signs and crowds of people in thick coats and moonboots ambling along the snowy thoroughfare. Above the bars and restaurants, tall blocks of flats towered up, hugging the cliff-face that rose up even higher immediately behind. With the wooden clapboard and uneven roofline, the flats almost managed to merge into the scenery. The buildings were ultra-modern and quite bizarre in the way the windows and balconies jutted in and out at crazily different angles. Luke wasn't sure if he liked the style of architecture but whatever he felt about it, it certainly wasn't bland.

He put the aesthetics of the resort to the back of his mind and looked at the après-ski delights on offer. Luke wasn't sure he wanted a beer in a noisy crowded bar full of strangers. He debated whether to walk round the village until he could be sure Pat and John had retired and he wasn't going to get accosted for a hand of cards, or give in and allow his ears to be battered by overloud music in some club.

If Julie had been with him he knew what she would have opted for – a crowded club where she could display her amazing dancing skills and be the centre of attention, but that really didn't appeal to him, especially not without a companion. He trailed along the main street, trying to find a hostelry that appealed. If he was honest with himself, none of them did. The bars and clubs on offer here weren't so dissimilar from the ones in London that he frequented for his job. As a gossip columnist for a major newspaper he seemed to spend a lot of his life in the company of the rich, young and beautiful, and bars and clubs were where they hung out.

He was weighing up his options when he saw a lone figure, blurry and indistinct in the falling snow, heading away from the crowds and lights to the other end of the resort. Millie, he was sure of it.

Without thinking he turned and followed her. It was only after he had gone fifty or so yards that the thought crossed his mind that she might be going to her own bed. He had no doubt that she wouldn't appreciate him tracking her to her room. What chalet host would want one of the guests, a virtual stranger, tailing her to her own private space? She might be the most intriguing person in the chalet but it gave him no excuse to follow her. If she found out he was on her tail she'd have him labelled as a stalker before you could say 'restraining order'.

He stopped and let her carry on. He wanted to get to know her better but he had a whole fortnight in which to do it. And getting to know her better didn't mean that he had to know where she lived. He was about to turn back towards the village centre when he saw her run up a flight of steps and disappear through a wooden door. By the door was a small neon sign proclaiming that she'd gone to the Husky bar. Funny, he didn't remember her mentioning that place when she'd given them the low-down on the village nightlife. Perhaps it was awful, he thought. But why would she be going there if that was the case?

Luke shrugged and turned away from the bar and down a side street. He reckoned he still had the best part of an hour to kill before Pat went to bed. He wandered along the snowy road, occasionally peering in the windows of the shops that flanked it, and thinking how much Julie would appreciate all this over-priced designer gear on display. She liked anything that was flashy and expensive. He reckoned that was why she'd first taken a shine to him – that, because of his job and the invitations he received, he'd be able to take her to all sorts of flashy and expensive venues in London. Sadly, though, most of the invitations were just for him. All she'd wanted was an entrée into the sort of circles where she'd meet the hacks from the glossy mags and her interest in him had begun to wane when she realised that he wasn't going to be able to provide it.

Luke turned onto another road without really being aware of where he was. For a small resort it seemed to have quite a maze of little streets but that was possibly because it was a car-free zone. He looked about him trying to get his bearings. He seemed to be back at the edge of the village again. And there was the sign announcing the Husky bar, just to confirm it. At this end of the village the music from the other bars was barely audible so when the door opened and a burst of applause flooded out into the quiet night air, it was quite startling. Luke was curious. What would merit such enthusiasm?

He tried to emulate Millie by running up the steps but hadn't reckoned on his lack of acclimatisation to the altitude. He had to stop for a second or two at the top to catch his breath, his blood pounding in his ears. He wondered what else Millie had in her repertoire that she could do superbly well – she could cook, she was kind, she was fit . . . He pushed the door open.

And he saw Millie on a tall stool with a guitar in her hands. She had her head bent as she re-tuned the strings and Luke took the opportunity to slip around the edge of the room to the far end of the bar. It was taking her a while to get the guitar tuned to her satisfaction and while she got herself organised, Luke ordered a *grande pression* and settled himself in the shadows, well out of her line of sight.

'*Eh bien*,' she said into the mic with a big grin on her face. '*On y va encore.*' She strummed a couple of chords, adjusted the mic and then launched into an old Bob Dylan number which had the audience clapping along. When she had finished and the applause had died down, she did a song Luke recognised as being by the Kinks, then several that he knew from his parents' record collection. As she played, the audience sang and clapped, and as each song ended they cheered until she played some more.

Luke listened to the old pop classics and sipped his beer. What a surprise Millie was. OK, so when they'd all pitched up to her chalet she hadn't exactly been shy but he wouldn't have imagined that the kid would have this sort of stage presence. She was amazing, and her voice! And the way the music just seemed to sweep her away. Where did all that come from?

As he watched her from his half-hidden position in the corner, he wondered more and more about her. The honest truth was that Millie just wasn't like any other woman he had come across. And he had sisters so he'd come across quite a few in his time. She was kind and caring and didn't seem to be the least bit self-conscious. She hardly bothered with make-up, her hair was just scraped back any old how and yet she still managed to look pretty. No, more than that – really lovely. He wondered idly just how gorgeous she might be if she did make an effort, but then again, it was impressive that she was so natural.

Julie hadn't been natural, that was for sure. She made use of anything to enhance her charms. Not that she had been very charming by the time things had come to a head.

'But you're never here in the evening!' she'd accused

shrilly, forgetting that, as a dancer, neither was she very much. What she meant was he wasn't around when she wanted him to be. 'You're always out meeting people and ignoring me.'

'For fuck's sake, Julie,' he'd yelled back at her. 'I'm a journalist. It's what I'm paid to do – go out and meet people.'

'But you don't have to be so nice to them. You're always taking people out to lunch or dinner. I never get a look in.'

'That's bollocks and you know it. I took you out last week. And the week before.'

'But you've been out heaps more often than that.'

'It's my job. The editor expects me to do it. I get *paid* to do it. I write a gossip column. Schmoozing people is how I get my material. And I'm sorry I can't always wangle an invitation for you. I do try, you know.'

'Not hard enough.' It was a few minutes after that that Julie, realising she was losing the argument, began to throw things. Luke had picked up his laptop and his coat and left. 'And don't come back,' Julie had shrieked down the stairwell as he'd made his escape.

'No chance,' Luke had muttered as he'd hailed a cab. It was only when he was heading across town to Archie's pad where he was hoping to find temporary refuge that he realised that he felt an overwhelming sense of relief.

He couldn't imagine Millie behaving like that – even if she did have red hair. From what he'd seen of her so far, she was simply too nice. She couldn't do bitter and screwed up if her life depended on it. Julie could do them as easily as breathing.

After a set of about ten songs Millie took a break. She climbed off her stool and headed to the bar where half a dozen people tried to buy her a drink. She shook her head and accepted a beer from the barman instead. Luke watched her lean on the bar and chat to the fans that surrounded her. He felt strangely voyeuristic as he observed her. This was obviously her place; the place where she wound down after a day's work; the place she escaped from the chalet guests.

Luke had noticed that the language spoken at the bar had been, almost without exception, French. Many of the customers seemed to know each other, greetings and fare-wells were exchanged when anyone arrived or left. The bar-man, whom he had gathered was called Georges, exchanged gossip and chat with people buying drinks as if they were old friends – which they probably were. Luke concluded that this was where the locals drank, where the resort workers – the ski-lift attendants, the ski instructors, the waiters, the shop girls and the like – got away from the interlopers. Interlopers like himself.

Suddenly Luke felt like a gatecrasher. This was the equivalent of a private party and he ought not to be there. He drained his glass and put it on the bar. Georges took it and raised his eyebrows. Another? Luke dithered. He'd made up his mind to go but Georges was happy to serve him. Well, perhaps he'd stay for just one more drink. Luke nodded and handed over the money.

Millie had finished her beer and was getting back on the stool. The room erupted with applause. She smiled her shy smile, spent a few seconds checking the tuning and then launched into 'Summer of Sixty-nine'. The bar pulsated to foot-stamping and clapping and the whole crowd roared the lyrics along with her. Luke watched her in awe. She was good – *really good*; she could sing, play the guitar and, what was most impressive of all, she knew exactly how to keep her audience enthralled. Not bad for someone who was little more than a kid.

Millie finished the song and the bar went wild. Luke thought she looked bemused as she gazed around at the cheering locals, as if she felt she didn't deserve this reaction. Suddenly she spotted him. He raised his glass to her and smiled. She lowered her eyes and checked the tuning of her guitar again – ignoring him. Damn, thought Luke. And who could blame her? She'd come here to get away from anything work-related and here he was. This was her bolt-hole. This was where she got away from the day job and now a reminder of the job was here, in her face. She was probably worried he'd go back and tell the others about the bar. He imagined that was the last thing she wanted. Well, the others wouldn't hear about the Husky from him and he'd slip away as soon as he'd finished his drink.

Millie began strumming again. This was going to be a slow one. Luke half recognised the tune. She began to sing and Luke's memory cleared. As she got to the words in the chorus of the classic Carole King number, she looked over to him from under lowered lids. God, she was beautiful, thought Luke, knowing what words came next and feeling a thrill of expectation and anticipation. Was this deliberate?

'You make me feel like a natural woman,' she sang.

Luke stared back at her. Millie lowered her eyes. Had he imagined it? Perhaps he had; the song continued and her gaze didn't reach him again. Luke was still staring at her when the song finished, willing her to look in his direction again, to give him a hint that what had happened hadn't been just a coincidence, not just a casual meeting of eyes across a crowded room. But she looked in several directions but not his, then she changed tempo again and began belting out a Bruce Springsteen song. Luke drained his beer and slipped away. Once out of the bar, he leant against the wall and allowed the chill night air to cool him before he made his way down the steps and walked thoughtfully back to the chalet.

'Had a good time?' inquired Archie when he got back to their room. Archie was lying on his bed idly flicking through a magazine.

'It was all right. Just had a couple of beers. How about you?' Luke began to undress.

'Perfectly grim. Old woman Barking-Loony was not amused when I suggested strip poker and said she was only going to play bridge. How's that for a fun-packed evening?' Archie threw the magazine on the floor and sat up in bed, rearranging his pillows as he did so.

'God, I didn't know you could play bridge. You sad git.'

'Of course I don't play bridge – and I don't intend to learn, which was what she suggested.'

'Shit, you're joking.'

'Wish I was.' Archie leaned forward and rested his elbows on his knees. 'We're going to have to keep out of the old bag's way. More than half an hour in her company and I might have to drive a ski pole through her heart.'

'Don't think she's got one. Did you see the way she bossed poor John around? She's a monster. Pat Barking-Loony, the undead.' Luke followed the statement with a hollow, melodramatic laugh.

'Point taken. That poor little bloke is being sucked dry as we speak. We'll find a desiccated husk in the snow in the morning.'

This time Luke really did shudder. 'For God's sake, Archie. The thought of Patricia sucking anyone dry doesn't bear thinking about.'

Archie blew his cheeks out and exhaled noisily. 'Ugh. Sorry. Quite the wrong metaphor to use there.' He grimaced. 'Anyway, what are we going to do to avoid her?'

'Easy, we always go out after supper. She won't come out if there's any danger that she might enjoy herself.'

'So what are the bars like around here? Find a good one?'

'They're OK. Pretty much what you'd expect in a resort.' He kept his face expressionless. Archie was his best mate. They'd gone to university together, they'd gone into journalism together, they worked on a tabloid together, got drunk together more times than either of them could remember, and hell, thanks to Julie, they now even lived together, but he didn't want to tell Archie about Millie's moonlighting just yet. He wanted to keep the information to himself for a bit longer.

Luke finished undressing and went into the adjoining cubicle which was their shower room to clean his teeth.

'Chelsea and Venice look like they could be fun,' Archie called to him.

Luke put his head round the door and removed the toothbrush from his mouth.

'Correction, what you mean is Chelsea and Venice look like they might be pullable.'

Archie shrugged and grinned. 'Maybe. Which do you fancy?'

'Neither,' said Luke firmly and went back to finish his teeth.

'Liar,' yelled Archie after him. 'Besides, I can't manage them both.'

'But you'll try.'

'Maybe.'

Luke rinsed and spat and returned to the bedroom.

'Just one thing, Archie.'

'What's that?'

'Let's not let on what we do for a living. Chelsea and Venice are nice enough but they look the sort who will pester us for connections. I can just imagine them thinking they would make a great feature in the lifestyle section. And you know what it's like, all the others will want to tell us stories that they think are hilarious or interesting, just because we write for a living, and you and I will end up losing the will to live.'

'Deal,' said Archie, who knew exactly what Luke was on about. He'd been cornered as many times as Luke by people who thought that as a journo he would be fascinated, even grateful, to hear their life story.

Luke switched off the main light.

'I'm bushed,' he said as he climbed into his bed and pulled the duvet firmly over his head. 'Night,' he said, muffled by the goosedown.

'Night,' said Archie good-naturedly. He switched his light off and both men slid into sleep, thinking about the women they had met that night.

At eleven thirty Millie played the last song of the night, despite the crowd in the bar baying for more. She took the guitar strap off her shoulder and handed the instrument back to Georges.

'Come on, Millie, just one more set.'

'I have to be up early, you know that. I'm tired out. I need my sleep. I'll play again tomorrow.'

'But they want you to play now.'

'I've been told that you should always leave the stage while the audience still wants more.'

George shrugged pragmatically.

'OK, Millie, you win. See you tomorrow.' He reached into the till and pulled out a fifty euro note. 'Here, you earned it.'

Millie took it gratefully and slipped it into her bag. 'Cheers. *À demain.*'

'*À demain,*' agreed Georges.

Millie slipped out of the bar and made her way to the bedsit she shared with Helen. The cramped bedsit was in a block at the other end of the village where the holiday reps stayed. No luxury accommodation with state-of-the-art ensuite showers and goosedown duvets for them. Most of the other kids in the block were there for the skiing and didn't give a toss about their rooms. Only Millie was there because her priority, when taking the job, had been having somewhere to live.

Wearily (changeover days were always the longest) she climbed the stairs to the third floor and let herself into the studio flat. The floor was strewn with piles of folded clothes because the cramped wardrobe was full to overflowing and there was nowhere else to store anything. The room was furnished to accommodate people staying for just a week or two, not four or five months. Millie and Helen tried to keep the place tidy but it was an uphill task and after a tough day cooking, cleaning and tidying up after their respective guests they had little energy left for their own domestic chores. Besides which, free time was for skiing and clubbing, right? Or in Millie's case, skiing, clubbing and singing.

Millie dumped her bag on her bed and slumped beside it. Then she took the fifty euro note out of her purse and shoved it into a bulldog clip of other notes which she took from the drawer in her bedside table. She counted them. Nearly a thousand euros now. She would put it all into her bank account tomorrow. That, plus the money she had already saved, would allow her to pay off the rest of what she owed Freya. Of course it would mean clearing out her bank account completely but at least she would be debt-free. For the first time in six months she wouldn't owe anything to anyone – well, except undying gratitude and a debt of friendship to Freya that Millie knew she would never be able to repay.

She flopped back onto her pillow, feeling a sense of relief at the thought of being debt-free. Not that Freya had hassled her for the money. In fact Freya had said there was no hurry but Millie's strict upbringing had left her with a horror of owing money. She'd had enough lectures from her father on the subject. Dear God, she'd had enough lectures from her father on *every* subject.

Millie sighed and wondered if she had been such a bad daughter. Compared to Helen, if Helen was to be believed, she'd been positively saintly in her youth, but, she thought wryly, when you were a bishop's daughter being saintly was probably the very least that was expected of you. Trouble was, with those expectations, if you slipped up, it seemed so much worse, so much further to fall, and Millie, as she had been told in no uncertain terms, was a fallen woman and no mistake.

Millie undressed and put her dirty clothes in the laundry bin. She brushed her teeth, set her alarm and climbed into bed. Was she so very bad? she wondered. She'd made one mistake, just one, and that had been enough for her father, the Bishop, to disown her. She wasn't the only girl in the country ever to have got pregnant by accident but the way her father had carried on, it was hard to believe.

It was a tough break finding out that you were really bad when you'd spent your life trying to be good, she thought. From the earliest she could remember, it had been clear to her that she had to try her very hardest at everything she did, as second-best simply would not do. Everything, from doing her homework to practising her guitar to keeping her room tidy, she'd slaved at to try and get his approbation. However, approbation just wasn't in the Bishop's psyche.

When her hard work at primary school had paid off and she'd got a scholarship to the cathedral school, her father hadn't even congratulated her. Her mother had given her a stiff little hug, the closest she got to showing affection, and said well done, and added that her free place would help with the family finances. But Millie had been hurt beyond belief that her father hadn't even acknowledged her success.

The girl given the desk next to hers on her first day at the new school had been impressed, though.

'Blimey,' said Freya Fairbrother when she'd found out a week or so later. 'Just how brainy does that make you? I am so pleased we're sitting next to each other. I'll be able to copy off you.'

Millie had felt her eyes widen at the enormity of the suggestion. Copying? Cheating?

'Go on,' said Freya, seeing her new friend's horror. 'I'm as thick as pig-shit so I'll be the class dunce if you don't help me. Dad will go fucking mental if I come bottom all the time. Especially on the money it's costing him to send me here.'

Millie, who hadn't heard a word stronger than 'gracious' in her sheltered life in the cathedral close, felt her eyes widen even more at Freya's profanity. Gosh, she thought, how amazing this girl was! She looked so innocent with her blue eyes and blonde pigtails but she was wearing nail polish and she said 'fucking'! Millie wasn't quite sure what it meant but she knew it was bad. How thrilling. How grown-up!

She'd fallen in love with Freya there and then and had willingly helped her out with her homework from then on. In return Freya had taken Millie under her wing and had swiftly introduced her to things that Freya felt were lacking in her protégée's life: Radio One, cider, skiing, horses and boys for starters.

Radio One showed Millie that there was music to enjoy

other than the tedious hymns she strummed at Sunday school and bible study classes. In the privacy of her room, when her father was out, Millie would quietly work out and practise the chords to the latest hits until she could play them perfectly. Freya was incredibly impressed at her friend's skill and encouraged her all the more by occasionally buying her the sheet music as a present.

The cider she could only indulge in on visits to Freya's huge house in the country. The two of them would swig it from bottles out in the tackroom when Freya's mum and dad weren't around. They never drank very much but they both felt deliciously naughty doing it all the same.

Freya's dad owned a snow dome in Westhampton, a place which was a mystery to Millie. On her first visit Freya had kitted Millie out with boots and a board, 'You don't want to be bothering with poncy skis – it's what the old people and the no-hopers use,' and Millie had been besotted with the experience of sliding at speed over the snow. After that Freya had arranged a pass for her friend so she'd been able to go and practise there when she was able to sneak off from her chores and duties at home.

The horses, however, Millie wasn't so keen on, although she was happy to watch Freya canter around and put her horses over jumps and would obligingly dash out into the paddock to replace the poles Freya knocked down. But, despite Freya's encouragement and exhortations, Millie was adamant about not getting any closer to the animals than several yards. They terrified her and she couldn't get used to their size and strength.

Unlike horses, Millie did get used to boys, despite being almost as terrified of them at first. The boys, members of Freya's pony club, accepted Millie as a friend even though she wasn't pony mad. Like Freya they seemed cool and sophisticated and also like her they were kind and friendly and included her in conversations, high jinks and, as the years slipped past, their parties.

Being Freya's friend had had other advantages too. Freya was undoubtedly the richest girl in the school and possibly the most popular so the fact that Millie was Freya's best friend made Millie popular by association. Millie knew it was shallow to enjoy the advantages it brought but she didn't care. For the first time in her life she felt almost happy.

But the best thing about Millie's friendship with Freya was that the Bishop admired and respected Freya's father, Jim Fairbrother, who had discovered religion late in life and was now an enthusiastic member of the Bishop's congregation. And, which was almost as important, he was a generous benefactor to the cathedral. Because the Bishop liked Jim so much he never once doubted that Freya wasn't being brought up within the same strict code of conduct as his own daughter. Thus he never questioned what Millie got up to when she stayed over at Freya's house, so Millie never had to lie. It was perfect.

It was also her downfall.

Millie fell in love.

Now, looking back, and with the perspective of the passage of time, it probably was little more than a teenage crush but Millie had felt it to be the real thing at the time. She had adored Alex and he had made her feel special. He'd told her she was beautiful, which she hadn't believed but he had insisted that she was. He'd bought her little tokens, he'd taken her to the cinema on Saturday afternoons and he'd kissed her. She still remembered the thrill of that first kiss; the way he'd tasted, the smell of his skin, the feel of his arms holding her tight, the feeling of being loved and cherished and valued. Perhaps if she had experienced those feelings at home she wouldn't have been so desperate to find it elsewhere. When Alex had told her that he loved her, she had believed him.

In her bedroom at night she would dream about the home they would make together, the children they would have, the holidays they'd take and it was all perfect and happy and forever. So when, after weeks of dating and innocent kisses, Alex said that if she really loved him she would have sex with him, she wanted to prove that she did. She was his for ever, they were going to marry, weren't they? So what did it matter if she jumped the gun just a little?

Millie squeezed her eyes to keep the tears at bay as she remembered the aftermath. Only a few weeks later she told Freya that she thought she was going down with some bug as she kept on being sick. Freya, hardly saying a word, had marched her straight to the nearest chemist in the school lunch hour and bought her a pregnancy testing kit.

'Oh God,' Freya said as they watched the blue line appear on the little stick.

Millie had sat down hard on the bench under the coat pegs in the sixth-form cloakroom. 'Shit. Now what?' she whispered.

'Well, for a start you've got to tell Alex.'

Millie nodded, dumbly.

'And you've got a few decisions to make. Do you want to keep it?' asked Freya bluntly.

Millie stared at her friend. Did she? Didn't she? She was only just eighteen, for heaven's sake. What did she know?

'And I think you should tell your mother. She ought to

know. She can help you decide what you should do for the best.'

Millie nodded. She was too shocked to be able to think straight; her mum would help her.

'So who are you going to tell first, Alex or your mum?'

Millie had opted to tell Alex. He loved her, he'd said so, hadn't he? He would support her in whatever decision she made. He would make it all right. But it hadn't been like that.

'You silly cow,' he'd yelled. 'When I asked if you were "all right" and you said yes, I thought you knew I was asking if you were taking precautions. Don't you know anything?' He'd turned away and Millie could see he was shaking, but whether it was from anger or shock she couldn't tell. He'd turned back. 'I can't help you. I've got an offer at York. I'm not messing that up, it's my big chance. There's no way I'm going to get a job to support some brat I don't even want, instead of funding my time at uni. You'll have to get rid of it and that's that.'

Shocked and distressed, Millie had run to her mother, expecting understanding, sympathy and a solution. Instead there had been an appalling row. Her mother had gone straight to her father and the Bishop's palace had reverberated with her father's stentorian bellows as he'd called her every name he could think of, belittled her musical talent, railed about her morals – or lack of them – insulted her friends and destroyed every scrap of self-esteem that, against the odds, she had managed to accumulate in her short lifetime. Then he disowned her. Her mother, cowering in the kitchen, had been no help and Millie had fled that day to her friend Freya, with nothing much more than the clothes on her back and her guitar.

'So much for Christian forgiveness,' Freya had said bitterly, as she thought about the way Millie's folks had reacted and watched Millie sob herself to exhaustion on her bed.

Eventually Millie, with no more tears to cry, had blown her nose and sat up. 'What am I going to do, Freya? Alex doesn't want to know. Neither does my mother. As for my father . . .' Well, nothing needed to be added there. 'I can't go home, I've no money, I've ruined my life . . .'

'And it's all my fault,' wailed Freya, her eyes glistening with tears at her friend's distress. Even Millie in her grief couldn't see how Freya could take the blame. 'I should have told you what boys are like,' said Freya. She kicked at the carpet angrily. 'They only want to get into your knickers. They'll say anything if they think they can achieve that.'

'But Alex wasn't like that,' snuffled Millie.

'Oh? He didn't say "if you really love me you'll go with me" then?'

'Yes but—'

'Yes but *nothing*. They're all bastards and I should have warned you but I thought you were too sensible. I thought you weren't like me, that you were good and moral and would want to be a virgin on your wedding day. I never thought you'd . . . Oh, bugger it.' She stared at Millie and shook her head in anger and frustration at the situation Millie had got into. 'And I didn't realise you and he had got so involved. Oh Millie, I've got to make it up to you. I'll do anything it takes to get you sorted out. Mum and I will help you find the right advice.'

Millie had dissolved into another burst of sobbing at this. It should be her own mum helping her, shouldn't it? Not Freya's.

But Freya had been a rock. She persuaded her parents that Millie had to stay with them for as long as was necessary.

'For fuck's sake, Dad, we've got ten bedrooms and use about two of them. What's the problem?' Her dad had muttered about undermining the Bishop's authority and Freya had let rip. 'If you don't support Millie I'll leave home and take her with me. I've got enough money of my own to do it so don't think I wouldn't.'

Millie had watched the exchange aghast. She would never have spoken to her father like that. But Jim Fairbrother hadn't raised his hand to his daughter or forfeited privileges. He'd backed down and Freya had smiled triumphantly.

'See? Putty,' she'd crowed after he'd left the room.

In the Easter holidays she took Millie to see a counsellor so she understood all the options available and when Millie had decided that with no home, no money and no prospects she had to opt for a termination, Freya had lent her the money for the op.

'And there's no hurry to pay it back,' she'd insisted as she'd accompanied Millie to the clinic and held her hand before and after.

If only the fallout from the abortion had been just financial. The money that Millie owed was an enormous sum but that was the least of her worries. Time, from when Freya took her to the clinic for the initial consultation and examination to the moment, a week later, when the op had been performed, had seemed to go so fast that Millie hadn't really stopped to think about all the implications and repercussions of what she was doing. Judy Fairbrother, Freya's mum, had had a long talk with her about her future and told her that she had to think of herself first and foremost, and it had made sense at the time. It dovetailed with what the counsellor had said. And anyway, what choice did Millie really have? But afterwards, as she lay recovering in her vast room at the Fairbrothers' house, feeling battered and empty, she realised that she had killed her baby.

Guilt avalanched over her, burying her in remorse and shame. How could she have been so selfish? The baby had done nothing wrong and she was responsible for the death of an innocent child. Herod, at least, had had the excuse of feeling threatened. What had this poor little mite done to her? She was so overwhelmed by despair that she couldn't even cry. But she knew that she would carry this burden for ever.

Despite Freya's assurances that no one, besides her own family and the Fairbrothers, knew about Millie's abortion, Millie was fraught at the idea of returning to school. She slunk into the sixth-form cloakroom on the first day after the Easter holidays, expecting everyone to be whispering about her behind their hands. Apart from the usual shrieked greetings exchanged by teenaged girls who have been parted for a couple of weeks, nothing was out of the ordinary. Until the deputy head requested that Millie report to the head 'before assembly'.

She was told that the governors and trustees of the school had heard about her appalling behaviour and as such a decision had been made to permanently exclude her.

'But what about my A levels?' stammered Millie, feeling numb with shock.

'If you can make arrangements to take them elsewhere I am sure you will do very well,' the head told her dispassionately, disapproval oozing from her.

With a burst of uncharacteristic defiance – what had she got to lose? – she demanded, 'So who told you? Who told you about me being pregnant?'

'You needn't concern yourself with that, young lady.' But the head didn't meet Millie's eyes. She looked guiltily at the desk in front of her.

Millie understood. Her father had told the school. He had shopped his own daughter. She turned and walked to the door. Just when she thought her life had hit rock bottom, she'd discovered it was possible to fall even further.

Freya instantly rang her father's chauffeur and demanded he take them both home. Millie sat rigid beside her in the limo. Betrayed by her boyfriend, let down by her mother, disowned and stabbed in the back by her father; she was beyond emotion now.

It had been Freya who had got her the job with the holiday company. Her dad had contacts in the ski industry and Freya knew exactly who they were. It didn't take much to sweet-talk one of them into it, and make him promise not to let Jim Fairbrother know. Millie sometimes wondered exactly what Freya had offered to seal the deal but Freya only giggled when she asked and tapped her nose.

'You'll have a roof, money, food, and what's more you'll have months abroad, right away from your dad, to get yourself back on track. This'll blow over and in a few years' time it won't seem as bad as it does right now.'

At the time Millie had doubted it. Her life was ruined for ever, nothing was going to change that, but getting away from Westhampton would be good. She never wanted to clap eyes on her parents or Alex ever again and a fresh start where no one knew anything about her was fine by Millie.

And what was more, she was determined that no one would find out about her. She was going to be the girl with no background. Besides, if she buried the past deep enough, she might be able to forget it occasionally herself.

Millie contemplated her life now. Not so bad considering; she had friends by the score at the resort, this room might be cramped but it was warm and cosy and her father wasn't around to berate her over its untidiness, she had her music and she had fun, and now that she'd earned enough to pay Freya back, she might even have some money for herself.

Good old Freya. It was one thing paying Freya back the money she owed her. It was going to be a whole other issue paying her back for her friendship and support. She'd never, ever be able to do that. And Freya had been proved right; things didn't look as bleak as they had previously. Life wasn't perfect and Millie knew the scars would always be with her, but the endless dark misery she'd been through seemed less dreadful now. Sometimes she felt almost happy. And besides which, she'd proved to herself she could get through this. Now she was going to prove to the world that it took a lot to get Millie Braythorpe down.

The fact that she'd even found an outlet for her love of music and singing had probably helped the most and it pleased her no end to think that she was devoting herself entirely to secular music. Her father would be apoplectic if he knew that she now only performed rock and pop music and hadn't sung a hymn in months. Millie smiled gleefully. Serve him right.

So, considering how well she was doing, how far she had come in the year since the row, what on earth had possessed her to flirt with Luke when she was singing? She felt the colour rise in her face when she thought about how she'd directed the Carole King number right at him. He'd have to be pretty oblivious not to read 'come on' into that manoeuvre. Hadn't she learned her lesson? Hadn't she sworn not to get involved with a man again? Hadn't she promised herself to be sure of a real commitment before she ever let another bloke touch her? And yet all Luke had had to do was flash his glorious deep brown eyes at her and send a couple of smiles in her direction and she was giving him the glad eye. Perhaps she was the cheap tart her father thought she was. No, she told herself with determination, mistaking a teenage romance for true love did not make her a cheap tart. Stupid, but not cheap – and there was no law against being stupid. Mind you, she thought, there wasn't a law against being cheap, either.

The door banged open.

'Hiya, Mil,' said Helen as she chucked her handbag across the room and onto her bed. 'Had a good evening?'

'Great, thanks.'

'Singing?'

Millie shrugged. 'Well, yeah. But I like to do it,' she added defensively.

'I never said you didn't. But it's work, isn't it? You never seem to just, well, enjoy yourself.'

'I do. I go out heaps with the gang.'

'What, once or twice a week.'

'Well, you lot could come to the Husky and support me when I'm singing.'

Helen wrinkled her nose. 'Not being rotten, Mil, but your music . . . I mean, you're bloody good and you've got a fab voice but it's not like the sound we get in the clubs, is it?'

Millie laughed. 'I was only joking, Helen. I can't see you and your mates singing along to "American Pie" or "Delilah".'

Helen laughed too. 'As if I've ever heard of the songs you've just mentioned. But seriously, Mil, even when you do come out with us you don't really let your hair down, do you? I can't remember ever seeing you bladdered. Or trying to pull a bloke or two. It's not natural, Mil. Not for a girl of your age.'

Millie lowered her eyes. She wasn't going to explain to Helen why she behaved as she did. She was the girl with no background.

'Besides,' continued Helen, 'I know you say you need to earn the extra but you never spend it, do you? I mean, you're not out on the pop most nights like the rest of us, the company feeds us, I've never seen you hit the shops since you've been here . . .' Helen tailed off and shrugged, clearly unable to make head or tail of her roommate.

'No, well . . .'

Helen laughed. 'It's no skin off my nose what you do with it. Honest, you don't have to explain yourself to me.' She went to the mirror and began to remove her make-up. 'What are your new lot like?'

'You know, the usual. A few nice ones and a few horrors. There's one old bag who thinks she's there to police everyone's morals, rationing how much they drink and wanting to know when room inspection is.'

Helen's eyes widened. 'You're kidding.'

'No.' Millie kept a completely straight face and looked a picture of innocence.

Then Helen grinned, realising she was being had. 'Right. But she doesn't want them enjoying the free wine.'

'Apparently not. But they will if I have anything to do with it.'

'Go for it, girl.' Helen slathered moisturiser on her face. 'Heard anything about the summer job from head office?'

'This week, they said. I really hope I get it. Just think, a whole summer in the south of France being a rep. No cleaning, no cooking . . .'

'Just sorting out delayed flights, dealing with complaints, dragging the tourists around the same sights week in, week out, keeping the hoteliers sweet when they mis-behave . . .'

'It'll be cool. In a couple of weeks I might be in Nice or Cannes.'

'But don't you want to go home? See your folks first?'

'No.' Millie said it with more venom than she meant. Helen looked at her via her reflection in the mirror and raised her eyebrows.

No, thought Millie, despite the fact that she had grown to really like Helen over the past months she wasn't going to explain to her that she'd had a fall-out with her parents. That might lead to other explanations. All Helen knew was that she was working overseas to improve her language skills and she'd never seemed to want to know more about her room-mate. Helen, in her turn, had told her she was working overseas for a good time. Millie grinned to herself.

That was Helen all right – the original ladette. Her father would have kittens if he met her!

Helen returned to cleaning her face and didn't pry, despite her obvious curiosity. She'd told Millie at the start of the season that she'd had so many jobs as a rep, shared so many rooms with so many others, she no longer gave a flying fuck what her colleagues were like as long as they pulled their weight and didn't nick her stuff. That suited Millie down to the ground and since then neither had asked the other much about their home life or past. Besides, if she needed to confide in someone she phoned Freya. Her mates in the resort, like Helen, were great company for a night out but they weren't real, deep-down friends – not like Freya.

'Right, bed,' Helen said breezily, climbing into the twin next to Millie.

'Yeah. Night-night.'

Millie switched the light off. Thinking about it, she wasn't sure she wanted to see her parents ever again. Her father was a bully, she'd known that all her life. But her mother, who had always promised she'd be there for her only daughter, her mother hadn't stood by her. She hadn't lifted a finger to stop her dad from throwing her out. Frankly, Millie wasn't sure she wanted a relationship with her either.

Luke was the first of the guests to appear in the kitchen the next morning, albeit still only in his dressing gown. Outside, fine snow was still falling and the sky was resolutely overcast. Millie saw him shrug disconsolately. Well, she thought, if they wanted good snow to ski on they had to be prepared for it to get topped up. She knew it would be preferable to have the snow fall overnight or in someone else's holiday week, of course she understood that, but the snow wasn't so heavy that they wouldn't be able to get out on the slopes. If they were keen.

'Tea?' offered Millie breezily. She wasn't going to refer to the previous evening. She didn't want to jog Luke's memory about that Carole King number. If she ignored the issue maybe he'd think he'd imagined it.

'Please.'

Luke pulled a chair out from the carefully laid table and took the proffered mug from Millie.

'Milk and sugar are behind you,' she said as she returned to stirring the porridge.

'You sing really well,' said Luke as he stirred his tea.

Millie remained standing with her back to him. She could feel the colour rise in her cheeks. 'Thanks,' she mumbled, cringing with embarrassment and not knowing how to react to the praise.

'Why didn't you tell us about where you perform?'

'Well . . . I don't like to sound as if I'm touting for business. The guests come to ski, not to hear me sing.'

'Your decision, of course.' Luke sipped his tea and Millie carried on preparing breakfast. 'So, do you ski or board?'

She relaxed slightly. Thank God he seemed to have dropped the subject. 'Board.'

'Been doing it long?'

'About eight years.'

'Lots of skiing holidays with your parents – or was it school trips?'

'Neither.' Millie had a momentary vision of her father, complete with crosier and mitre, on skis. She suppressed a smile. 'I had a mate at school whose dad owned the

Sno-Zone Lair in Westhampton. She used to get me in for free.'

Luke whistled. 'Lucky you. Some friend!'

Millie nodded. 'Freya is the best mate anyone could wish for. So, do you know the Sno-Zone?'

'Everyone knows the Sno-Zone. It's got the best indoor snow park in the country.'

'So I was told by Freya's dad.'

'So did you ever try skiing or did you go straight to boarding?'

'Freya said skiing was poncy and I'd get more fun from boarding. She got me doing all sorts of tricks as soon as I could stay upright.'

'Cool. So your parents don't ski.'

'No.' Millie wasn't going to elaborate. Her parents were off limits as far as she was concerned. She turned round to put the porridge pan on the table and saw that Luke was staring at her thoughtfully. Millie looked away and concentrated on getting breakfast sorted.

Luke finished his tea and returned to his room. The other guests appeared in ones and twos and by eight o'clock everyone was round the big table tucking into porridge or French bread with butter and jam. As they were finishing, Jack arrived with their lift passes and a handful of piste maps. He handed out the passes and collected the deposits for the little oblongs of plastic and explained that if they got lost they could not be replaced for free. The guests all took note of what was said and zipped them carefully into pockets.

Jack then shoved the bread basket to one side and spread a piste map out over the table.

'For the boarders amongst you the best places to go are

here.' Jack indicated some runs on the map and pointed out the snow park where they would find half-pipes and ramps and anything else they needed for getting some serious air. Archie and Luke leaned forward to get a better look. 'As for the rest of you, just get out there and have fun. For those of you who have booked lessons I'll show you the ski school meeting point when we go to the hire shop. I know the weather isn't fab at the moment but I've checked the forecast and the word is that it'll clear up later today and then should be fine for a few days.' A buzz of excitement ran round the table. 'OK, we need to get you lot kitted out. If you get your jackets and hats on, and make sure you're wearing thick socks, we'll go down to the hire shop. May I suggest that those of you who are having lessons go first, as you have to be at the meeting place at nine thirty.' The group nodded.

'I'll come down with you,' said Millie. 'Then when you've got your boots and skis you can get straight out on the slopes. I'll bring all your shoes back here.'

'Cor, that's sweet of you,' said Venice, nudging Chelsea to emphasise the point.

'Very kind,' said Pat, although she didn't sound grateful.

Old bag, thought Millie, wondering if she could get away with forgetting to bring back Pat's shoes. Probably not.

'Right then,' said Jack, looking at his watch. The guests took the hint and left the table to get themselves ready for a day on the slopes. 'You shouldn't spoil them by bringing their shoes and boots back for them. None of the other kids do that.'

'It's no big deal, Jack, is it?'

'Well, I hope they tip you well at the end.'

'Me too.' The pay for the chalet hosts was less than

generous and the tips could make a lot of difference. And she was only doing for this group what she'd done for other groups that season. It had nothing to do with the chance to spend another few minutes in Luke's company before getting on with her chores for the day. At least, that's what she told herself.

5

It was nearly eleven o'clock by the time Millie got back from the hire shop, cleared up the breakfast things, whizzed round the bathrooms, made a cake for tea, prepared a pud for dinner and tidied the living room. Normally she could get that list of tasks squared away by ten but playing the Good Samaritan and carting the guests' shoes back had held her up. She looked in the veg rack to see what she had available to serve with that night's supper. There didn't seem to be much of a selection. Down in the cellar, in the cool and dark, she had a great rack of stuff.

She took an old carrier bag with her and made her way down the cellar steps. She picked over what was there and made her decision. Carrying her booty in the bag, she switched off the light and began to return to the kitchen. Her shoes were soft and the steps concrete and she made no sound as she returned to the ground floor. She was several steps short of the top when she heard a noise. There were people in her kitchen. Well, that was nothing new. The guests could come and go as they pleased but there was something odd about these noises and Millie stopped to listen.

The voices were low, furtive, and she could hear cupboards being opened and closed quietly. Whoever was there was looking for something. Millie tiptoed to the top step and pressed her eye to the crack in the door jamb. Deedee and Cuthbert were busy rifling through her cupboards. Now, if it had been Pat, Millie wouldn't have been the least bit surprised. The old bat was exactly the sort, in Millie's experience, who would check up to see how clean the chalet was, if any of the jams or dry goods were past their sell-by dates (which Millie was totally sure they weren't), but Deedee and Cuthbert? It didn't make sense.

She pushed open the door. Cuthbert looked round. He didn't look the least bit surprised; perfectly innocent in fact. Millie decided she was going mad. Obviously, she thought to herself, this was the paranoia that set in as a result of being a chalet host for an entire season.

'Hello,' said Cuthbert. 'We got cold and thought we could do with a hot drink. We hope you don't mind. We just don't seem to be able to find the tea bags.'

Millie smiled and showed them the storage jars of tea and instant on the counter, labelled quite clearly with what they contained. She thought she'd told everyone where they were last evening. It was just typical that half the guests never seemed to listen. 'Not at all. Help yourself.'

Deedee and Cuthbert flashed her a smile and got out a couple of mugs.

'Well,' said Millie dumping her load of veg in the rack, 'I'm off now. Just make sure the door is properly shut when you leave. You'll be the last.'

She took a last look round the chalet to make sure she'd missed nothing and then went back to her own flat. When she let herself into her room, Helen was already there, lying on her bed.

'Not skiing today?'

'Can't be arsed. The weather's too shitty. What about you?'

'I've got a couple of odds and sods to do but I'll probably hit the snow park for an hour or two.'

'Even in this muck?' Helen threw a filthy glance at the weather outside the window.

'I shall wrap up well. 'Sides, Jack reckons it might clear up later.'

'Nah. Betcha it's set like this for a couple of days.'

'Oh well.' Millie went to the drawer where she kept her money and removed the wadge of notes.

'Going on a spree?'

Millie laughed. 'Me? No, I'm paying it into the bank.'

Helen leaned up on one elbow. 'What is it with you? Have you got a secret family you're supporting? What do you do with your pay because you sure as hell don't spend any of it?'

'Well . . .' Millie shrugged.

'I know,' said Helen with a sigh. 'It's none of my business.' She flopped back on her bed again. Finding out what made her room-mate tick was far too much like hard work.

Millie mumbled something about not being long and, stuffing the money in her pocket, she fled.

It wasn't that she didn't like Helen, she did, but she had no intention of telling her about having to borrow a load of money from a friend for an abortion. An *abortion*, for heaven's sakes. It was such an awful thing she'd gone through – *done*. Not that, realistically, she'd had much choice but not everyone would see it like that. People had really strong views on the subject and Millie was still too raw to want to defend her actions to someone with an axe to grind. If she could she would blank the whole thing from her mind but it wasn't as easy as that. Every day she saw something to remind her that she'd got rid of a baby. If she hadn't it would have been about six months old now, and every time Millie thought about it she was filled with such a sense of loss. It didn't matter how often she tried to tell herself she'd had no option, part of her also argued that maybe there had been one. Surely, if she'd looked hard enough, she could have found somewhere to live, found some means of supporting herself, until she'd given birth. It would have only been for six months or so, not that long. Perhaps she should have insisted that Alex or his parents help bail her out. Perhaps she shouldn't have accepted his denial of responsibility quite so readily. If she'd been stronger maybe she could have managed. Maybe having an abortion had been the easy way out.

Millie left the warmth of the apartment block and turned onto the road that led to the centre of the village. The falling snow had the effect of deadening what little sound there was in the near-deserted street. Those who were hardy enough to hit the slopes regardless of the conditions were up on the surrounding mountains, while those who had decided to give skiing a miss until conditions improved were either tucked up in their chalets or sampling the local patisserie in the cafés. The street was almost deserted and Millie trudged through the ankle-deep snow towards the bright yellow neon sign of the local bank.

A wall of warmth hit her as she opened the door and she stamped her feet and slapped her coat to get the worst of the snow off in the foyer rather than tramping it into the main body of the building. It only took her a few minutes to deposit the cash and make arrangements to transfer it to Freya's bank account. She was tucking the paperwork into her wallet as she left the bank when she cannoned into a man who had just made a withdrawal from the cash machine. She would have fallen if a pair of strong arms hadn't gripped her and held her upright.

'Millie?'

'Luke!' Her ribcage felt as though it was being squeezed in a vice and her heart flip-flopped around in it, battering against the sides. Her breathing seemed to be all over the place. What was it with this bloke that he had such an effect on her? She pulled herself together and made herself breathe normally. In, out, in, out. See, she told herself, you can do it. 'Sorry, I wasn't looking where I was going.'

'That makes two of us. Still, no harm done.'

Luke let her go and Millie stepped backwards so she wasn't actually touching him. She wondered if he had been aware of her thumping heart under her jacket. 'Not skiing?' She hoped she sounded casual.

'Archie and I tried it but the visibility is awful. It was a white-out in the snow park. Impossible.'

Millie knew exactly what he meant. With white snow falling from a white sky onto white ground and with the light so flat that there were no shadows to give any shape or definition to the terrain, it was impossible to see any lumps and bumps in the snow. It made skiing a nightmare and downright dangerous if you wanted to do jumps or tricks.

'That's a shame. I was just about to go up there.'

'I wouldn't bother till after lunch. If what Jack says is true it'll be great later – and heaps of fresh snow.'

Millie considered what Luke had said. It was no fun skiing when you had to spend every scintilla of your time concentrating on staying upright, but when, *if*, the sun came out, the fresh powder would be heaven on earth.

'Look, Archie and I are going to have a drink. Why don't you join us?'

It was a very tempting offer. If she didn't join them, what else could she do? The thought of going back to her tiny room didn't appeal. She could take shelter in the chalet but there was a distinct possibility that the other guests might have also jacked in skiing for the time being. Did she really want to get cornered by Venice and Chelsea, nice as they were, and be forced to sound interested in hair and nail extensions? Or, heaven forefend, Pat and John? But – and it was a big 'but' – if she spent more time with Luke she might end up wanting to get to know him even better. She just couldn't ignore the effect he had on her and spending time with him in close proximity might be dangerous. She made up her mind to refuse.

Sensing her indecision, Luke said, 'Come on, what else have you got to do?' He smiled at her. 'Or am I so horrible that you'd rather disembowel yourself than spend time in my company?'

'No. No! Absolutely not.' Oh shit, she thought, that was way too enthusiastic. She sounded pathetically needy.

'Good. Then that's settled.' Luke slipped his arm through Millie's and began to lead her out of the bank. Unless she fought and struggled she didn't have a choice now.

Oh God, she thought, this shouldn't be happening. No getting involved with men, she reminded herself. But I'm not getting involved. I'm just going for a drink. But even Millie thought she was lying.

Luke steered her into a nearby bar and pulled out a chair at a table in the window.

'What's your poison?'

'Hot chocolate please.'

'Coming up. Keep an eye out for Archie. He's joining us in a minute. He's gone to buy some goggles.'

Millie unzipped her jacket and stretched out her legs. The bar was warm and not too crowded. Behind the hubbub of voices Millie could hear a current pop hit playing on the radio. She made a note to herself to download the song onto her MP3 player so she could learn the chords and the lyrics. She needed to keep abreast of the charts.

Luke was still at the bar so Millie passed the time staring out of the window at the mesmerising swirls of snow dancing and twirling along the main street of the resort. Not so attractive now with the clouds lowering across the mountains and no sun to bring colour to the scene. Millie suddenly felt a yen for the sea and sun and warmth. The skiing had been great, she'd enjoyed her time here but she felt ready to move on. A job in the Midi would be just the ticket after this; the perfect contrast. She wondered how long she would have between finishing here in the Alps and starting her new job.

A movement beside her jolted her back to the present.

'Hiya.' It was Archie, smiling down at her, looking at her as though she was the person he most wanted to see.

'Hi.' Millie smiled back at him. She couldn't help but like him. 'Luke is getting in the drinks.'

Archie bounded over to the bar, reminding Millie of a big puppy, and asked Luke to get him a beer too. He returned to Millie, hooked a chair away from the table with his foot and plumped down on it.

'Shitty weather,' he said, turning down the corners of his mouth to emphasise the point.

'We need the snow.'

'I know. But . . .'

'But it'll clear up this afternoon.'

Archie fiddled with a beer mat. 'S'pose. I was looking forward to getting out there this morning.'

Millie thought he looked just like a toddler who had had a favourite toy taken away. She laughed. 'Yeah, I know it's disappointing. If I could make the snow fall at night and the sun shine during the day I would. It's rotten when you look forward to one skiing holiday a year and then the weather isn't perfect.'

Archie looked sheepish. 'I'm just being greedy. I was skiing only two weeks ago.'

Millie's eyebrows shot up. 'Lucky old you,' she said hurriedly to cover her surprise. 'Tell me if it's none of my business but if you ski so much, how come you don't have your own kit?'

'You've heard the old joke about flying: breakfast in London, dinner in Aspen, luggage in Moscow?'

Millie nodded, the penny dropping. 'So your ski kit is in . . . ?'

'Your guess is as good as mine. The airline can't find it. I should get an insurance cheque any day now but until I have it in my sticky hand I don't want to splash out.'

'What? In case they don't cough up?'

'Have you ever dealt with an insurance claim?'

Millie shook her head.

'There are always strings, problems, reasons why it was your fault, why they can't – or won't – pay, why your policy didn't actually cover you for this eventuality.'

'That sounds like the voice of bitter experience.'

'God,' said Luke, putting the drinks on the table, 'you haven't got him onto the subject of insurance companies, have you? I should have warned you.'

Millie grinned. 'It's his specialist subject, is it?'

'Amongst others.' Luke took a pull of his beer, leaving a frothy moustache on his top lip. He wiped it away with the back of his hand.

Millie pulled her cup of chocolate towards her. 'This is really kind of you.'

'Not at all,' said Luke with his easy charm. 'I just hope it's not against company regulations.'

Millie smiled. 'No. I don't think so.'

'So fraternising with the guests *is* allowed.'

'Actually it isn't really, but . . . Anyway, there's fraternising and just having a social drink together.'

'I imagine it depends on the guests,' said Archie.

Millie lowered her eyes. If she looked at him she'd giggle. Archie was so right.

'Thought as much,' said Archie. 'Looks like we've been accepted by the management, Luke.'

Millie took a sip of her hot chocolate.

'So, when you're not doing this, what do you do?' asked Luke.

Millie put her cup carefully back into the saucer. 'This?'

'Slaving away for a pittance, looking after ungrateful plebs like us.'

'More of the same,' she answered slowly. She didn't want to enter into a discussion about her private life. 'I'm after a summer job near the Med. And what about you?'

'Oh, we work for a big firm in London,' said Luke easily. 'Desk jobs. Dull stuff.'

'That's right,' said Archie. 'But it pays the bills so can't complain.'

'Right,' said Millie. God, whatever they did sounded tedious. Funny, she thought, they didn't look like City types or accountants or whatever. But then, she thought, she wasn't exactly sure what City types or accountants did look like. On the other hand, it made sense. If Archie earned enough to have more than one skiing holiday a year he had to be doing something that paid well.

Archie took a pull of his beer and stretched his legs out under the table. 'So, Millie, what do you do for fun in the evening? I mean, where's your favourite spot to chill out?'

Millie glanced up at Luke. He gave her the merest hint of a shake of his head and the tiniest of shrugs, as if to let her know that he'd not mentioned anything. Millie traced her finger along the edge of her saucer. Even if Luke hadn't told Archie about the Husky, he was bound to find out sooner or later. And it wasn't that big a deal anyway. She just liked to keep bits of her life in separate boxes; it stopped people getting too close to her. But, hell, it was the end of the season, she'd be gone from here soon, what would it matter if people knew?

'There's a place I go to. The tourists don't go there much. It's just an ordinary bar. Down that end of the village.' Millie indicated the general direction of the place with a small jerk of her head. 'It's called the Husky.'

'But the music's great,' said Luke.

'Music?' said Archie, perking up. 'Live music?'

Millie nodded.

'Local band?' asked Archie again.

'No,' said Luke quietly, with a gentle smile. 'Just one amazingly talented girl.'

Millie stared hard at her chocolate, knowing that her face was burning.

'So you've already been to this joint?' asked Archie. 'How come you've already found it?' He sounded put out.

'I just sort of stumbled on it when I was out for a walk last night.'

'And the girl that sings? A local?'

'Sort of,' said Luke. 'It's Millie.'

Millie could feel her innards squirming with embarrassment.

Archie put his beer slowly down on the table. 'My, my. What a dark horse you are. So young and yet so multi-skilled.'

Outside the window the light was brightening. 'Look,' said Millie. 'I think the weather's perking up.' She knew her change of subject was so obvious as to be verging on the painful, but she really, *really*, didn't want this sort of attention. Goodness only knew where a conversation, with her as the main topic, might lead and the very idea made her feel sick.

But Archie wasn't to be deflected. 'So is this part of the deal? Are you the après-ski entertainment? Is it in your contract with the tour company?'

Millie shook her head, but somehow, breaking her own rules, she found herself telling them all about it. 'I just happened to go into the place shortly after I arrived and there was this really beautiful guitar hanging behind the bar and it was all dusty. So I asked Georges, the owner, why it was never played as it obviously hadn't been for ages. Apparently he'd been given it as payment for a bar bill someone couldn't clear. He asked me if I could play and when I said I could, he asked me for a couple of tunes. Said I could have a beer on the house in exchange. It sounded like a fair swap. Somehow I've been playing there ever since.'

'I hope Georges gives you more than a couple of free

beers,' said Luke fiercely. 'Your playing is worth far more than that.'

'Yes, I get paid.' She sipped her chocolate and wished the conversation would move on.

As if Luke sensed this he said, 'I wonder how Chelsea and Venice are getting on.'

'Knowing them, and knowing what ski instructors are like, I should think they're having a grand time, but not necessarily doing much skiing,' said Archie with a grin.

Millie hid a smile. 'That's a bit unfair,' she said. 'They seemed quite keen on hitting the slopes this morning.'

'You're right,' said Archie. 'But even you will admit, they don't look the jolly hockey sticks type.'

'They certainly don't believe in hiding their assets, that's for sure,' added Luke.

'But that's the fashion, isn't it?' said Millie, keen to defend the two girls. 'Spray-on tans, bags of make-up, fake nails and boob jobs?'

'So what about you?' asked Luke.

'No, well . . .' Millie finished her chocolate. Time for her to clear off, things were getting personal again. 'Thanks for the drink.' She pushed her chair back. 'I've got stuff I must get on with if I'm going to get a couple of hours' skiing in as well.'

Luke frowned. 'Going already?'

Millie nodded. 'Busy, busy, busy,' she said brightly, pulling on her gloves and hat.

Archie stared thoughtfully after her as she left the café. 'Is she really that good?'

'Sensational.'

'And what about her guitar playing?' Archie raised an eyebrow.

'God, but you've got a filthy mind. Seriously, I reckon she's got something.'

'Maybe I'll come along and check her out this evening. I mean, if she's *that* good there's chaps on the paper who might be able to give her a leg up.'

'Not if she doesn't work in the UK. I get the impression she doesn't do "going home". She's working here, then going to a job in the Med.'

'She's probably on a gap year,' said Archie. 'She'll be back home in a few months.'

Luke shrugged, not convinced. He was intrigued by Millie and he was sure there was more to her being out here than met the eye. She was utterly unlike any holiday rep he'd come across before.

As Millie left the bar, watery sunshine illuminated one of the peaks across the valley. Suddenly, out of the murky clouds, she could see this towering monochrome pyramid set against a milky sky. Jack had been right; the weather was going to brighten up. She noticed the snow had almost stopped. Time to hit the slopes and reap the benefit of all the fresh powder. Millie raced back to her apartment, pulled on her boots and grabbed her board.

Half an hour later she was climbing off the ski lift at the top of the mountain above the resort and staring at picture-book snow slopes that led off from the lift station. Right on cue, the sun burst out from behind a cloud and the light was so intense Millie felt it was bruising her eyes. The snow sparkled like a jeweller's showcase and where there were shadows, in the dips and creases in the snow, they had a wonderful opalescent bluey tinge. Millie caught her breath at the beauty of it all, despite the fact she'd seen it dozens of times before. She pulled her sunglasses off the top of her head and settled them on her nose before flopping down onto the piste to secure the bindings on her board. She ratcheted the levers to tighten the straps and then she pushed herself upright and jumped her board around so she began to slide down the piste.

In seconds she was skimming over the surface, her arms held slightly away from her body for balance, perfectly poised, a picture of elegance even in her bulky trousers and jacket. Her auburn hair escaped from its constraining band and flew out behind her like a fiery comet's tail and the wind whipped past her face, bringing colour to her cheeks. To her right, as she floated over the surface, Millie could see a field of perfect deep snow, unpisted and unspoiled. With a graceful and almost imperceptible change of weight, her board altered direction and Millie zoomed off the marked slope and onto the deep powder. Fine granules of snow sprayed out behind her board like the wake behind a waterskier as she skimmed down the slope, leaving flawless, even curves drawn over the surface. With a swoop and a whoop she took off over a small bump, landing with a muffled 'flump' a couple of seconds later and then she allowed her board to take her back onto the piste. Ahead was the lift to take her back up the slope and she steered and slowed her board so as to join the back of the small queue. With a flourish and a scrunch, she kicked the board sideways and came to a perfect stop just a foot behind the tail of the line.

Panting slightly, she bent down to undo her bindings and as she did so she became aware of an ironic handclap. She looked up to see which poor fool had made a mess of getting on the lift, or maybe someone had done a spectacular fall. As she straightened up she looked right into Luke's face. She felt her heart somersault and her breathing went out of the window again. Running into him, almost literally, twice in one day – was it too much of a coincidence? Bloody hell. Was he following her? Was he a stalker? Unlikely if Archie was with him but she couldn't see him. Where was he?

Then she spotted him, about five people ahead in the queue, chatting up some slinky woman with masses of make-up and designer gear. She felt a sense of relief and returned her attention to Luke.

'You're good,' he said.

'Not really,' said Millie, embarrassed. 'Can't I get away from you?' Oh, shit. That wasn't what she meant to say at all. 'I mean . . . I don't mean . . .' What on earth did she mean? She sighed and bent down to finish taking off her binding, hoping Luke would think her cheeks were red from exhilaration, not embarrassment. 'I'm sorry,' she said, still bent double, 'that came out all wrong.'

'No offence taken. I'm not following you, honestly.'

Millie stood up. 'You did last night.'

'Yeah, well. And I'm glad I did.' He grinned and Millie's insides went to mush again. 'Honest, this is just sheer coincidence. You left way before we did, remember. I had no idea which lift you took.'

The queue shuffled forwards a few feet. Archie turned round and caught sight of Millie.

'Hiya, babe,' he yelled over the heads of the others in the queue and the noise of the lift machinery. 'Coming to ski with the dunces?'

Millie laughed in spite of herself and noticed that the woman Archie had been chatting up looked distinctly put out. She gave Millie a disparaging look and then turned away from her. Obviously she didn't like any competition and she certainly didn't seem to appreciate it when the competition came from someone dressed in unfashionable ski kit. Millie was amused. She couldn't give a stuff what she wore as long as she was warm and dry. It didn't matter a jot to her that her kit was Freya's cast-offs and definitely last season, if not the season before. And neither was she after Archie. If Ms Snobby wanted him, Millie wasn't going to stand in her way.

'Not if you'd rather I didn't. You seem to have company already,' she yelled back.

The woman with Archie shot Millie an even more vile look – if Archie wasn't good enough for Millie and her tatty gear, he certainly wasn't good enough for her – and pushed forward in the queue to ease her way through the gate that regulated the flow of passengers onto the lift. Archie, distracted by Millie, was left behind on the wrong side. He looked at his fast-disappearing near-conquest and shrugged and then grinned. He waited by the automatic barrier for Millie and Luke to catch him up then they all caught the same chair. Once they were settled and had lowered the safety bar, Archie leaned forward to chat to Millie.

'Thought I might be about to pull there.' He didn't look the least bit upset with his lack of success.

'Thought so too. I really hope she didn't think I was cramping your style.'

'No matter. She only seemed to have one topic of conversation – herself.'

'And was it fascinating?'

Archie rolled his eyes upwards and let his head drop onto his shoulder, his jaw open slackly – a caricature of a man in a coma.

Millie laughed. 'Right, I get the picture. So you're not devastated to lose her.'

'Nah. So what are you doing here? Can't stay away from us, eh?'

Millie gave a snort of good-natured laughter. 'Dream on.'

'Millie,' said Luke, 'is going to show us the best slopes. Aren't you?'

'Am I? Why would I want to do that and have the good pistes cluttered up with a couple of losers like you two?'

The banter continued to the top of the lift and then, as soon as they had got themselves sorted and their bindings were secured, Millie led them, at breakneck speed, down the back of the mountain. At the bottom, panting only slightly, she waited for the two boys to catch up.

'For God's sake, Millie,' gasped Luke as he came to a stop beside her. He bent double as he eased the stitch in his side and tried to get his aching, trembling muscles to recover.

'Ohmigod, that was awesome,' panted Archie when he arrived a couple of seconds later. 'Where did you learn to board like that?'

'I told you, Westhampton.'

'But you've done loads of boarding in the Alps since then, right?'

'Not till this season.'

Archie gave a groan and flopped backwards into the soft snow at the edge of the piste. 'I can't believe I've just been beaten by a girl who learnt to board in England. Oh, the humiliation.'

Millie grinned and scooped up a handful of snow. Before Archie realised what was going on she lobbed it accurately into the open V at the top of his jacket. Then before he could retaliate she sped down the last hundred yards of the piste to the next ski lift.

He was still extricating snow from his jacket when the three of them piled onto the lift. 'I'll get you back, Millie,' he growled.

'Got to catch me first,' said Millie, smiling at him broadly and blowing him a kiss.

'A valid point,' said Luke, raising an eyebrow, sounding slightly jealous.

Archie glanced at Luke and then at Millie and lapsed into a thoughtful silence.

As the lift swung them back up the mountain, Millie glanced at her watch. 'I've only got time for one more run, then I'm going to have to make tracks.'

'Oh,' said Luke. He made a moue of disappointment.

'Sorry, folks, but if you want to eat tonight someone has to have their shoes off and get shut in the kitchen. I think that someone should be me.'

'So where did you learn to cook as well as you do?' asked Luke.

Millie snorted. 'I don't think you can really judge my cooking yet, you've only had one proper meal and breakfast. And I don't think Raymond Blanc is looking over his shoulder at the competition.'

'Come off it, Millie. Most girls of your age can just about manage a Pot Noodle – toast if they've done the advanced course.'

Millie smiled at his outrageous exaggeration. 'Well, I did the advanced course when I got the job as a chalet host. A couple of weeks' learning how to cook lasagne and fish pie – things a little more sustaining than Pot Noodle and toast.' She didn't mention that she could cook perfectly well before the course. No mention of the fact that she'd had to help her mother out in the kitchen for all the interminable dinner parties they'd cooked for the various members of the diocese that her father had felt duty bound to entertain. Or tell him that before she went to the cathedral school she could turn shin of beef into something edible, something that wouldn't cause her father to fly into a rage because it wasn't 'good enough for dogs'. Or tell him about the endless sandwiches she'd cut in countless church halls for one worthy cause or another. Or the gallons of soup she'd helped make for the soup kitchen down by the canal. Or . . . Her past was no one's business but her own, and no matter how much she liked Luke and enjoyed his company, it certainly wasn't any of his business.

Once off the lift they raced down the slope, carving perfect turns, flying over the bumps, with Millie beating the boys easily again.

'Blimey, you are hot on a board, Millie,' said Luke when he'd got his breath.

Millie flushed. 'Well, I was lucky I had that free pass to the Sno-Zone.'

'Don't go all modest,' said Luke. 'You're a genius. Admit it.'

Millie shook her head but inside she was fizzing with pleasure. She gave herself a little shake and told herself not to be so shallow. A couple of nice words didn't mean anything, did it? Besides, men weren't to be trusted. She remembered what Freya had said about men just wanting one thing. Well, she wasn't going to fall for that old trick, even if Luke was far too nice to be included in Freya's sweeping generalisation.

'Right, that's it,' she said, checking her watch again. 'Time for me to head back. Thanks for the company.' She sped off with a wave.

'Right,' said Archie, still panting. 'Round again?'

Luke was watching Millie speed off, deep in thought. 'Sorry. What did you say?'

'I said,' said Archie with exaggerated enunciation, 'round again?'

'What? No.' Luke shook his head. 'I think I'll head back too.'

Archie gave Luke a lascivious wink. 'Oh yeah. What, you fancy joining Millie for après ski by the kitchen sink?'

Luke shook his head. 'Christ, but you've got a one-track mind, you filthy bugger. No. Absolutely not.'

'Me thinks the gentleman doth protest too much.'

'Fuck off,' said Luke without a hint of malice. 'If you must know I want to grab a few minutes in the internet café.'

'Oh, you're not missing work already.'

'Do I look that sad?'

Archie considered the question. 'Well . . .'

'Did we all have a good day's skiing?' asked Pat Barkham-Lumley when most of the group was gathered in the big living room, sipping wine. There was a vague murmur of assent but it was plain that no one really wanted to engage in conversation with her. But Pat Barkham-Lumley wasn't going to be so easily dissuaded. 'Chelsea, Venice? How did you find it?'

'God, it's difficult,' said Chelsea, with a theatrical sigh. 'And isn't the snow slippery. Me and Ven thought we were goners more times than you'd believe possible.'

'If it weren't for our instructor . . .' The pair shrieked with laughter. 'Ooh, how we had to grab hold of him.' Venice caught sight of the horrified look on Pat's face. 'Only for support. Honest.' She scanned Pat's face to see if she believed her but then fell around laughing again. 'But I dunno why he grabbed us back. Do you, Chel?'

Millie, putting jugs of wine on the table, said, 'Perhaps it was your magnetic personalities,' and winked good-naturedly.

Venice dissolved into giggles again.

Pat sniffed and wandered over to look out of the window, turning her back on the merriment.

Sour old cat, thought Millie.

Luke came into the room, stamping snow off his boots. He caught sight of the look on Millie's face as she eyed the dirty puddles of melting snow splattered on her shiny tiles.

'Oh God, I'm sorry. Here, give me a cloth and I'll clear it up.'

'You'll do no such thing. More than my job's worth to allow a guest to mop the floor.'

'I won't tell if you don't,' offered Luke with a devastating smile.

Millie felt herself melting like the snow on the floor. Instead of handing Luke a cloth she passed him a glass brimming with red wine and then grabbed a handful of kitchen towel off the roll. In a couple of seconds the floor was pristine again. 'There,' she said, straightening up and admiring her handiwork. 'Now, don't do it again,' she added with mock severity.

'Or what?' asked Luke hopefully, a smile playing round his lips. Millie threw the damp tissue at him which he caught and threw back.

'Children, children,' said Archie, catching the soggy paper in mid-flight as he entered the room. 'Detentions all round if you can't behave.'

Millie took the tissue from him and returned to the kitchen.

'Where the blazes have you been?' Archie asked Luke.

'I told you. At the internet café.'

'For all this time?'

Luke shook his head. 'I went and found a beer after, but my investment in an hour on the internet was money well spent.'

Archie was intrigued. 'Why?'

'Later,' said Luke firmly.

Dinner was over, the guests were lounging around the living room sipping coffee and feeling replete and Millie had just about finished clearing away and had gone to the cellar to fetch some more dishwasher tablets. Archie and Luke were still sitting at the table and Archie was wriggling with impatience.

'So when are you going to tell me?' he hissed to Luke.

Luke shook his head. 'Not yet, but if you come out with me for a drink in a minute, I might.'

'Ooh, going out,' called Venice from across the room. 'Can Chel and me come?'

Luke, his back to the room and the girls, looked at Archie in horror.

'Why not?' said Archie smoothly. 'Luke and I would love you to join us.'

Luke's eyes narrowed. 'In which case I shan't tell you what I found out.'

'Right,' said Millie, coming back into the room. 'I'm off again now. Is there anything else I can get you folks before I disappear?' She popped the tablet into the dishwasher and shut the door, the last chore done.

Deedee looked up. 'Actually, there is something. I don't suppose you know anyone who might be able to do a sewing job for me. I ripped my jacket today – got it caught up on one of my poles when I took a tumble and if it's fixed

quickly it won't get any worse. A stitch in time and all that.'
She smiled rather wetly as she gazed at Millie.

'How bad is it?' asked Millie.

Deedee went into the hall and fetched her jacket in.
'See.' She pointed out a three-corner tear on the sleeve.
'But it'll fray dreadfully if I leave it.'

'It's not so bad,' said Millie. 'I'll bring up a needle and
thread tomorrow. I'll do it for you before breakfast. Leave it
on the back of a chair in here so I can find it first thing.'

'Gosh,' gushed Deedee. 'That would be so kind of you. I
mean, I wasn't expecting you . . . I didn't mean to hint . . .
I'll pay,' she finished rather lamely.

'No problem. Right, well, if there's nothing else?' Millie
looked around the room. 'Goodnight then.' And she headed
for the door.

'So where are you two hunks going to take us then?' said
Venice, leaning over the back of the chair next to Luke to
give Archie the full benefit of her charms.

'A surprise,' said Archie. 'Get your coats. You've pulled.'

7

Millie walked along the snowy road that led to the centre of the resort. After about five minutes she glanced behind her and was disappointed to find Archie and Luke weren't hot on her heels. They're finishing their coffee, she told herself, they'll be along later. She came up with all kinds of excuses as she walked the last stretch to the bar and was irritated with herself for caring enough to do so. But even so, she couldn't resist a momentary pause at the top of the steps that led to the Husky to scan the street again.

In the distance, at the far end of the resort, she could see the distinctive orange of Luke's jacket – there couldn't be two that colour in the resort, surely – and with him were several other people. Millie stared and realised that one was Archie (obviously – he and Luke seemed joined at the hip) and the others looked suspiciously like Venice and Chelsea. Maybe Freya's comment about men should include Luke after all. And after all the fun they'd had that afternoon too. Well, thanks, boys. She snorted in anger, annoyed with herself for caring and flounced in the door.

'Qu'est-ce qui c'est passé?' asked Georges, sensing her mood the instant she stamped up to the bar.

'Rien,' snapped Millie.

Georges understood enough about women to know that this was not the moment to quiz her further. He just handed over the guitar from its shelf under the bar and shrugged.

Millie tuned it up, arranged the two mics, checked the levels and thundered into 'I Will Survive'. Georges, behind the bar, shook his head knowingly. Something had upset Millie and no mistake. And the thought that someone had made her unhappy made Georges sad too. He'd watched her when she wasn't performing, when she wasn't projecting the image of a confident, happy singer, and had seen the sadness in her eyes. Once, early on in the season, he'd even casually asked her if there was anything the matter and she'd shaken her head, laughed, and asked if it was in his gift to do anything about her hours, pay and accommodation. He knew she'd deliberately misunderstood him and he hadn't asked again, respecting her desire for privacy. But it hadn't stopped him wondering.

For twenty minutes she belted out the loudest and angriest songs in her repertoire until she knew that if she didn't have a drink her voice would give out. She put the guitar on its stand and made her way through the applauding throng to the bar.

'Better now?' asked Georges tentatively.

'Yes, thanks.' She grinned at him. 'Was I that much of a cow when I came in?'

'Yes,' said Georges flatly.

'Sorry.'

'Want to talk about it?'

'No.'

Georges nodded. Fair enough. Her answer came as no surprise. For a young woman she was a breath of fresh air;

no dramas, no tantrums, no endless chit-chat and self-obsession. In fact she was very mature and likeable – even if she was English. And the paternal side of him worried about her more than he cared to admit.

Over the rim of her beer glass Millie saw Luke and Archie enter the Husky. Deliberately she turned her back on them, not waiting to witness the arrival of Venice and Chelsea too. They could go to hell. She flipped through her mental collection of songs. Kiki Dee's 'Don't Go Breaking My Heart' was a bit obvious. And anyway, Luke wasn't 'breaking her heart'. She hadn't fallen for him. She just liked him and she hoped he liked her. It wasn't as if she was fantasising about him waiting for her at the altar. As if! She went back to thinking about what she was going to play next and suddenly the perfect song came to mind. OK, it was a cliché but, heck, it was an ideal cliché. Serve him right. She finished her beer and made her way back to her stool. A quick check of the tuning and she launched into an old Carly Simon number.

'You walked into the party,' she sang, 'like you were walking onto a yacht . . .' Her audience whistled and clapped their appreciation and Millie looked directly at Luke to see if he was making the connection. Luke raised his glass to her and smiled. Millie felt another buzz of irritation. Her jibe was missing its mark. Then she noticed two things: first, the blondes weren't with them; second, Luke's expression had altered to one of total bafflement. He now seemed to have twigged that her song contained a message aimed at him but he was at a loss to know why. Millie lowered her eyes. She'd wanted him to see her hostility, and he had. And she had misjudged him. Perhaps the boys had just been escorting the girls into town and had never meant to spend the evening in their company. Whatever it was, she'd leapt to entirely the wrong conclusion. But how was she to know? Men! she thought.

Luke studied Millie. What had he done? Was it something to do with the blondes? But he couldn't understand what. He'd only spent about half an hour in their company and surely Millie couldn't have known about it. She'd been here, singing, while he'd been trying to escape. He'd have to make it up to her as he'd obviously upset her. His thoughts were interrupted by Archie nudging him in the ribs to get his attention.

'Do you think Chelsea and Venice'll come looking for us?' he asked. He obviously hadn't picked up on Millie's choice of song, which amused Luke.

'Did you see the way they latched onto those two ski instructors? I don't think so.'

'But it wasn't very gentlemanly of us to just lose them like that.'

'I don't suppose they've even noticed we've gone.'

'Maybe.' Archie took a thoughtful sip of his beer. 'So, now it's just you and me, why don't you tell me what you were up to this afternoon and what fascinating facts you found on the internet?'

'OK.' Luke put his beer glass down on the table. 'For a start, Millie, for all that she can only be about eighteen, nineteen tops, is a paragon. She cooks, she sews, she plays the guitar, she's nice, she's helpful . . .'

'And?'

'How many girls do you know who do "mending", or any of those other things I mentioned?'

Archie shrugged. 'I don't know. It's not something I ever

ask. I mean, do the girls you date ask you if you can change a fuse?'

Luke ignored the question. 'Take it from me, I've got sisters and there are precious few girls these days who can sew on a button let alone do complicated stuff like darning.'

'I still don't see where you're getting at.'

'Doing mending is what you do if you're seriously strapped for cash. Lots of girls these days don't bother. They chuck the spoilt stuff and buy new.'

Archie nodded. It made sense.

'Another pointer that Millie isn't loaded is that she wears second-hand ski kit.'

'How do you know that, Sherlock?' challenged Archie.

'Because someone else's name is sewn into her jacket and is stamped on her snowboard.'

Archie looked contrite.

'As I was saying,' continued Luke, 'Millie doesn't seem to be loaded but she has a friend who is. That snowboard cost a fortune. Have you clocked the make?'

Archie nodded.

'And it's not just that. Loaded girls go on ski holidays, they don't work in ski resorts. Anyway, her friend is *so* wealthy that she, or rather her dad, could probably buy, not just the chalet we're staying in, but the entire holiday company, and not even notice the dent in the bank balance.'

Archie whistled. 'Who?'

'James Fairbrother.'

'Blimey.' Archie's eyes boggled. 'You *do* mean the Jim Fairbrother of Fairbrother Conglomerates?'

Luke nodded.

Archie let out another whistle then his forehead creased into a frown. 'So how do you know this?'

'Because the name in Millie's ski kit is Freya Fairbrother.'

'But that doesn't mean it's got anything to do with Jim Fairbrother.'

'It does when you remember she has a friend whose dad owns the Sno-Zone Lair.'

'And Jim Fairbrother is the owner.'

'Got it in one. Plus his daughter is called Freya.'

'How do you know that?'

'I had a look at Google.'

'So Millie and Freya are friends. So what? I really don't see what you're driving at. If you ask me you're obsessed.' Archie took a pull at his beer.

'Well . . .' Luke realised that his interest in Millie did look a bit weird. 'But I'm not obsessed. Honest.'

Archie snorted.

'Well, not very. However, this is the really interesting bit. Remember where the Sno-Zone is?'

'Westhampton.'

'Give the man a coconut. And what's Millie's surname?'

'Jesus, what is this? Mastermind?'

'It's Braythorpe.'

'How do you know that?'

'You haven't read the nice comments about her in the visitors' book in the chalet then. There's a postcard from a grateful guest stuck in there with her full name on it.'

'Oh. But I still don't get the significance.'

'How about Bishop Braythorpe? The Bishop of Westhampton. Have you heard of him?'

Archie's jaw nearly hit the floor. 'Fuck a duck,' he said. 'Blood and Thunder Braythorpe.'

'That's Millie's dad. I Googled him too, to check out the name of his daughter. Which is Millie, by the way. And I'd bet good money that both kids went to the same school, hence the friendship.'

'A nice kid like Millie having a dad like him? Surely not. And she's so normal. Her dad is barking. Raving. Completely off his trolley.'

'And against holidays, any form of waste, buying clothes rather than making your own, watching TV, drinking, enjoyment of any kind. In fact, you name it or enjoy it, he hates it. He's shot his mouth off on just about everything under the sun that involves people spending money or having a good time and, if the press is to be believed, he practises what he preaches. Which fits in with Millie's charming skills.'

'So what's she doing working here of all places? And singing in a bar in a ski resort! Her dad must be having forty fits.'

'I'd love to find out, but I'll bet good money old Blood and Thunder doesn't know. Can you imagine his face if he found out?'

Archie laid a hand on Luke's arm. 'But you wouldn't, would you? You wouldn't do that to Millie.'

'No,' said Luke, looking Archie in the eye. 'I may want to know why, but I wouldn't hurt Millie. Whatever I find out is just to satisfy my own curiosity. Why on earth would I want to tell her dad?' He looked over at Millie and saw a beautiful redhead, swept away with the music she was playing, looking contented and happy. But he doubted if life with her father could have been anything like contented and happy if his reputation for austerity and a ferocious temper was to be believed. And if, by working here she was attempting to escape from her father, he wasn't going to wreck things for her.

'Good,' said Archie.

For hard-bitten reporters, thought Luke, they were both being amazingly protective about Millie, which all proved how likeable she was. And possibly how vulnerable.

Millie looked across the bar and saw Luke and Archie deep in discussion. Then they both looked at her. She wondered if she was the topic of their conversation and then felt cross with herself for even thinking such a thing. I am *not* interested in Luke, she told herself firmly, or what he talks about. But she knew she was kidding herself. She played on, making a conscious effort not to look their way again. She finished another set and wandered over to the bar. Georges was ready with a beer.

'Only a couple of weeks to go,' he said, 'and you'll be finished for the season.' As he talked he poured drinks for the press of customers who had taken the opportunity of the break to surge to the bar.

Millie, sipping her drink, nodded.

'Will you be coming back next year?'

'I don't know, Georges. I've got no plans beyond getting a job for the summer.'

'If you came back I could find you better rooms. The holiday companies always give their staff rubbish accommodation.'

'It's worth considering,' said Luke beside her.

Millie jumped. She hadn't noticed him. 'This is – *was*,' she corrected, 'a private conversation. Anyway, I didn't know you could speak French.'

'You didn't ask me,' retorted Luke with a grin. 'There's no law against it, is there?' He held two glasses out to Georges for refilling.

'There should be if it stops people like you from eavesdropping.'

'Sorry.' He didn't look it though. 'Let me buy you a drink.'

'No thanks, I've got one. Besides, a few beers each evening is part of the deal.'

'So,' said Luke casually, 'what do you think you'll be doing next winter, if you don't come back here? Uni?'

Millie shrugged. 'Don't know. I'll be somewhere I can get a job.'

'So this isn't just a gap year thing.'

Millie put her beer on the bar. 'No.' She narrowed her eyes. Was he interested or prying? It was a fine line between the two and she wasn't sure she could judge it. Defensively she said, 'It's not really any of your business though, is it?'

'Just wondered,' said Luke, holding his hands up in surrender. 'I mean, it's a reasonable assumption you're on a gap year.'

'Yeah, well . . . Sore subject.'

Georges came back with Luke's beers. Luke rummaged in his pocket for some cash and swapped a few coins for two full glasses. 'I really don't mean to pry. Honest. Look, when you've finished here, how about a drink with me somewhere else?' He looked her straight in the eyes.

Millie weakened. He seemed so genuine; concerned about her even. And he was everything she had ever dreamed about in a man and here he was, offering to take her out. And she couldn't deny to herself that she liked him. But was it wise? Would he get the wrong idea if she agreed? Supposing he was after more than just a casual, friendly drink? And what if . . .

'I won't jump on you, if that's what you're worried about,' said Luke with a smile.

Millie gave a rueful smile. 'No, I wasn't worried about that,' she lied, wondering if he could mind read. 'And it'll have to be a quick drink. Some of us have to be up with the lark.'

'So where do you want to go?' asked Luke as they left the Husky.

Millie led him across the way to a small café. Luke ordered the drinks while Millie found a table.

'What did you tell Archie?' she asked when Luke joined her with a small brandy each.

'To get lost.'

Millie grinned. 'Didn't he mind?'

'Don't know, don't care.'

'That's a bit cruel.'

'He owed me a favour.'

'Must have been a big one.'

'It certainly was. He invited Chelsea and Venice out for a drink tonight. It wasn't my idea at all and it took us an age to dump them.'

So that's what had happened, thought Millie. 'Those poor girls. How mean. That was no way to treat them.' Millie sipped her brandy, enjoying the warm glow it gave her.

'They'll be OK. I saw them consoling themselves with a couple of ski instructors.'

'I take it back then. Girls like that bounce back.'

'Especially if they fall on their fronts,' said Luke.

Millie couldn't stop herself laughing. 'You are dreadful.'

Luke made a mock bow. 'So,' he said, serious once more, 'why aren't you going to uni?'

'Life got in the way.'

'You mean you screwed up your A levels.'

'Pretty much.' Millie stared at the brandy bubble she was cradling in her hands.

'You can take them again.'

'I didn't take them in the first place. I had to leave my school rather suddenly. It happened just after the Easter holidays so I didn't have time to find somewhere else to sit them. Bit of a blow really as I'd got a good offer from Bristol. For once I'd even managed to please my father. Of course he wasn't very pleased once the school expelled me and it all turned to ashes.' Why, wondered Millie, was she telling this guy any of this? She barely knew him. She'd probably never see him again after next week. Maybe, she reasoned, that was why. She was unburdening herself to a stranger. It was probably why people spoke to the Samaritans who worked in the cathedral crypt. When things had been really bad, when she'd had the abortion, Millie had considered ringing them herself but she was afraid that someone might recognise her voice. That was the problem with being the Bishop's daughter, anyone who had anything to do with the cathedral knew who she was. But Luke wasn't associated with the cathedral and despite having only met him that week, she felt she could trust him. It was almost as if she'd known him for years.

Luke was staring at her, stunned. 'They expelled you? The Bishop's daughter!'

Millie froze. She felt as though someone had just poured cold water right over her. 'How did you know that?' Her voice was shaking, she knew it but she didn't care. 'No one here knows that.' A terrible thought struck her. She put her glass down on the table. 'Did my dad send you here to find me? Did he?'

Luke looked as horrified as Millie felt. 'I can't believe I said that,' he mumbled.

'You still haven't told me how you found out,' Millie said, her voice shrill with anger. A couple of people looked round to see what the commotion was about. She lowered her voice again. 'How did you find out?' she hissed.

'Your surname is in the visitors' book, on that postcard you stuck in. And you told me you came from Westhampton so I wondered if you were related to Bishop Braythorpe. That's the problem with having an unusual name. If you'd both been called Smith I wouldn't have made any connection. I thought it would be a bit presumptuous to ask you outright but a couple of clicks on the internet and I found out that Bishop Braythorpe has one daughter called Millicent.'

Millie had never thought her name was that unusual, and it probably wasn't in some parts of the country but in a small southern cathedral city . . . She sighed, defeated. Luke was right about her name. They were the only Braythorpes in the area. 'Please don't tell anyone else. I don't want people to know who I am. It's not easy being my father's daughter.'

'I can imagine.'

Millie shook her head. 'No, I really don't think you can.'

'Do you want to tell me about it?'

She'd already opened up to him once, telling him some more wasn't so hard. So she told him a little about life in the palace; about the lack of heating, the lack of appliances, the second-hand clothes and how difficult it was to please her father. 'And when I got expelled . . .' She gulped, forcing the tears back, and looked at her drink to hide any possible trace of her hurt. 'Well, it wasn't pleasant.'

'Tell me,' said Luke very gently and quietly.

Millie shook her head again, still not daring to look up in case Luke saw how raw it all still was. 'Not yet. One day.'

She downed the last of her brandy and got to her feet. She took a deep breath to steady herself. 'Thanks for the drink. Sorry for the overreaction. I'm still a bit sore about what happened.'

Damn, thought Luke, worried that he'd scared her off.

He rose to his feet too. 'I'll walk you home.'

'There's no need.'

'I'd like to.' He paused. 'Really.'

His look was so concerned and tender, Millie felt her resolve melt. She smiled and zipped up her jacket. As they left the warmth of the bar, Luke slipped his arm through hers. Millie contemplated removing it. She hadn't been touched by a man in an affectionate way since Alex. Somehow, though, this wasn't intrusive or suggestive of Luke wanting more than just friendship. It was comforting rather than sexual and Millie found herself enjoying the contact. They walked through the snowy street, arm in arm, until they came to Millie's apartment block.

'Well,' said Millie, turning to face Luke, 'here we are. Thanks for the escort.'

'My pleasure.' He was standing close to her. Their smoky breath mingled above their heads as it rose into the still, freezing night. 'Goodnight.'

Millie noticed he was staring at her lips. Did he want to kiss her? She stared at his in return, wondering what it would be like to kiss him. If she moved forward six inches she would find out. She hadn't felt this way about anyone for over a year. Then, after that dreadful last encounter with Alex, she would have run away rather than get this close to a man again, but Luke seemed different – safe. And she couldn't deny to herself that she wasn't attracted to him. She'd found him occupying her thoughts almost constantly since he'd arrived at the chalet. She'd kept telling herself that she wasn't interested but her body and her heart weren't paying any attention to her head. And now they were alone and almost touching and her body was controlling her. She leaned forward a fraction, lessening the gap.

'Goodnight,' she said, licking her lips in anticipation.

Luke leaned too and their mouths touched. Warm and soft and chaste. And electric. Then, a moment later, it was over. Millie, scared by the thrill that shot through her, turned away abruptly to hide her reaction.

'Goodnight,' she said again as she bolted through the front door.

Luke stared at the door slowly closing behind her. Now he'd really scared her off.

Luke, an habitually early riser, was first up again the next morning and wandered into the kitchen in search of tea.

'Morning,' he said, perching on a stool by the counter in the kitchen. He noticed that Deedee's jacket had already been neatly mended.

'Hi,' said Millie, breaking the last egg out of a trayful into a bowl. She wiped her fingers and then ran water into the kettle. As she plugged it in she said awkwardly, 'About last night . . .'

'Yes?'

'Thank you for the drink.'

'My pleasure.'

'Can I ask you to forget what you know about me? You know, about who my dad is.' She began to beat the eggs rhythmically with a fork, not looking at him.

'I can't do that,' said Luke gently. 'It's impossible; you can't forget things just like that. But I will promise you that I won't tell anyone else. And I'll ask Archie not to mention it to anyone either.'

Millie groaned. 'You didn't tell Archie!'

'Sorry, I really am. I told him I knew who your dad was before you and I went out for a drink. He's my oldest friend,

I tell him everything. I didn't think. Sorry,' he said again.

Millie sighed and shrugged. 'I don't suppose it matters. It's almost the end of the season and then I'll be moving on from here.' She sprinkled salt and pepper into the eggs and put them by the hob for scrambling later.

'He won't tell anyone. In fact he told me it might be a kindness to keep it to myself. And certainly not tell . . .' Luke stopped himself. 'Doesn't matter.'

The kettle boiled and Millie made a pot of tea. 'What doesn't matter?'

'Nothing.' He smiled at Millie, willing her to trust him. She didn't need any more worries. She had enough with a madman for a father. 'Look, how about you ski with Archie and me today? We had fun with you yesterday. We'd really like to do it again.'

'I don't finish here till at least ten o'clock.' She poured the tea into two mugs. 'You don't want to hang around waiting for me.'

Actually, thought Luke, he didn't mind the idea of waiting for Millie at all, whereas he'd resented hanging around waiting for Julie – which he'd done constantly, as her idea of being 'on time' was to arrive on the right day. 'We could meet you up the mountain. There's that café at the top of the six-man lift. How about it?' Luke gave her his most appealing smile.

'Well . . .'

'Oh, go on.'

'OK. I'll meet you there at eleven.'

Luke smiled happily and took his tea off to his room to get ready for the day. Millie, wondering if she was being entirely sensible, poured the beaten eggs into a saucepan and began to heat them slowly.

*

Millie slid off the chairlift, slithered forward a few yards to clear the arrival point and took off her snowboard. She carried it over to the rack outside the café and propped it up amongst the muddle of skis, poles and other boards. It was nippy at the top of the mountain as there was a stiff breeze blowing and the terrace outside the café was empty. Luke must be indoors. She searched the windows and spotted Luke watching out for her. She gave him a cheery wave. Mustn't appear too keen to see him, she reminded herself.

Warm air smelling of chocolate and hot chip fat swept over her as she pushed the door open. Her boots clumped across the rough wooden floor, scarred and splintered from years of heavy ski boots clattering over it. The café was already crowded with skiers warming up over a hot drink or quenching their thirst with a cold beer. The noise of dozens of people all talking excitedly about their morning's activities filled the air along with the clatter of waitresses clearing tables and serving others; they had to push past the customers crowded onto the long benches around the tables.

Millie picked her way carefully between the tables till she reached Luke who was nursing a large café crème and, judging from the crumbs on the plate in front of him, had just demolished some sort of pastry.

'Hi, there. Sorry I'm late,' said Millie as she hauled off her gloves and jacket.

'Only a few minutes. What can I get you?'

'No, I'll do this. You bought the drinks last night.'

'And I'm willing to bet good money that I earn several times more than you do a year.'

Millie gave him a wry smile. 'Well, you don't do this job for the pay, that's for sure.'

'So, what'll it be?'

'Just a hot chocolate, thanks.'

Luke went off to place the order and Millie admired the sun sparkling on the distant, jagged peaks, the skiers sweeping down the slopes and the deep blue of the sky. She would rather have been gazing at Luke but made a deliberate effort not to. Mustn't be too obvious.

'Here you are,' said Luke, sliding a mug onto the table in front of Millie. 'Thought you might like this too.' He passed a pain au chocolat to her. 'They are exceptionally good here.'

'And at about four times the price of anywhere else in France, exceptionally expensive.'

'Yeah, well, but worth it for the view. And the company.'

Millie could feel herself blushing. She covered up her embarrassment with a large bite out of the pastry. Besides, he was just being nice. She wasn't stupid. What did a man ten years older than her, who earned enough for proper regular skiing holidays, see in a kid like her? Nothing, that was what. He was just kind and considerate and after some company. But she didn't mind. She could pretend to herself that it might be more than that and she could enjoy the wonderful warm feeling it gave her.

'Where's Archie?' she asked indistinctly through a mouthful of flaky pastry.

'He sloped off to chat up some bird he met on the chairlift coming up here.'

'Another one?'

'That's Archie. Always chasing talent.'

Millie smiled. 'Does he catch it?'

'According to Archie he does.'

Millie nodded. 'Right,' she said slowly, with a sceptical expression. She ate some more. 'Is he coming back to ski with us?'

'Why? Don't you feel safe without a chaperone?'

'Don't be silly.' A muffled boom reverberated around the mountain tops. Luke looked at Millie questioningly. 'It's just the local authorities, bringing down the loose snow. All that snow we had the other night and now this fine weather has made the chances of avalanches more likely. It's just a safety precaution.'

'I hope they know what they're doing with that explosive.'

'I should think so. They do it all the time.' Millie finished the last of her hot chocolate and mopped up the few remaining crumbs on her plate. 'Come on. You mustn't forget I have to be back on duty at five and I have to shower and change first. It doesn't leave us a lot of time.'

Luke pushed his chair back. 'So where are you taking me today?'

'Just round and about. We'll ski over to the next valley and see what the snow is like there. There's a terrific run down with some great off-piste skiing to be had. And it generally isn't too busy.'

'That was fantastic,' said Luke as he kicked his snowboard to a halt beside Millie. He was panting and his cheeks were pink from exertion but the smile across his face was broad and genuine.

'I love this run,' agreed Millie. 'Come on. But this time keep close behind me and we'll find some deep stuff.' She shot off down the slope and Luke had to use all his skill to stay in her tracks. After a couple of minutes Millie stopped again, at the edge of the piste. Luke joined her and stared at the almost sheer drop that led down into a virtually perfect bowl. There were half a dozen tracks that led down through the deep snow into the bottom of it but, other than those, the slope was almost untouched. The piste proper swept around the side and they could see it falling gently away down the far slope to the thin black line of the drag lift in the distance.

'What do you think?' asked Millie.

'How do you mean?'

'What do you want to do? Take the wussy route down or go the quick way.'

Luke stepped forward to get a better look at the 'quick way'. He peered gingerly over the edge.

'You've got to be joking!'

'No.'

'So what's it like?'

'Dunno. I've not done it myself yet. But it looks fun.'

Luke gulped. 'Fun' wasn't the word that had sprung to his mind. Suicidal was the one he'd thought of. 'So what is it? A black?'

'I wouldn't know. It's too steep for the piste machines so it can't be graded. It's got to be worth a go though, hasn't it?' Millie looked at him, challenging him.

Luke wasn't convinced.

'Well, I'm going to do it. You can go round by the piste. I'll meet you at the lift at the bottom.' And with a whoop Millie let her snowboard drop over the precipitous edge.

'Fuck,' muttered Luke as he watched her plummet. Then with his heart thudding and his hands shaking he followed her over the drop.

The snow was deep and soft. At least, reckoned Luke, as

he struggled to control his turns, if I fall it won't kill me.

Ahead of him Millie was turning and swooping, her board floating over the deep drifts. She seemed to be managing it with no effort at all. Not so for Luke. He felt his balance was in jeopardy every time he made the least move. His legs were shaking after only a few turns from the effort of staying upright and forcing his board round in the calf-deep powder. He let his concentration slip for a second and he felt himself lose it. He pitched forward into the snow and in a split second found himself sliding, face down, through it.

The steepness of the slope, coupled with his own body weight and the momentum he'd carried into the fall had knocked the wind out of him and now he was careering down the slope on his nose, with snow being forced into every opening of his jacket, front and back. It seemed like an age before he finally stopped, thanking his lucky stars that the drifts had been deep enough and soft enough to prevent any sort of injury. However, he lay still for a few seconds gathering his wits before he attempted to stand up again. Warily he rolled onto his back so he was facing the sky but he was still lying with his feet up the slope, head down it. At least, he thought, he seemed to be all in one piece.

He lifted his feet, board still attached, and brought them down and round in an arc, so his board was on the same level as his head. He really wanted to get the blood flowing back in its normal direction. He also reasoned that it would be easier to stand up again like that. But while it would have been relatively easy on hard snow to lever himself upright and back onto his board, on this stuff Luke found himself floundering around. Trying to push himself upright just resulted in his arms sinking into the snow up to his armpits.

He thought about taking his board off but he realised that his feet would just sink in the same way. It was like being in quicksand and probably, though he'd never experienced it, just as exhausting. He lay back in the snow panting with his exertions and wondered what he'd do if he couldn't get back on his feet.

Millie, he could see, was down and waiting for him and judging by the way her body was moving she was in fits of giggles. With a super-human effort he managed to get his board under his knees. He knelt there for a couple of minutes panting. It would have been hard enough at sea level but at this altitude his heart was thundering and his lungs were aching with effort. Once he had recovered, it was a relatively straightforward business to stand and get moving again but this time Luke didn't risk the fancy stuff. He traversed across the slope until he hit the piste on the far side of the bowl.

Millie, still rolling around laughing, was making clucking sounds when he finally joined her. 'Chicken,' she said with a grin.

Luke, concentrating on extracting lumps of snow from the back of his neck and the wrists of his sleeves, ignored her jibe.

'Do you want to do that again?'

'No way. Once is definitely enough.' Luke finished shaking the snow out of his jacket. 'Come on. I need to find somewhere to thaw and dry out.'

In the little café at the top of the drag lift they had taken out of the bowl Millie watched Luke being served from under her eyelashes. He was so gorgeous he must have hoards of women to choose from back in the UK. She reasoned that he was only being kind and attentive because she was around and available. The blonde cousins seemed to be besotted with the local ski instructors; Deedee only had eyes for Cuthbert; the same had to be said about Bella and Mike; and Pat was just plain scary, besides being ancient. It was really the only logical explanation as to why Luke continued to hang around her. And he still wouldn't let her pay for anything. She'd offered yet again in this place but he'd refused. Gratefully she thought that for once it didn't seem like charity, and charity was something she was an expert on. With a father like hers who had such decided views against consumerism, it was difficult to get by in the modern world without an awful lot of charity.

Nearly everything she had in her wardrobe that was nice and moderately fashionable was a cast-off of Freya's. In fact about the only things that she owned that actually had been bought for her were her bras and pants. Her mother had drawn the line at the family wearing second-hand undies and even her father had agreed to that. Millie fiddled with a teaspoon and wished that just a few of her clothes were ones that she had chosen herself. Not that she resented Freya's generosity but she just wondered what it would be like to go shopping and be able to pick and choose. She tried to imagine what it would be like to have the sort of money to shop in the boutiques in the resort. She'd stared in the windows often enough but the price tags were terrifying – and anyway, she had plenty of clothes. Even if they were cast-offs. They might not be ones she had chosen but they fitted and they were warm. What more did she need? Except that it would be nice . . .

Luke turned round and saw Millie staring into space, looking utterly wistful. He wondered what she was thinking about. He couldn't get over what she had told him the night before about her austere upbringing. And there had apparently been an appalling row because of her being expelled. So what had caused that? he wondered. He couldn't imagine Millie doing anything that bad. But whatever it was, her parents obviously didn't know what she was doing now. Frankly, he couldn't blame her. Her childhood had sounded pretty grim, which made it all the more commendable that she had turned out such a balanced, normal individual. He didn't think many kids her age would have managed to stay sane after such a bizarre start in life.

He paid for the two hot chocolates and returned to Millie.

'Penny for them?'

'Oooh,' she said in mock wonderment. 'A whole penny – riches! But too much for my thoughts.'

'What were you thinking about?'

'Shopping.' Millie blushed as she admitted this.

Luke laughed. 'I don't see you as the sex and shopping type.'

Millie looked up, a frown creasing her brow. 'And just what do you mean by that?' she asked icily.

'God, nothing. I didn't mean . . .' Luke was confused. Surely Millie realised that he knew she wasn't a frivolous airhead, especially after their conversation last night. 'I mean I thought you had more substance to you than most girls who spend their lives buying more clothes than they are ever likely to be able to wear. Besides, after what you told me about your childhood . . .'

Millie sighed. 'Sorry, I shouldn't have bitten your head off. It's just once in a while it might be nice to be frivolous and not frugal. I haven't done shopping but it doesn't mean that it's never going to be on my agenda.' She didn't mention the sex. How could she, she thought sadly, given what had happened?

Luke was intrigued. Julie had blown every penny she ever earned and filled the flat with clothes, some of which she had never worn, so he couldn't quite grasp the concept of a female with a frugal gene. 'So what do you spend your salary on?'

'Well, there's not much of it in the first place, but what there is I have had to use to pay back a debt.'

Luke took a sip of his chocolate. 'What, all of it?'

Millie nodded. 'And it's taken me all season. But now I've done it.'

'Wouldn't your parents help out with the debt?'

Millie shook her head hard.

'Right,' said Luke slowly.

Millie stared at him and let out a small sigh. 'Not that it's any business of yours, but at the moment I don't care if I never see them again.'

Luke inhaled deeply. 'Blimey. As bad as that. I mean, I know your father has a bit of a reputation . . .'

'A bit!'

'But he is your dad.'

'Well, sometimes I wish he wasn't. And my mum took his side. Or rather she didn't see my side.'

'So it all got a bit heavy.'

'Yeah, well . . . Anyway, like my debt, it's all behind me now and I'm moving on.'

'And doing normal stuff like shopping.'

'I've only got one more week of paid employment to put in the kitty. Hardly enough for a spree.'

'No, I suppose not.'

'Well, there may be some bonuses at the end of the season to be divvied up, plus tips and my final pay packet.'

'I'm glad to hear it. What are the bonuses for?'

'Stuff like the commission from the hire shops for putting custom their way. And the money we make on the lift passes.' Millie's hand flew to her mouth and she turned even more scarlet than she had a few minutes earlier. 'No. I didn't say that. Forget it,' she mumbled.

'Oh, come on. You can't leave it like that,' said Luke. It was his turn to inject a little ice into his voice. 'Besides, I bought a lift pass, remember. And sodding expensive it was too. I think I have a right to know if I've been ripped off.'

Millie shook her head vehemently, but she didn't look him in the eye. 'No, none of the punters are out of pocket. You've got to believe me on this. Honest.'

'I'm not sure I do.'

Millie raised her eyes and looked at him. 'Look, if I tell you, you've got to promise it doesn't go any further.'

Luke didn't respond. He wasn't sure he wanted to hear any excuses. He felt a nasty sense of betrayal, and the fact that he felt it was Millie who seemed to have betrayed him just made it so much worse. She toyed with the handle of her cup. Luke thought she looked desperately uncomfortable but he didn't feel inclined to put her at ease.

'Remember we asked you to pay us a deposit for your lift pass?'

Luke nodded. 'So you forget to give us it back? Is that it?'

'No, nothing like that. What we want is your lift pass back. We don't want the punters keeping them as souvenirs.'

'Well, that's harmless.' Luke really didn't see what possible advantage the reps got from gathering some used bits of plastic in at the end of each week.

'But that's the scam.' Millie took a deep breath. 'You know how people who travel a lot get frequent flier points?' Luke nodded. 'Some ski resorts operate a similar system. If you use your lift pass more than once a season, or for consecutive seasons, there are substantial discounts to be had. Most holidaymakers from the UK go to a different ski resort each season so they don't get the benefit – most of them don't even know the discount system exists anyway. So the price we charge you for your pass is the standard price. But because we recycle all the lift passes, because the punters give them back to recoup their deposit, we get all the passes at the lower rates.'

'Which you don't pass on.'

'No,' she agreed barely audibly. 'But how could we? The guys who bought the original passes had to pay full whack so it's a bit unfair on them. Besides, what you pay is the price listed in the brochure, which is the standard resort price.'

'That makes me feel so much better.'

'You don't have to get your passes off the reps,' said Millie defensively. 'You could get your own pass, come to the resort again next year and get the benefit.'

'Yeah, well . . . Whose idea is this?'

Millie shrugged. 'No idea. The system seems to run from year to year. Jack got handed a stack of last year's passes when he got out here and I imagine he'll make sure that the passes we have left at the end of the season get handed on to next year's reps.'

Luke whistled and sat in silence for a few minutes. 'So, suppose the saving is ten euros per customer, and there are one hundred guests here each week, that's a thousand euros a week you lot are making. Over a whole season, say sixteen weeks, that's a lot of money.'

Millie nodded sadly. 'But it's more than that, more than ten euros – nearer thirty – and we have about two hundred guests here at a time.'

Luke did another mental sum. 'My God, that's over ninety thousand euros. So how much is your cut?'

'A couple of grand.'

'Euros?'

'Pounds.'

'Good grief.'

Silence descended again. Millie silent with embarrassment and Luke silent as he absorbed the scale of the scam.

'You could do a bit of serious shopping with that,' he said after a bit.

Millie nodded. 'It makes it sound really awful. Like I'm fleecing the guests.'

'Aren't you?'

'No! Honestly, ninety-nine per cent wouldn't qualify for a discount anyway. We're just providing a service and we're, well . . . We're reaping the benefit,' she finished quietly. 'But please don't tell anyone about this. Head office doesn't know and the other reps would go ape-shit if this got out.'

'I can imagine,' said Luke drily.

'So do I have your word?'

'Yes,' said Luke. 'I promise.' Although if it had been anyone other than Millie telling him this, he wouldn't have felt obliged to honour his word – not in the slightest.

Millie dished up mashed potatoes and put the big casserole of coq au vin on the table.

'Tomorrow is Thursday again, in case you've lost track of time,' she announced, 'and therefore my day off. So I'm afraid, once more, you'll be fending for yourselves. If I can just ask one of you to make sure the dishwasher is loaded and run at the end of the day . . .' Millie looked around the room hopefully. Predictably, Pat put her hand up. 'Thanks. The bread will be left by the bakery at the door for breakfast, just like last week. You know the form.' She smiled at her guests. Just a few more days and the season would be over. Then bye bye snow and hello sun and sand, thought Millie happily. 'So is everyone OK with that?'

Inside she wasn't that bothered if they were or not. She was taking the day off regardless. She wondered if Luke would want to ski with her and the rest of the gang again. She really liked being with him, aside from his other obvious attractions he was such good company and fun to be around. She was perturbed, however, that he hadn't made another move after that kiss. Part of her was glad, as it made her determination not to get involved with anyone that much easier to stick to, but another part of her couldn't help being disappointed. Still, regardless of that, she had a whole day free for skiing with no tedious duties to muck it up, such as carting all the company bedlinen and other washing off to the laundry and bringing the bundles of fresh stuff back. Then, last Monday, she'd had to go down to the big supermarket in the valley and do the weekly shop for all the chalets. As a rule Millie didn't mind shopping for food but this was something else. This wasn't so much a shop as a military resupply exercise. The list had included nineteen chickens, a dozen hands of bananas, five kilos of mince, to say nothing of the catering packs of mayo, tins of tomatoes the size of small oil drums and a sack of carrots. The first time Millie had had to do this, the scale of the task had been utterly daunting. Now she was used to it but it was still a lot of hard work.

At least on the last Saturday she'd been excused the airport run, as her guests were staying put, even though strictly speaking it had been her turn. However, these extra duties weren't all bad news. She liked the trip down the valley, where winter was suddenly left behind and spring was visible everywhere – in the drab grass showing signs of greening up with fresh, vibrant shoots pushing through, in the primroses on the banks and the carpets of wood anemones on the valley floor, in the brilliant forsythia providing splashes of chrome yellow and the pale pink cherry blossom clashing cheerfully with it.

But tomorrow she had no duties, no chores to get in the way of her skiing. The forecast was good and she planned to spend the whole day on the slopes. It would be even more fun if Luke and Archie wanted to join her. Her thoughts were interrupted by Pat.

'Of course I'll make sure it all happens,' she said briskly, as usual answering for everyone. 'Don't you worry, Millie.

I'll keep an eye on things for you.' Behind her Luke and Archie rolled their eyes. Chelsea and Venice saw their expressions and giggled. Pat shot the girls a look. 'I'm sure no one wants you to have any extra work when you come back off your rest day, do they?'

A few of the guests mumbled no. They reminded Millie of a Sunday school class who had been caught out misbehaving. She wondered if Pat would hand out detentions if they left dirty mugs around the chalet. Would she come back to find some poor soul in a pointy hat standing in a corner?

'I can't believe a fortnight could go so fast,' said Chelsea. 'Wednesday again already. Blimey.'

'So are you and Venice expert skiers yet?' asked Millie as she returned with a bowl of salad.

'We've been moved up a class but we're still not much cop at it. My thighs don't 'alf ache, I can tell you. It's all that falling down and getting up.'

'But you're enjoying it.'

'It's lovely,' said Venice. 'Mind you, it wouldn't be 'alf so much fun without Claude.'

'Is he your new instructor?'

'He is for skiing. We've found out we can teach him a thing or two when it comes to having fun off the piste. Bless him, he's not much of a drinker for a froggy geezer. He's a real lightweight. Can't keep up with us girls at all.'

'We're giving him private lessons,' giggled Chelsea.

Venice snorted with laughter.

Pat Barkham-Lumley went red and looked apoplectic. 'Really!'

The two girls shook with laughter and completely ignored Pat.

Millie turned away to hide her own amusement. Poor old Pat, she thought as she returned to the kitchen. If it hadn't been for Deedee and Cuthbert who played the odd game of bridge with her and John each night they would have been pretty well friendless. As it was, Millie suspected that Deedee and Cuthbert were glad to escape after a couple of rubbers and were just playing to be polite.

Millie returned to the table with a jug of water and helped herself to a plate of casserole. She returned to the kitchen to eat hers, where she kept an eye on the chocolate soufflé in the oven. She'd just sat down when an icy draught ripped around her ankles. Someone had opened the front door. She looked up, her fork halfway to her mouth.

'Jack! What a surprise. I wasn't expecting to see you tonight.' Then she noticed the look on his face. It was thunderous. 'What's up?'

Jack plonked himself down on a stool and shot a look at the chalet guests. They were all busy chatting amongst themselves and eating Millie's delicious food.

'The shit has just hit the fan,' he hissed.

Millie lowered her fork. 'What shit? What fan?'

'The lift pass scam. Head office has found out.'

Millie felt her blood drain down into her toes. 'No!'

'Yes,' said Jack with venom. 'Some stupid git has let the cat out of the bag and the news has got back to the management.'

Millie thought she was going to be sick. It couldn't be her fault, could it? Luke had given her his word that he wouldn't tell anyone. Surely he wouldn't have betrayed her? She looked across the room at him. He looked up and smiled at her. Millie forced herself to smile back at him, willing herself to be normal. She had told him and someone had told the management, so it had to be him. Who else could it be?

Millie took a deep breath and prayed her voice would hold steady. 'So what's happening?'

'All staff have to attend a meeting tomorrow at the Hotel Bellevue – ten o'clock sharp. We'll find out what's going to happen then.' Jack shook his head. 'Frankly, I expect we'll be told to work this last week and then our services will be dispensed with.'

Millie thought she was going to cry. 'But they can't sack us. I need that summer job. The company has as good as promised it to me.'

'I think you can kiss that goodbye.'

'But I've got nowhere else to go. I was relying on it.'

'You'll just have to do like the rest of us and move back home.'

Millie pushed her plate away, her appetite completely gone. She had been counting on the money from the lift passes to set her up – that and the summer job. She'd hoped that at the end of the summer she'd have enough to get herself a small flat somewhere, to be independent and to make a new life for herself. But with barely a penny in her bank account and no job, she wasn't sure what she could do to survive over the next few weeks.

'Well,' said Jack, standing up. 'I'd better get on and spread the glad tidings further. Can you tell Helen when you see her?'

'Yeah,' said Millie tonelessly. 'I'll make sure she knows. Great day off tomorrow is going to be.'

'I'll see myself out,' said Jack, but Millie was staring out of the window, lost in her own thoughts. She weighed up her options. In less than a week she was going to be jobless and homeless. Freya was at uni and living in halls so she wasn't going to be able to help with accommodation. Going home was absolutely not on. She couldn't think of anywhere else she could go. Then there was the job issue; it was almost certainly too late to get a job with another holiday company as a rep for the summer. And anyway she was unlikely to get a reference from this job. Sackings generally didn't come with letters of appreciation for services rendered. Millie wondered, not for the first time in her life, why her? Other people floated through life without a care or a woe. All she had ever tried to do was be nice to people, work hard and get on and yet at every turn something had always managed to put a sodding great spanner right in the centre of the works. And here it was again. She could almost cry she felt so miserable.

'Penny for them,' said Luke appearing at her side, a pile of plates in his hands.

Millie shook her head and snatched the plates, hoping she didn't look as close to tears as she felt. Besides, he was the last person she wanted to talk to. 'Huh,' she snorted. 'They're costing a sight more than that right now.' Two grand, in fact. How did the bastard have the effrontery to behave like this when he'd shafted her and the other reps? And he'd promised not to tell! She was beside herself with anger and indignation. She wanted to scream and throw things, she was so cross. But she just had to content herself with shooting him a filthy look.

Something other than Luke caught her attention. The smell of chocolate cooking. 'Shit, the soufflé!' She dumped the plates and flew to the oven, grabbing an oven cloth on the way. She pulled open the door and peered inside. 'It might just be edible,' she muttered to herself.

'Looks all right to me,' said Luke.

'And what do you know about cooking?' she snapped back.

Luke put his hands up and took a step back. 'Just saying . . . No need to go for the jugular.'

Millie glared at him and Luke backed off further, looking hurt, and returned to the table. Serve him right, thought Millie bitterly. Bastard. She put the soufflé on the table, ignoring the complimentary comments about how well it had risen and how delicious it smelt, and slammed back into the kitchen for the vanilla ice cream to accompany it. She banged around, getting out serving spoons and plates and then thumped them on the table. The guests' conversation died away as the poisonous atmosphere leeched from Millie into the room at large.

'Is there something the matter, dear?' asked Pat, obviously out of curiosity rather than concern.

'No,' said Millie. She dug into the soufflé and dolloped a helping onto a plate. She almost threw it at Luke.

'Not bad news I hope,' said Pat, refusing to give up.

'No.' Another spoonful whacked onto a plate

'If there's anything we can do . . .'

'You can't.' She dished out another helping, scoop, slap, and pushed the ice cream down the table so the others could help themselves.

'I was just wondering.'

'Well don't.' Dollop. Followed by a glare.

Pat looked as if she had been slapped. She sniffed and stuck her chin out. 'Really.'

The rest of the soufflé was served in silence. Millie took the empty dish and returned to the kitchen. She knew she shouldn't have spoken to Pat like that. She was being very unprofessional. It wasn't the stupid old bag's fault that she was insatiably curious. Nor was it her fault that head office had rumbled the lift pass business. No, she could blame Luke for that – she was certain of it. Angrily she started the washing up, crashing the pots and pans around in the sink.

The conversation began at the table in a quietly anxious sort of way. The atmosphere was distinctly nervous. Not surprising, thought Millie, considering what a mardy cow she'd just been. Perhaps she should apologise. But then she dismissed the idea. If she did that she'd have to explain and what could she tell them? That she was angry because all the guests could have paid nearly thirty euros less for their lift passes and she was pocketing the difference? No. It wasn't an option.

She loaded the dishwasher and got on with the coffee. Venice and Chelsea brought the pudding plates into the kitchen and gave her a nervous smile. Millie flashed a smile back but she knew it looked false. The two cousins scuttled out again.

Millie felt like a heel. The poor girls were only trying to be nice, trying to make things better. Millie knew she had to make amends. She poured boiling water on the grounds in the cafetière and then rummaged in the cupboard. There at the back was a packet of rather smart chocolate biscuits she had bought out of her own meagre earnings for personal consumption. She looked at them longingly, they were seriously delicious. No, she had to be strong. With a sigh she tipped them onto a plate.

'They don't half look nice,' said Venice with relish when Millie put the tray on the table.

'Yeah, well,' said Millie. Just because she was in a bate

with Luke it didn't give her the right to take it out on the others. 'Enjoy.'

'Thanks,' said Pat, coldly. Millie gave her a smile but Pat didn't return it. Millie couldn't really blame her. She had been well out of order. She hoped the guests wouldn't mention her dreadful behaviour outside the chalet. She was in enough trouble as it was without piling on more. Being vile to the guests was definitely against company regs.

'Blimey,' said Venice as Millie left the chalet. 'Someone put a spike up her arse and no mistake.'

'She was in a shit mood,' agreed Luke, still smarting from Millie's inexplicable anger and wondering what on earth could have happened.

'The girl was insufferable,' Pat spat. 'No one has ever been so rude to me before.'

Oh, come on, thought Luke, they must have been. But he said, 'Whatever it was, it's serious. Millie's usually such a sweetie.'

There was a murmur of agreement round the table.

'I'm going after her,' said Luke. 'See if I can't buy her a drink and cheer her up.'

'But you don't know where she's gone,' said Pat sniffily.

'I think he does,' said Archie. Luke was already halfway out of the room. 'Tell her from us, if there's anything we can do to make it better . . .'

Luke nodded as he shrugged into his jacket. A bitter draught whipped through the room for a moment as he left the chalet.

'Well, girls,' said Archie, beaming at Chelsea and Venice. 'How about we cheer ourselves up too? Let's go and find some fun.' The girls beamed back.

A couple of minutes later only Pat and John, Deedee and Cuthbert, Mike and Bella were left in the room.

'And then there were six,' mused Bella. She poured herself a glass of wine from the carafe on the table and offered it to the others. Pat shook her head but the others pushed their glasses forward.

'Well, I feel sorry for her,' said Bella, looking at Pat as she said it. 'She's been wonderful till now. Look at the way she mended Deedee's ski jacket. She didn't have to do that.'

'She wouldn't take any money for it,' said Deedee thoughtfully. 'I did try to pay her.'

'And she brought our shoes back here for us on the first day and saved us all a trip,' said Mike.

Pat sniffed. 'It doesn't excuse the way she talked to us tonight.'

'It wasn't meant personally,' said Mike.

'Huh! It wasn't you she spoke to like that.'

'It wasn't me that wouldn't let the subject drop,' he retorted.

Pat looked daggers at him. 'Well, I am going to write to head office about it when I get back. Mostly this holiday has been satisfactory but when one has paid the sort of prices we have, that is only what we expect. What I don't expect is to be spoken to like that by the hired help.'

Bella rolled her eyes.

'It could do Millie a lot of harm,' said Deedee. 'Head offices take that sort of thing pretty seriously.'

'Too bad.'

There was a far from companionable silence round the table. Pat got up and wandered over to the window.

'Well, I think I'm going to turn in,' said John, taking the

opportunity of his wife's back view to pour another slug of wine into his glass and quaff it. 'Are you coming, dear?'

A sniff emanated from her direction. 'In a minute.'

John took his glass to the kitchen and then left the room. A minute or so later Pat followed him. The atmosphere lightened considerably.

'Cards, anyone?' offered Deedee.

Bella and Mike declined. 'I think we'll go and do a recce to find somewhere to eat tomorrow,' said Mike.

A couple of minutes later it was just Deedee and Cuthbert in the room.

'Well, that was a jolly evening,' said Cuthbert.

'Not one of the best,' agreed Deedee. 'Poor old Millie.'

'Pat has got her knife stuck into her and no mistake.'

'I expect there'll be other testimonials that will counterbalance whatever the evil old trout has to say. Have you read the comments book?'

Cuthbert nodded. 'I had a look at the start of the holiday.' Even so he went over to the table by the easy chairs and picked it up to remind himself of what the other visitors to the chalet had had to say about their host. He flicked through it again. 'All very positive. Loved by one and all, one might say.'

'Not by Pat, she isn't.'

'But whatever she says to head office, Millie has dozens of other people contradicting it.'

'And we could tell them she was goaded into losing her temper.'

'We could indeed. We're going to be meeting the management tomorrow anyway. We can tell them when they've finished sacking everyone.'

'Just as long as none of the reps see us there. We really

don't want them to know they have a couple of quislings in their midst.'

'It's not a problem if they do see us at the hotel. We're doing a recce for dinner tomorrow night.'

Deedee smiled. 'You think of everything.'

Luke strode along the snowy road towards the Husky. Something had really upset Millie, something Jack had said obviously, as she'd been fine till then, and Luke wanted to find out what it was. Partly it was his journalist's curiosity but more than that he could see Millie was deeply hurt and angry and he wanted to help her. Oddly, she had seemed angry at him specifically. But why? He'd done nothing. Luke puzzled over the incident, rewinding the events in his mind. Jack had come in, he'd said something to Millie and then she'd let rip at anyone within range but her initial venom had been directed at him. Was it just because he had been there? Certainly she'd had a go at Pat but under the circumstances a saint would have been hard pressed not to have cracked.

But he still didn't have the first clue as to what Jack had said. Luke reasoned that if it had been bad news of a personal nature, the holiday company would have sent a senior rep down to break it to Millie, not the resort dogsbody. And it didn't seem likely to Luke that she would have been allowed to carry on working if she had just been informed of some sort of personal tragedy. They would have had someone else finish serving the meal, surely.

So what on earth could Jack have told Millie? That her father knew where she was and what she was up to? That he was ordering her back home? It had to be something of that nature.

Luke arrived at the wooden steps up to the Husky and loped to the top. What a difference from his first encounter with them. Several days' hard skiing with Millie, and a number skiing rather less energetically with Archie, had toned muscles made flabby by his sedentary job. He peered through the door; she was nowhere to be seen. Luke was surprised. This was Millie's place. He knew she didn't sing here every night but she had a whole slew of friends here and he was certain she'd want to find someone to unburden herself to. He pushed his way through to the bar. Georges looked up.

'*Bonsoir*,' Luke hollered over the hubbub of voices in the crowded room.

'*Bonsoir*,' Georges replied, glowering.

'*Je cherche Millie. Est elle ici?*' asked Luke. He was wrapped up in his own thoughts and didn't notice the less than cordial reception.

Georges shrugged. '*Non*,' he replied flatly.

'Hasn't she been in then?'

'Not tonight. Want a beer?'

Luke thought about it, then shook his head. 'Do you know where she might be?'

'*Non.*'

Luke shrugged and turned to go, then changed his mind and turned back. 'Look, if you see her, can you tell her I was looking for her? I think something bad may have happened. I wanted to make sure she's all right.'

'OK.'

Luke left the bar to search for Millie elsewhere in the resort.

Georges watched him go then slipped into the back room.

'Hey, Millie. He's gone.'

'What did he say?'

'He thought you might want to talk to a friend about the shit that's happening in your life.'

'Well, I have plenty of friends to talk to, but he's not one of them. Bastard.'

'You going to sing tonight?'

'Would you mind terribly if I don't? I'm really not in the mood. I think I'll just go to bed.'

Georges nodded and put his arm paternally around her slim shoulders. 'You do that, *chérie*. And don't worry about the meeting tomorrow morning. It probably won't be as bad as you think.'

Millie shook her head, unconvinced. 'I think the very least I can hope for is the sack, along with the rest of the reps.'

'That's all they can do to you.'

'It's enough,' said Millie gloomily. 'Trust me, it's enough.'

The next morning Millie sat on a bench outside the Hotel Bellevue and flipped open her mobile. She hit a couple of buttons and put it to her ear.

'Freya? Hi, Freya, it's me, Millie.'

'Millie, good to hear from you. Are you well?'

'Yes, yes, I'm fine. Actually I'm not.'

'Oh God, Millie, you haven't gone and got yourself knocked up again?'

But Millie could hear the laughter in her friend's voice

and knew it was meant as a joke. 'No, I bloody well haven't!' she retorted, trying to sound cross but all she could hear was a gurgle of laughter from Freya. 'And it's not funny.' Only Freya could have got away with a comment like that. Coming from anyone else, Millie would have been horrified but Freya . . . Well, Freya knew her better than anyone else in the world, probably even her parents, and Freya had been there for her through the worst of the dark times, had sorted her out, had comforted her, had listened to her and, finally, had made her see that she needed to move on and put it behind her. And then she had made Millie laugh again. Millie would always be grateful to Freya for making her see that life was for living and enjoying and everything was so much easier to bear if you could just see the lighter side of it.

'No it isn't. Sorry, Mil.' But she didn't sound sorry – well, not very.

'Apology accepted.'

'So what's wrong? You been and gone and broken something?'

'No, it's nothing like that either, although it'd be sod's law that I break something now. No, I've been sacked.'

'What!' Freya's loud squawk of disbelief made Millie wince. 'But you are a paragon. How could they sack you?'

'It's not just me. All the reps have been fired.'

Another squawk shrilled out of the earpiece. 'But they can't. Can they?'

'They have. But it's complicated. I'll explain when I see you.'

'Bloody hell. What a bitch. Fuck, Millie, that's the last thing you need. And on top of everything else.'

'Yes, it's a bastard. Actually it's *much* worse than that. But I need a favour. Can you lend me a grand again?'

'Sod lending, I'll give it to you, Mil. Just tell me where to send it.'

'No, not *give*, absolutely not. I'll go somewhere else if you talk any more about *giving* it. I only do borrowing.'

'Well, borrow then, if it'll make you happy. Text me your account details and I'll get it transferred.'

'You are a star. I'll be home quite soon. Can I come and see you and doss on your floor for a night or two?'

'Like you have to ask.'

'God, Freya, I love you so much. You are such a friend.'

'And you're a great friend too. You know I'd walk through flames for you. Now you take care and don't worry. Any more problems and you know where to come. Big hugs.'

'Yes, and hugs back to you. Bye.'

Millie closed her phone and stared at the bustling street in front of her, hardly seeing the happy holidaymakers in their bright jackets and sunglasses. Thank God for Freya. At least she had somewhere to go when she landed back in England. OK she would only be able to stay for a few nights at the most. She couldn't stay for more or Freya would risk getting chucked out of the hall of residence, but the chances of the authorities finding out she was kipping there if she only stayed forty-eight hours were slim. Millie just hoped that she'd be able to find a bedsit or room really quickly. Of course the advantage of wanting somewhere to stay in a university town was that there were usually lots of cheap digs to be had. And hopefully not all of them would be occupied.

Millie sighed and blessed the day she and Freya had met. They'd been soul mates since. And now, yet again, Freya was being a total rock. One day she'd pay back the favours. Millie didn't know how or when but one day, she vowed she'd manage it somehow.

A shadow fell across her, making her look up.

'So there you are! I've been searching high and low.'

Luke was the last person Millie wanted to see. 'Sod off,' she said, leaping to her feet. Her phone catapulted out of her hand and into the snow. Luke bent down to pick it up just as Millie did and their heads clashed with a sickening thump. Millie reeled, clutching her temples, tears spurting from her eyes. The pain compounded with being sacked was just the last straw. Angrily she snatched her phone from him and stumbled off.

'Millie, wait,' Luke called.

'Don't you *ever* get the hint?' she yelled over her shoulder, mad with anger and pain. 'I never, *never*, NEVER want to see you again.' Millie knew her voice was shrill and that passers-by were staring but she didn't care. 'Now get out of my life.' She stormed off, leaving Luke looking stunned and hurt and bewildered in equal measure.

A couple of minutes later she reached her room. Helen was already there, lying on her bed staring at the ceiling.

'God, you look rough. Have you been crying?'

Millie nodded, not sure if she should risk speaking.

'Head office weren't that bad. I mean, none of it was personal. We're all in the same boat after all.' Her implication was obvious. She wasn't crying so why on earth should Millie?

'It wasn't them.' She grabbed a tissue from the box by her bed and blew her nose hard. Then she took a few breaths to make sure she was steady enough to speak. 'I've had a fall-out with one of the guys in my chalet.'

Helen sat up and took an interest. Millie was confiding in her. This demanded that she pay attention. 'What, did he come on to you or something? Or didn't?' Helen was eager for the lowdown.

'Nothing like that.' Millie paused. She couldn't let on the whole truth. Things were bad enough without the other employees knowing that everything was entirely her fault. Her and her big mouth's. 'I told him something in confidence and he told someone else.'

'What?' Helen was agog.

'It's not important.' Wow, what a whopper that was, she thought, with not a shred of remorse. But considering all the other crap that had happened to her recently it was hardly going to matter. If hell and eternal damnation really existed, as her father completely believed, then she was doomed anyway. Another lie wasn't going to make eternity less long or the pit of hell less hot.

Helen wasn't fooled. 'Come on, Millie, he made you cry. Whatever it was is hugely important to you.'

Millie shook her head.

'So what are you going to do tomorrow?' Helen wasn't one to give up easily. 'You can avoid him today but on Friday you've got to see him over the breakfast table.'

Millie nodded glumly. She'd already thought about that. 'I'll just have to cross that bridge when I come to it.'

'How?'

Millie shrugged. Didn't Helen ever give up?

'I suppose,' began Helen, then she paused and shook her head. 'No, it wouldn't work.'

'What wouldn't work?'

'If you and I swapped chalets.'

'Why not?'

'The company wouldn't like it.'

'And? They've sacked us. What else can they do? Stop our bonuses and commission? They've done that.'

'They might make us all walk home,' said Helen.

'Even *they* wouldn't do that,' said Millie with the ghost of a smile.

'You think we could do it?'

'Why on earth not? We're both looking after ten guests. As long as we swap what menus we've got planned for the last night, what can go wrong?'

'And you'll never have to see that bastard again.'

'No. No, I won't.' She felt her jaw tighten, her throat constrict and the pricking sensation start again at the back of her nose. Shit, she was going to cry again. She turned away quickly so Helen wouldn't see. But she wasn't sure if it was the thought of what Luke had done that hurt so much or the thought of losing him.

'I just don't understand women,' said Luke as he and Archie shared another chairlift.

'What's happened to you now?' said Archie.

'Millie. She's mad at me and I don't know why.'

'You've got to learn not to get involved. Be like me – no commitment. Love 'em and leave 'em, it works.'

'But I didn't *do* anything.'

'Should be quicker off the starting grid then. You only have yourself to blame if you didn't get past first base.'

'I didn't get past any base. I didn't want to. I wasn't after Millie for her body.'

'More fool you then.'

'Not all of us are controlled by our libido.'

'And what is wrong with that? If you've got it, share it, I say. I've made a lot of women very happy.'

Luke sighed. Didn't Archie ever think of anything other than his next conquest? 'Look, on Wednesday, one minute she was fine – happy, chatty, cheerful – then she goes ballistic. Why? She said I should get the hint and that she never wants to see me again. I mean, why? Did I miss something yesterday? Did I have a temporary spell of total deafness and not hear an entire conversation?'

'Search me, mate. She's a woman, so there's no need to look for logic. Wrong time of the month? It's the usual reason.'

Luke shook his head. It was no good talking to Archie about anything serious. He was a terrific friend and a great laugh but not someone you would choose to confide in – not even in an emergency.

'Ask her what it's all about when you see her on Friday,' suggested Archie. 'After all, if she's as mad at you as you say she is it's not going to make things worse, is it?'

'I don't know. And she wasn't playing at the Husky last night.'

'Maybe she doesn't on a Wednesday. Come on, Luke. Think about it, the kid has to have some fun some time.'

The lift reached its destination and the two men slid off the seat onto the snow. As Luke sat on the ground and did up his bindings he kept his eyes peeled for Millie. He was worried about her. Something was wrong and he wished he could help. Well, he'd see her tomorrow at breakfast and ask her point-blank then. As Archie said, it wasn't going to make things any worse.

*

'Hi, I'm Helen. Millie has been unavoidably detained so I am going to look after you for the rest of the holiday.'

'What do you mean?' said Luke who had come into the kitchen for his customary early morning mug of tea.

Helen gave him a level stare, hoping to God that he didn't guess the effect he was having on her insides. Wow! This had to be the guy Millie had got herself so worked up about. And no wonder. A stud or what!

'Personal stuff,' she said.

Millie had forbidden her from mentioning that they'd done the swap because of him. She'd been quite adamant about it.

'If he gets so much of a hint why we really swapped I'll seek you out and . . . and . . . and do something unpleasant,' she'd finished lamely. She didn't do threats as a general rule.

'Why on earth don't you want me to tell him?'

'Because I don't want him to flatter himself that I give him any thought at all.'

Helen had decided that Millie wasn't just trying to lie to the mystery man but to herself as well. It made her even more intrigued about what had gone on between the two of them. All the more so because Millie seemed, well, a bit of a prude, if Helen was entirely honest. She'd never got legless, she didn't spend money on clothes, she didn't go with men, she did extra stuff for her guests. All in all she was a bit too good to be true so it was a racing certainty that she hadn't been laid by this bloke. Or maybe Helen was completely wrong. Maybe she had. God, Millie might be a prude but she was also human. You'd have to be a robot not to feel some kind of desire for this bloke. And Helen was feeling a darn sight more than 'some kind of desire'. A judder of lust ripped through her as her mind wandered into a fantasy involving the hunk with his kit off. She cleared her throat to steady her voice.

'So what do I call you?' she asked casually.

'Luke.'

'Luke,' Helen repeated.

'That's right. Like the saint.'

'Practically divine then.' He most certainly was.

Luke raised an eyebrow at her, amused. 'Your predecessor didn't seem to think so.'

'No? Well, I wouldn't know anything about that.' And, irritatingly, she didn't either. It had to be something to do with sex, surely? Even Millie, Millie with her concrete knickers, must have weakened where this god was concerned. Perhaps her story about confiding in him and having her trust betrayed was just a load of bollocks. No, Helen made her mind up that sex had to be at the bottom of it.

'I hope it's nothing serious,' said Luke.

Helen stared at him, uncomprehending. 'Sorry, you've lost me.' She flashed him one of her best smiles. If Millie didn't want him any more then Helen was prepared to step into the breech.'

'Millie. The personal stuff that's stopping her from working. I hope it's nothing serious.'

'Oh no.' Whoops, that didn't sound right, far too casual and dismissive. 'Well, it's serious but not desperate, if you get my drift.'

'Not really.'

Helen turned away and began slicing a baguette into chunks. Luke switched on the kettle.

'Is she still here?' he asked.

'Millie? Yes.'

'So she hasn't had to go home.'

'No.'

'So where is she?'

'I don't know,' lied Helen. Luke gave her a hard stare and Helen dropped her gaze. He was annoyed, she could tell.

Luke made his tea in silence and took it back to his room. Helen stared after his cross back view. Millie was going to have to keep a low profile if she didn't want to have anything to do with him. Still, thought Helen, she might be able to provide some diversionary tactics. Anything to help a friend.

Luke sat outside one of the many cafés in the resort and scoured the main street with his eyes. Millie had to be somewhere around. Tomorrow, like the rest of the chalet guests, he would be flying back to Gatwick. If he didn't find Millie he'd probably never see her again.

Would that be so bad? he wondered. He'd soon forget about her. She was a sweet, charming girl with a bizarre father. A sweet, charming girl who had cast a spell over him. That was all. The spell would be broken in time and he would find someone else who he would be just as smitten by. He sighed. But would he? Millie had got under his skin in a way that even Julie, for all her seductive charms and sexual expertise, had never managed. He kicked at a lump of snow in frustration.

Across the road Luke spotted a red jacket. Millie? His heart gave a bound and then the figure turned round and it thudded down into his moon boots. No. This is madness, he told himself. He'd paid a fortune for his lift pass. He should be tearing the arse out of it, squeezing every last expensive euro from it but instead he was mooching around like some

lovesick teenager waiting for a glimpse of his squeeze.
Squeeze! That was a joke. He'd hardly even touched the
girl. He should sack this search and get his backside up the
mountain but . . . He glanced at his watch. He'd give it
another half hour. He caught the eye of the waiter and
ordered another coffee.

Millie took her key from her pocket and let herself into her shabby flat. She was dog-tired from her shift at the supermarket and her feet ached horribly. She dropped the heavy carrier bag full of reduced items, dented tins and veg on its 'sell by' date, and kicked off her shoes. Despite the warmth of a May evening outside, the flat felt cold and she shivered. It was cheerless, sunless and damp but with the budget she was on it was all she could afford. Freya had been horrified when Millie had shown her the estate agent's description.

'You can't live there,' she'd expostulated. 'The area's shite, even by Saltford's standards, and the place is a tip. Frankly, the whole estate should be condemned and has a reputation for crime and violence that beggars belief. And as for the sort of people that live there . . .' She'd paused meaningfully. 'Millie, the place is crawling with lowlifes, drug dealers and God alone knows who. You won't be safe.' A worried frown had creased her brow. 'Let me sub you some more so you can afford a flat where you aren't likely to get raped or mugged – or worse,' she'd finished, pointedly.

But Millie had refused the offer, reassured Freya that she'd be fine and had signed the contract. Besides, she'd already slept on Freya's floor for nearly a week and she was terrified that the authorities would rumble that Freya was breaking her residency agreement. She couldn't risk hanging around any longer in the hope that something else within her budget would turn up. Millie was fraught about getting her friend into hot water so she'd ignored Freya's concerns and signed the contract, paid the deposit and moved in. And now it was home and it had been for over a month.

Millie padded into the tiny kitchenette and flicked the switch on the kettle. She'd deal with the shopping in a minute but what she needed now was a cup of tea. The sound of her mobile ringing escaped from her handbag. Wearily she trudged back to the front door and extracted it.

'Hi, Freya,' she said.

'Hi, Mil. How's tricks – and the job?'

'All right. I can't say I love my work but it's better than being an office cleaner. Besides, at least I work almost normal hours now. And it pays the bills.' Just.

'You OK for tonight?'

'Yup. I'm going to grab a bite to eat and have a kip for an hour. Being on your feet all day is knackering and I want to be fresh for tonight. I don't want to let you down.'

'Look, I know you'll be fine. When has your playing ever done anything but bring the house down?'

'Yeah, but it's one thing playing to a bunch of holidaymakers or drunks in a pub and quite another thing playing to students. You've had some class acts at the Union. They're used to proper entertainment.'

'Which is exactly what you're going to provide. Now stop worrying and tell me what time you want me to pick you up.'

'I can walk. It's only a mile or so to the campus.'

'Don't be daft. You're on at nine. How early do you want to get there?'

Millie gave in. 'About eight-ish? I like to get an idea of the venue first, see what the set-up is like, get a feel of the audience, work out where I can take cover when they start to throw rotten tomatoes.'

'You'll be fine. See you later.'

Millie closed her phone and tried to ignore the butterflies in her stomach. She didn't normally get very worked up before she performed but this was more like a concert than the stuff she'd always done on a casual basis in the past. Good old Freya. She'd got her the gig at the uni by lobbying the Students' Union reps until they'd given in. It had been to her advantage that Freya was actually dating one of them – a chap called Tim. But even so Millie was now scared that she wouldn't be up to snuff, that the students would hate her and Freya would get grief about it. Millie wasn't so fussed about getting booed off the stage herself but if Freya had a hard time as a result she would feel so guilty. The students were probably into rap and hip hop and garage and stuff, not the sort of singer-songwriter music that she performed. Well, it was too late now to back out. The posters had been up round the campus for the past fortnight, the tickets had been sold and Millie had been promised a couple of hundred quid for the night – money she desperately needed to whittle away a bit more of her debt to Freya, and to pay for a few essentials in her life, like the electricity bill.

She gathered up her carrier bag and went back to the kitchen to make her longed-for cuppa and put the shopping away. Having done that, cradling her mug to warm her cold hands, she went into the one other room in the flat and sat on her bed. She looked at her surroundings; tidy but squalid. How she hated this place but, to be honest, her room in the Bishop's palace had hardly been warm and comfortable. Her father had very decided views on central heating and luxuries so, like most of the rest of the house, her room there had had the bare minimum of furniture and been freezing cold. But it hadn't been as horrid as this place. In particular, the carpet made her flesh creep. The day she'd moved in she had scrubbed it with soapy water but it still had marks and stains on it that made her shudder. When she had some spare cash she was going to buy a rug or two to disguise it. At least if she couldn't see it she might be able to put its nauseating appearance out of her mind.

When she'd finished scrubbing the carpet she'd washed as many surfaces as she could reach with a disinfectant solution. Better that the flat smelt like a hospital ward than it caused her to end up in one, she thought as her hands became wrinkly and sore. But no amount of scrubbing and rubbing could disguise the peeling wallpaper, the chipped skirting boards, the yellowing paint and the vile curtains. At least with Freya's money she'd had enough for the deposit on the place, the first month's rent and sufficient left over to put in a new bed and armchair. She had even been able to afford a portable TV and radio, and kit out the kitchen with a few pots, pans and other essentials. But even knowing she was sleeping on a clean mattress and eating off new plates didn't prevent her from feeling grubby about five minutes after she came in through the front door after a hard day at work.

Millie drank her tea and then, having set the alarm on her mobile, allowed her eyes to shut. Please, she thought, as she slipped off to sleep, please don't let me dream about

Luke yet again. It was ridiculous, she knew it, but she was unable to rid herself of the image of his face; the hurt look when she had screamed at him like a banshee to get out of her life. It was just a pathetic teenage crush. It was stupid and she needed to get over it. He had probably never given her another thought. Why should he? She was just a stupid kid who had shared a couple of weeks of his life as the hired help in a ski chalet. So maybe they had shared a couple of drinks too, and a few runs down the mountain, but why on earth was she kidding herself that she meant anything to him? And he was ten years older than her. And a bastard who had betrayed her.

Crossly she turned over on the bed and tried to get comfy. Stop it, stop it, she commanded her brain, but the image of him refused to fade.

How, thought Millie, could anyone ring a doorbell exuberantly – but Freya managed it. Millie flung open the door and greeted her friend with a broad smile.

'Hi, Freya. Did you manage to avoid the louts who normally hang around in the stairwell?'

'Piece of piss.'

'Piss and stairwell – hmm, why do those two words seem to belong together?'

'Yes, I had noticed,' said Freya, wrinkling her retroussé nose. 'You know, I could lend you more money if you want. I hate you living in this shithole. It really is rank.'

'No,' said Millie. 'I have got to manage on my own. I can't keep running back to you every time something goes wrong. It's ridiculous.'

'No it's not.'

'Yes it is. If I didn't have you I'd be forced to manage.'

'But that's my point. You do have me. You don't have to struggle.'

Millie shook her head. 'No. Thanks but no thanks. This place may be shabby, but it's getting there.'

'Getting where exactly? The municipal tip?'

'You're exaggerating.'

Freya didn't answer; she just looked pointedly at the state of the carpet and the cracks in the ceiling.

'The answer is still no,' said Millie, ignoring Freya's expression of disgust.

Freya shrugged. 'Well, if the roof falls in, you know where to find me.'

'Please,' said Millie in mock horror. 'When you're here will you *not* use phrases like "if the roof falls in". You're just tempting providence.'

Freya grinned and glanced at her watch. 'Look, I don't like to hurry you.'

'You're right. Besides, you don't want to leave your car unattended for a minute longer than necessary. The little scrotes round here will have it up on blocks and the wheels off in no time.'

'They wouldn't dare.'

'They would.'

'No they wouldn't. I flashed my library card at them and told them I was police.'

'You never! Surely they didn't believe you.'

'It seemed to work. Let's face it, none of them are going to have the first idea what a library card really does look like and I flashed it very fast. We'll know the truth if I still have tyres on my car. Now get your guitar and come along.'

Millie grabbed her kit and followed Freya back onto the landing. She locked the door carefully and ran down the stairs behind her friend. At the bottom, Freya was gulping in air.

'I had to hold my breath the whole way down. How can you stand it?'

'I guess I'm used to it. Besides, there are worse smells.'

'Yeah? Name three.'

As Millie could only think of one she kept silent. Freya scored a point in the air with her index finger, then set off again at a brisk pace to where her car was parked. A gang of young lads in baggy jeans and hooded sweatshirts were eyeing her Audi TT from the grandstand of a set of nearby concrete steps.

Millie heard her murmur that at least it still had all four tyres. With a confidence that hadn't been apparent from her last comment, Freya strode towards the vehicle and plipped her key.

'Thanks for keeping an eye on it, lads,' she said cheerfully to the youths. A couple shuffled their feet in embarrassment.

Millie opened the passenger door, shoved her guitar into the back and climbed in beside her.

Freya started the car and pulled away from the kerb. As she drove, the houses and flats that flanked the roads became steadily bigger and less rundown, the gardens tidier, the verges wider and greener, and the lighting better until they reached the big red-brick Victorian villas, ideal for student accommodation, that indicated they were almost at the campus.

'I wish—' began Freya.

But Millie interrupted her before she could finish the sentence.

'You may, but I don't.'

140

'What?' said Freya, sounding hurt and aggrieved.

'You want me to live somewhere like this. And you'll provide the cash.' Millie shifted around in the car seat so she could look at Freya. 'Don't think I don't appreciate this. I do. But I've lived on charity and handouts all my life. I want – *need* – to be free of all that. I've done with being beholden.'

Freya shot a smile at her friend. 'OK, OK. I'm just offering for the sake of my own conscience. After all, I don't have to live there.'

Freya swung the car through the main entrance to the university car park, found a slot and killed the engine.

'Ready to rock and roll?'

'Maybe not rock and roll. Not quite my style.'

'Whatever. You'll knock 'em dead.'

Millie grinned nervously. This gig meant more to her than she wanted to admit, even to herself. If it went well, maybe, just maybe, she'd get more work and be able to supplement her dire supermarket earnings. At the moment her wages allowed her to exist. She wanted to be able to *live*.

12

'Now I've softened you up with some old favourites, I thought I'd try something I wrote myself,' said Millie into the mic. So far that evening the audience had been attentive and appreciative but she wasn't entirely sure how much it was due to her choice of songs and how much the cheap beer. She peered through the lights that held her in their glare. From the small podium that had her raised above the students crammed round tables in the Union bar, she could just see Freya who was giving her the thumbs up. Well, of course her best friend thought it was a good idea. That's what friends did. Here goes nothing, thought Millie as she nervously checked the tuning and strummed a chord or two.

Flashing a smile at the audience, Millie launched into the first performance of the song she'd written in the quiet evenings in her slummy flat. This was new territory for her and her nerves were vibrating like the strings on her guitar. Suppose they loathed it? Suppose they booed?

'I was lost, I was alone, I needed help and there was none . . .'

She looked through the lights again at Freya. Freya nodded and smiled. Yeah, but she would. Millie had rehearsed this song so much she could sing it on autopilot and let her thoughts stray to judging reactions. She carried on to the end of the first verse and noted that the audience were still paying attention and not rummaging around for things to throw.

She changed key from minor to its relative major and began the refrain.

'I felt so low, I felt so blue, all the good times had bid adieu . . .'

Millie nervously stared through the lights again. She wondered briefly whether she resembled a rabbit caught in headlights. The room seemed to be still. No one was nodding or tapping their feet. That's it, thought Millie. The song is lame. The words don't work. She was pretty confident about the quality of the music. She understood enough about the mechanics of harmony and melody to know the tune worked. In fact, she would even go as far as to say she was proud of it. But the lyrics? What did she know about songwriting? They were probably completely dreadful. The thought only increased her nervousness as she sang on.

'Then through the clouds the sunshine poured. You smiled at me; I felt loved, adored.'

Millie could see Freya staring at her. A wooden, frozen expression on her face. Millie looked away, horrified. Oh bugger! It was worse than she thought. But she knew she couldn't just stop mid-verse. She had to carry on to the end. She determined not to wait for the reaction but to swing straight into something more acceptable; a spoonful of sugar to make the medicine go down.

'We lived, we loved, we laughed, we played, nothing could rain on my parade . . .'

Millie sang on, thankful that her voice remained steady

and her fingers were finding the frets and strings on their own. The thought that Freya, her best friend and biggest fan, was hating the song had completely knocked her sideways. She focused her gaze on the mic in front of her so she didn't have to look at anyone in the room. She probably looked cross-eyed as a result but that was the least of her worries.

'But life can be unfair, unfeeling, hearts get broken, love lies bleeding . . .'

A bit like this sodding song. She should have killed it at birth. It would have done the world a kindness.

'I must be strong, I can go on, I'm not broken, I'm not done . . .'

Except with this fuck-wit song. I'm done with that, she thought. Feeling ever more embarrassed by her lame-brain song, Millie wished that the last verse would be the next. She didn't dare alter anything, like skipping a line or two – if she did, her brain would be sure to seize right up and then she would look even more of a tit. As if that was possible. No, best she just concentrated on keeping the tempo steady, however tempting it was to let the whole thing career wildly out of control and over the cliff like the train smash that it was.

Thank God, the last refrain. Just a few more tortured seconds and the self-inflicted horror would be over – just like her career as a singer-songwriter.

'And I'll feel good and I'll feel high, I'll take my chances, I'll throw the dice . . .'

One last repeat and she could sing something good, something decent, something written by anyone but her.

She let her hand drop as the final chord hummed out.

Silence.

Well, no surprise there. She was about to launch into an old Neil Diamond number, always a crowd pleaser, when the applause started. And it built from a ripple to a wave to a tsunami that crashed over her. Claps, shouts, whistles, cheers, stamps . . . Millie looked up from the mic, bewildered. What the hell . . . ?

Then she saw Freya, charging across the room to her, tears streaming down her face. She had to fight the last few yards as, by then, the audience was on its feet and also surging towards Millie, but Freya, elbows jutting, barged through.

'Millie, Millie,' she yelled over the cacophony. 'Where did that come from? It was shit hot. Fab!'

'But I thought you hated it. When I caught sight of you at the start, you looked horrified.'

'I didn't. Couldn't have done. I was trying not to cry.' Freya dashed a hand across her face. 'The state of me. I must have mascara all over my face.'

Millie shook her head. 'You're fine.' She still felt dazed. This wasn't the reaction she was expecting. Freya's tears were catching. Millie felt her own eyes stinging. 'You really thought it was good?'

Freya gestured to the room. 'God, you're dim. Listen!' Around them the students continued to applaud and bay. 'You're going to have to do something, hon, or there's going to be a riot.'

Millie nodded. She found she was shaking. Not from nerves now but from excitement. She'd never had such approbation before. Her father had expected 'perfect' as standard. He'd never really praised her for anything and yet here was a roomful of strangers lauding her to the rafters. And she loved it. But how did she handle it?

'What should I do?' she yelled in Freya's ear.

Freya looked at her in astonishment. 'Sing, you moron. Sing.'

'What?'

'Your song. Sing it again. For fuck's sake, Millie, for someone with a Rolls-Royce talent you've got a Fiat Punto brain.'

Freya jumped off the podium, leaving Millie there alone. The applause began to subside.

'Thank you. You're very generous,' she almost whispered into the mic. Whoops and more applause greeted this. 'Right.' She took a deep breath, gathered herself and strummed a chord. 'This is a personal favourite of mine . . .'

'Stuff your favourite,' yelled a heckler. 'Give us that last song again.'

Millie shyly shook her head and began 'Cracklin' Rosie'. The bar erupted with whistles and catcalls and then a slow handclap. Millie stopped. A chant began in one corner and swept through the room to the front.

'Again, again, again, again . . .'

Millie held up her hand. 'You really did like it, didn't you? You weren't just having me on and being kind.'

The place erupted again. Freya smacked her forehead with the flat of her hand. What would it take to convince Millie?

Millie was still shaking when she sat in the staffroom at the back of the bar after her final set. Freya gathered up her things for her and put her guitar in its case.

'Millie Braythorpe, you are a dark horse. When did you learn to write a song like that?'

Millie shrugged. 'Dunno. I was messing around and it sort of came to me.'

There was a knock at the door and a tall, thin man with dark curly hair and a wide smile looked round the door.

'Can I come in?'

'Tim! Of course you can.' Freya turned to Millie. 'Millie, I want you to meet Tim.'

So this was the gorgeous man Freya had told her so much about and judging by his proximity to Freya and the body language between them, there was a lot more going on than Freya had hinted at. Millie was glad for Freya; Tim looked like a really nice guy. No one whose eyes twinkled like that and had such a friendly smile could be a complete bastard. Well, other than Luke of course.

Millie held out her hand. 'Hi.'

'You were awesome. Just fantastic. It takes a lot to impress that rabble. They've all been to the V festival and Live Aid and the like. They've seen all the big names, they've seen all the light shows that go with the gigs. I had my doubts about a bird with a guitar. I mean, I know Dido and K.T. Tunstall can pull it off . . .'

'Yeah, but they're pretty special,' said Millie.

'And so are you. You need more material. You're too good to sing cover versions.'

Millie blushed. All this praise in one evening. It was doing her head in.

'Anyway, I just popped in to say I'd like to book you again, maybe in the autumn.'

'Gosh,' said Millie. 'I'd love to come back.'

'And here's your fee.' He handed over a fat envelope.

Millie looked at it for a second before putting her hand out and taking it.

'I hope it's right. Do you want to count it?'

Millie glanced in the envelope. It contained a thick wad of tenners. 'Shit. Sorry, it can't be right. It's far too much.'

'Call the extra a bonus to make sure we get the repeat booking. Take it. You earned it.'

'You certainly did. Except for trying to get away with not playing that song a second time.'

'I thought they were taking the piss.'

Freya rolled her eyes. 'Trust me, if they were you'd have known about it. I've seen what was left of an act that died here. Not pretty.'

Millie stuffed her earnings in her bag. 'Well, thanks for getting me the gig. I'd buy you a drink but you've got to drive me home.'

'That's where you're wrong.'

'Oh. Right.' How presumptuous of her to expect Freya to chauffeur her both ways. Anyway, she had some cash now. She smiled brightly. 'Well, I'll get the drinks in and then order a taxi.'

'You'll do no such thing. I'm not driving you home because you and I are going to celebrate and I'm not risking my car after dark in the shithole where you choose to live. You're staying in my room tonight. I'll take you home in the morning.'

'Oh,' said Millie in a small voice.

Freya zipped up the guitar case and slung it over her shoulder. 'Coming, Tim?'

'Stuff to do here. But thanks for the invite. Enjoy your celebrations.' He loped out the door.

'Nice bloke,' said Millie.

'And a fantastic shag,' said Freya with a sigh and a wistful look.

'Really? So you and he . . . ?'

'I should coco. Took a bit of work though. Thought I'd lost my touch. Still,' she added cheerfully, 'it's nice to know he's not easy.'

Millie nodded sagely. But what did she know?

'Come on,' said Freya. Millie followed her friend out of the room and into the bar which was almost empty now. A couple of students who were clearing away glasses and mopping tables shouted some compliments to Millie as she made her way to the exit.

'Where are we going?' she asked Freya.

'My room. I've got some fizz on ice.'

Millie grinned to herself in the dark as she walked beside her friend. No beer or cheap Alco pops for her mate Freya. And knowing Freya, it was probably going to be Krug or Cristal. Yum. When she had gone to live at Freya's, her friend had been shocked to discover that Millie had never even tasted Cava let alone quality champagne and had taken the matter in hand. Millie now had a great stock of knowledge about proper champers although sadly she could not afford to apply it – except when Freya was around.

Freya unlocked the door of her room and switched the light on. Standard student room it might have been but Freya had added expensive touches that made it anything but standard; and the lighting certainly wasn't. Millie was sure that dimmer switches weren't normal, for a start. Nor was the small fridge that sat on the corner of the desk.

'Ta-dah,' said Freya opening the fridge door and pulling out a champagne bottle. Millie noted it was Cristal and that there were several others beside it. Bliss. 'Do me a favour, get the glasses down.' She waved the bottle in the direction of the top shelf where Millie could see a selection of cut glass. She climbed on Freya's bed and picked up two lead crystal champagne flutes. Obviously Freya hadn't been kitted out from Ikea like the rest of the student population in the country.

Freya got the cork off without spilling a drop and expertly filled the two glasses. Then she raised hers. 'To Millie – superstar.'

Millie giggled. 'Hardly.'

Freya gave her a steely stare. 'But you're going to be. Trust me on this.' She chinked her glass against Millie's, took a large swig and then flopped down onto her bed. Millie pulled the chair out from under the desk to sit on.

'So,' said Freya. 'Who was the inspiration?'

'How do you mean?'

'Come off it, Mil. Who was the heel that broke your heart?' A thought struck Freya. 'Ohmigod. Tell me it wasn't Alex-the-arsehole.'

Millie shook her head. 'No, it was most certainly *not* Alex-the-arsehole.'

'Thank God for that. Hideous thought.'

'What, that he broke my heart?'

'Don't be stupid. That you are still carrying a candle for him after what he did to you, the sod!'

Millie shook her head.

'So who was it?'

'No one.'

'Don't talk bollocks. That song was really heartfelt. You don't make up feelings like that, you experience them. *Like you did.* So who was the bastard who broke your heart like that?'

'No one.'

Freya took a sip of her champagne and tapped her beautifully manicured fingernails on the headboard of her bed. She leaned forward. 'Please don't bullshit me, Millie. I'm the one doing a degree. That means I am officially "not dim". This was someone you met when you were skiing, right?'

Millie nodded. 'I made a fool of myself.' She recounted the tale of liking Luke and confiding in him, so much so that it had ended with the mass sacking.

'The bastard. The utter prick.' Freya was livid. Incandescent. 'The total and complete shit.'

'I shouldn't have fallen for him. I wouldn't have confided in him if I hadn't.'

'Whoa.' Freya held up a warning hand. 'You are NOT taking the blame for this one, Mil. Alex-the-arsehole was your mistake. You fell in love with a guy you thought was a nice lad and who loved you back, when all he really wanted was a shag. You were such a sweet innocent that you thought him asking you if you were "all right" meant exactly that and wasn't an oblique reference to your contraceptive arrangements. And even afterwards you were too dim to take the morning-after pill. You were stupid.' Millie was used to the fact that Freya shot from the hip but what she said still stung, even if it was entirely true. 'But this time you did nothing wrong except confide in a guy you thought you could trust. This was out-and-out betrayal. Which doesn't make it your fault.'

Millie sipped her champagne and wondered why it happened to her. What was it about her that made people she thought she could trust let her down so badly. She'd always been a good, dutiful and loving daughter to her mother and she felt she had been a friend to Luke and that he liked her. So why had both of them thrown it back in her face? First her mother, now Luke. She felt that somewhere along the line there might be a third person waiting to do the dirty on her. Didn't bad things always happen in threes?

13

'You've got to forget about the girl,' said Archie, stifling a yawn. They'd been in the pub round the corner from Luke's new flat in Chiswick, the one he'd finally moved into after his protracted stay with Archie, for almost an hour now and all Luke had done was bang on about Millie. Archie wouldn't have minded so much if he'd been able to see the big screen over the bar showing Wimbledon highlights but there was a pillar between him and it so he had nothing to distract him from the monotony of Luke's moaning. He was seriously thinking of sloping back to his own pad and leaving Luke to it.

Luke stared into his pint of bitter as if the answer could be found in the froth at the top. 'Easier said than done. I mean, she's just disappeared. If I knew where she'd gone, if I knew she was OK, I wouldn't worry so much.'

'No, you'd be out there chasing her and trying to lay her. Come off it, Luke, the only reason you're obsessed by her is that you didn't score.'

Luke pushed his beer away angrily and it slopped on the table. 'Now just a minute—'

'Joke, joke,' said Archie hurriedly, holding his hands up.

Luke snorted, still cross. 'But she just disappeared.'

'So you've said. About a hundred times.'

'Something upset her in France. It wasn't me, I'm sure of it. I mean, I couldn't have done. I didn't say anything to her before she just vanished. I want to know what it was.'

Archie took a pull of his beer. 'So she had a row with one of the other reps. She was embarrassed about what she said to Pat and couldn't face her. She got outrageously drunk and shagged her boss.' Luke glowered at Archie for suggesting such a thing. Archie shrugged. 'Does it matter?'

'It does to me.'

'Then do something about it. Stop moping around.'

'As I have just said, easier said than done.'

Archie seriously considered leaving Luke to stew. He was no company – hadn't been for weeks now. That was the trouble with Luke, when something needled him he was like a terrier with a rat. Nothing would induce him to drop the subject.

He'd been tedious about Julia and her hang-ups but at least when the end came Luke had managed to move on. But this Millie business had left him in limbo and Luke obviously needed closure. Archie scratched his head. He had to think of something to stop Luke driving him nuts, moaning on about the sainted Millie and her mysterious disappearance. Obviously now was not the moment to suggest to Luke that Millie had discovered he had a tendency to be a single-issue bore and had changed her identity to escape his clutches.

Although, right now, it was tempting.

'What about tracking down her mate Freya Fairbrother?'

'How?' said Luke, not even giving the matter consideration.

'I don't know. You're the gossip columnist. Surely a rich bitch like that gets noticed about the place.'

'She's not living at home at the moment, that's all I know.'

Archie sighed. Gawd, this was like pulling teeth. 'Then find out where she is living. The Fairbrothers have staff, don't they? There's never been a char lady yet who wouldn't spill the beans for a wad of notes.'

'Trouble is, if Millie and Freya are as close as I think they are, Freya is hardly likely to tell me anything, is she? That is, even if I track her down. I mean, she'll have only heard Millie's side of the story.'

'But you don't know what Millie's side of the story was, you pillock. You have no idea why this bird has gone to ground. It may have nothing whatsoever to do with you, which you have already assured me is the case. She may have been abducted by aliens, or welcomed back into the bosom of her family.'

Luke snorted at this second idea as being even more preposterous than the first one. Millie had had a steely glint in her eyes when she'd told him she didn't want to see her parents again. He didn't think she had looked or sounded as if she was going to change her mind in the near future.

Archie ignored the snort and carried on. 'She may have seen the light and taken holy orders. She may have been offered a recording contract and is currently working in a studio in LA. You have no idea.' Archie sat back, hoping against hope that his speech would mean an end to it.

'That's just it. I have no idea.'

Archie finished his pint and stood up. 'Well, I've got a deadline and an early start – oh, and I also have a life – so, much as I would love to spend the rest of the evening speculating on the whereabouts of young Millie Braythorpe, I'm off.'

'Yeah, bye.' Luke didn't even look up as his mate left the

pub. Millie couldn't just disappear into thin air. She had to be somewhere. And Luke was determined to find her. He'd been obsessing about Millie since she'd disappeared. She'd got under his skin like no other woman he had ever met and he kept imagining that he saw her everywhere he went; every redhead he spotted he stared at, just in case. In bars or clubs, on the tube or across the street, he kept thinking he saw her and then . . . If he was going to retain his sanity he had to think of a plan.

Maybe her parents knew something. Millie hadn't sounded as though she'd been close to her dad, but what about her mum?

He decided he had to find a way of getting hold of Mrs Braythorpe. If he just pitched up there she might well be suspicious. If he was supposed to be a friend of Millie's he'd know she'd left home and there would be no use trying to find her in Westhampton. If he wasn't, then why was he snooping? Anyway, it was unlikely that any mother would tell a complete stranger the ins and outs of a family row, let alone the wife of a man who got quite as many column inches as Bishop Braythorpe. The Bishop might have always been in the press but as far as Luke was aware Millie and her mum had managed to avoid any exposure at all. This probably meant they were both very wary of the press or talking to anyone apart from their closest friends. No, Luke reckoned Mrs Braythorpe would be very suspicious of any approach from a stranger. He had to find a way of getting her to come to him. And there was a method he'd used before as a hack and it might work again.

Hannah Braythorpe dried her badly cared for hands on her apron and hurried towards the front door. She glanced nervously at her husband's study as she passed it, hoping that the doorbell hadn't disturbed his meeting. They weren't expecting visitors but that didn't stop people just dropping by. That was the trouble with being the Bishop's wife, the inhabitants of the entire diocese all thought they could pitch up when they felt like it. She stopped by the mirror in the hall and pushed her fingers through her lank mousy hair to get it out of her eyes which stared back at her miserably. There were shadows under them and her cheeks were hollow. The pretty looks of her youth had long since faded and since Millie's disappearance she now looked positively haggard. At least in the past Millie had given her a dozen reasons to smile each day but her smile lines had gone and her mouth now had a permanent droop. When was the last time she'd felt happy? she wondered. Certainly not since Millie's abrupt departure. She turned away from the mirror and lifted the heavy latch.

'Hello,' she said to the complete stranger who was studying the ancient architecture of the house. Neither the presence of a stranger nor his interest in the house was a surprise to Hannah; half the people who came to the house were unknown to her and the Bishop's palace was a particularly fine building to look at. A nightmare to live in but the visitors didn't care about that; as far as they were concerned, Hannah was incredibly lucky to live in such a beautiful property. Huh, if only they knew the reality.

The young man shifted his gaze from the mullioned windows and ornate Tudor brickwork and transferred it to her.

'Hi,' he said. 'I'm looking for Millie Braythorpe.'

Hannah stared at him and wondered who the man was. He didn't sound like anyone she would expect Millie to be friends with. But then who were Millie's friends these days?

'I'm afraid she doesn't live here any more.'

'Oh, bugger.' There was a short pause, and no apology for the profanity, Hannah noticed. 'Can you tell me where I can find her then?'

'No,' said Hannah flatly. As if she'd tell a complete stranger such information, even if she knew herself. 'Why do you want her?'

The bloke gestured at a white van parked in the gravel drive. 'Got a package for her.'

'I can take it in for her.'

'Sorry. I need her to sign. Personally.'

'Then I can't help.'

'Never mind.'

The man walked away.

Hannah had a thought. If Millie was getting a package, perhaps it was from someone she'd had recent contact with. Glancing hurriedly behind her to make sure her husband was still occupied with his meeting, she swiftly made up her mind. 'Stop,' she called out. The delivery man turned and ambled back.

'What is it, love?'

Hannah bridled. She hated strangers being familiar. 'What'll happen to the package if you can't deliver it?'

'Search me, love. I take it back to the depot and after that, who knows? I'm just paid to drive and deliver. But I expect they get rid of the unwanted stuff somehow – return it to the sender, I expect.'

'Who is that?'

The man gave her a long stare. 'You're asking a lot of questions, ain't you, lady? If Millie Braythorpe doesn't live here then it's no concern of yours, is it?'

'No,' said Hannah. But it was. Despite the fact that her husband had said that Millie was never to set foot in the house again, Hannah was shrivelling with anxiety that something dreadful had happened to her only daughter. Despite being expressly forbidden by her husband, she'd asked Jim Fairbrother if he knew anything about Millie's whereabouts but he was as clueless as she was. He in turn had quizzed Freya who only said Millie had gone to work abroad. She refused to be more specific. Abroad? So just the whole world to search.

'I would just like to know. I . . .' she paused to control her voice. 'I haven't seen my daughter for a while. I'm worried.' She couldn't completely disguise the catch in her voice, despite her efforts.

The delivery man seemed to take pity on her. 'Look, it's against company rules to let the wrong people sign for stuff but I don't think there's anything to say you can't look at the return address. How about that?'

'Thank you, you are most kind.'

The man went to the van and fetched a padded envelope. 'Just don't tell anyone I let you do this.'

Hannah read the name on the envelope. Luke Hastings. It didn't mean anything to her. 'Just a minute.' Hannah nipped inside again and grabbed the notebook from beside the phone in the hall. She copied the name and address down carefully and handed the package back. She wasn't sure what she was going to do with the information but maybe it might lead to something.

She shut the door behind the delivery man and glanced again at the shut door of the study. The voices emanating from behind it rumbled on. The meeting was obviously still in full swing.

Hannah climbed the wide shallow stairs to the second floor of the rambling house. She let herself into Millie's bedroom and sat on her daughter's bed, gazing at the muddle of belongings her daughter had left behind when she had fled after That Row: the pinboard with pictures of her friends from school, the half-read books by the bed, the bits of cheap jewellery she'd picked up at jumble sales spilling out of a box, her teddy on the pillow. At least now she could sit here without being overwhelmed by tears. For the first few weeks Hannah had been unable to set foot in the room without grief sweeping through her. As the days went by she found the courage to search the room, rather than sit and sob, in the hope that she might find something that would give her a sign as to where Millie might be. Every article she'd picked up or turned over, every drawer she'd opened had brought back a memory of Millie: Millie reading; Millie doing her homework; Millie going to the Sno-Zone. And each memory had been as painful as being dragged through barbed wire. Now, after all these months, she knew there wasn't a single clue to be found. Millie was gone and Hannah didn't have the first idea where. And worse than the sense of loss and the memories was her guilt. She ought to have stood up to Malcolm. She should have sided with Millie. But she'd been weak and pathetic and refused to believe that her husband, the father of her only child, would actually carry out his threat to throw her out.

Hannah came here now, not to try to find some overlooked morsel of evidence as to where her daughter might be, but just to feel close to her. These belongings of Millie's were the only contact she had with her.

Having tried to commune with her missing daughter, she thought she might try communing with God, although she wasn't sure that there was any point any more. None of her prayers for months had been answered – not that she told the Bishop any of this. He would have just snorted and said that she was being foolish and selfish and she ought to be praying for more important things. But what was more important to a mother than her only child?

She clasped her hands and prayed that Luke Hastings might hold a key. Then she tiptoed downstairs to the kitchen and phoned directory enquiries.

Luke looked at the flashing orange light on his answer machine when he got through the door. Could this be the call he wanted? A week ago, he and a snapper had hired a white van, to try to get access through the tradesmen's entrance of a country house hotel so as to get some shots and gossip regarding a big celeb wedding that was taking place there. It hadn't taken much to convince the snapper that Luke needed to get to the venue via Westhampton. They didn't get the wedding story or any usable shots but it had been a fun day out and they'd had a laugh over a pint before heading back to London in the afternoon. Not that Luke cared one way or another about the celeb wedding; all he was interested in was whether Mrs Braythorpe would take the bait of the fake parcel.

It had worked like a charm and seemed to confirm his hunch that Millie's row had been more with her Puritan father than with her mother. He'd also had a hunch that whatever the reasons for Millie not wishing to go home, her mother would be worried sick by the lack of contact. Under the circumstances it would be only natural for her to grasp at any straw floating past. He pacified his conscience – it was a bit of a mean trick to play on her worry – with the knowledge that he could tell her lots about how Millie had been in France and assure Mrs Braythorpe that her daughter was very much alive and well and in good health. Also, although he wasn't planning on engineering a reconciliation, at least he could act as a go-between if he made contact with Millie and if both parties were amenable.

He pressed the button and a hesitant voice stumbled over an initial sentence. His heart jumped as he recognised the soft voice.

'Hello . . . er . . . Mr Hastings. You don't know me but . . . er . . . I am hoping you know my daughter, Millie Bray-thorpe. I am . . . er . . . sorry to bother you but you tried to send her a parcel the other day. I traced you from the return address on it.' There was a pause. 'Look . . . er . . . Mr Hastings, I really need to talk to you. Could you give me a ring?' She left a number. 'Er . . . Sunday morning would be good . . . er . . . if you could manage it. I look forward to hearing from you. Bye.'

Luke played the message again, this time jotting down the number. He reckoned he'd been right, that she was desperate to talk to anyone who might have a lead. Not that he did, but as a gossip columnist he could bet his bottom dollar that he might be able to make far better use of any information she might have than she would herself. If he could just winkle that information out of her . . . Once he had it, he might have a chance of finding her daughter. Of course, whether or not Millie would want to re-establish contact with either of them was a moot point.

Still, at least her ringing him indicated that she wanted to talk – and if he called, as she had requested, on a Sunday morning, it seemed likely that she didn't want her husband to know about any of this. In which case she might be ready to tell him more than he'd hoped for.

Luke recognised Mrs Braythorpe's voice as soon as she answered the phone, but he played dumb. He was pretty certain that she wouldn't associate the estuary-English vowels and dropped consonants of the yob deliveryman with the slightly more educated tones of the real Luke Hastings.

'Can I speak to Mrs Braythorpe, please?' he inquired politely. He imagined her standing in the hall of the monstrous old building, probably feeling cold, despite the fact that it was summer – blimey, Millie hadn't exaggerated the awfulness of the palace. When he'd met Mrs Braythorpe he'd been struck by her likeness to her daughter. She must have been pretty in her youth but now she looked careworn and gaunt. Was that the result of age, Millie's departure or living with the Bishop? However, one thing Luke was now certain of, the message on his machine confirmed it – Mrs Braythorpe was worried sick about her daughter.

'Speaking.'

'You asked me to call you.' Luke left a pause. He wanted to emphasise the fact that he was doing her the favour and that she had instigated the dialogue. 'I'm Luke Hastings. You left a message on my phone.' Luke heard a little gasp of relief. 'You said Sunday morning.' He wondered what excuse she had given her husband for not attending matins.

'Oh, Mr Hastings. I am so glad you got my message. This is awfully kind of you.'

'What can I do for you? I gather you want some information about Millie.'

'Yes. Yes I do. You know her?'

'A bit. I met her in the Easter holidays. She was working abroad.'

'How . . . how was she?'

'Fine.' Luke gave her a rundown of how Millie had appeared to him, omitting the bit about singing in the bar. Mrs Braythorpe might not be quite so Puritan as her husband but he didn't want to make life for Millie any trickier than it already was. As he finished, he injected a puzzled note into his voice. He didn't want to sound as if he knew more than the bare facts. 'Tell me . . . No, sorry, it would be prying.'

'Mr Hastings . . .'

'Luke, please.'

'What is it you want to know?'

'Well, I just wondered why you are asking me about your daughter?'

'Millie left home last year. She . . . er . . . she had a falling out with her father.'

'The Bishop.'

'Yes. He's not an easy man and he has his position to think of. Well, he and Millie had a difference of opinion and she left. I've heard nothing from her since.'

'But surely she has friends. Don't they keep in touch with her? Don't they know how she is?'

'Yes, but I think she told them not to pass on any information.'

'I see.'

'I was wondering . . . I thought they might talk to you.'

Yessss! He hoped his voice sounded impassive; bored even. 'Yes, but I don't know any of them.'

'Supposing I gave you some names and addresses?'

Luke pretended to think about it. 'But is it ethical?' he asked. He didn't want to sound too keen.

'Oh.' Mrs Braythorpe sounded flustered. 'Oh, I hadn't thought of that. I just thought that as her mother I wouldn't be doing any harm just wanting to know how she is.'

'I'm sure it's OK,' said Luke smoothly. Shit, he just wanted to sound a bit reticent, he hadn't wanted to frighten her off. He was desperate to get hold of Millie again. He was losing sleep over the girl, he was besotted with her and he was beside himself with worry over her sudden disappearance. He had to know it wasn't anything he'd done. He couldn't bear it if she had suddenly found she had reason to hate him. Why else would she have turned on him like that? Of course he wasn't going to add to Mrs Braythorpe's worry by telling her that Millie had done a disappearing act a second time. 'Is there a special friend that she had? Maybe if I started there.'

'Freya Fairbrother. That's who you should ask first. She's gone to university. The secretary at the cathedral school says she won a place at Saltford. She's studying history.'

'Saltford's a big place, Mrs Braythorpe.'

'It's all I know. Freya's . . . well, she's very outgoing. I expect people will know her there.'

'I'll see what I can do. I can't make any promises. I'll call you when I know anything. Is any particular time convenient?'

'Sunday mornings are good for me. I really appreciate this, Luke.'

'No promises, Mrs Braythorpe. I may not get anywhere at all.'

14

Millie pulled her mobile out of her pocket and hit the answer button.

'Hi, Freya. What can I do for you?'

'Fancy coming for a drink tonight?'

Shit, that was a tempting prospect. Trouble was, she knew she didn't have enough money for a drink *and* supper. It was a case of either or.

'And before you say you can't afford it, you won't be paying. I have a proposition to put to you.'

Millie had heard this sort of line from Freya before. The propositions were usually something along the lines of Freya wanting to borrow back a piece of clothing that had been hers in the first place and which she had given to Millie. And then deciding that whatever item it was had never suited her so Millie might as well keep it anyway. But by that time it was too late, the drinks had been bought and Millie was once again left with the feeling that she should have made more of an effort to stump up for a round herself. But Freya had an expensive taste in booze and Millie, if she were scrupulously honest, was always faintly relieved she had escaped the bar bill again.

'Look, if I come out for a drink I'm going to pay my way.'

'No, this is a proper proposition. Honest.'

Millie wasn't convinced.

'Tim's going to be there too. Actually, it's his proposition really.'

Millie felt a stirring of curiosity. 'I'm still getting a round in,' she said defiantly.

'Good. Whatever.' Freya didn't sound as though she'd been listening at all. 'We'll pick you up at eight.'

'Eight then. Bye.'

Millie slipped her phone back in her pocket and got back to shelf stacking. Strictly speaking the staff at the supermarket weren't supposed to take personal calls in the company's time but as Millie was aware that the manager valued her magical abilities with handling stroppy customers, he wasn't going to sack her for a peccadillo like that. And both he and Millie knew it.

She glanced at her watch. Three o'clock. Only a couple of hours more and she was finished for the day. Thank goodness for that. She had an idea for another song that had been plaguing her all day and she really wanted to get home and try it out on her guitar. Since her success at the Union bar she'd been spurred on to try out a number of other ideas. She wasn't sure about these ones either, no more than she had been with that first attempt which had been such a wow, but that glimpse of public acclaim had given her a tiny seedling of faith in her ability. Furthermore, she was determined to make something of it now that she was shot of her father's withering opinion of her and her musical ability. That huge rolling wave of applause that she had experienced – applause from complete strangers – had given her more of a lift, more confidence than any amount of kind words from her friends.

'I don't understand it,' Freya had said. 'You must have

had tons of applause when you worked in that bar in France.'

'But I thought they were applauding songs they liked, not my playing.'

And Freya had shaken her head and told Millie to 'get a grip and believe it now', which Millie, to her amazement, found she really could.

The rest of the afternoon crawled, as did the bus ride home. Finally Millie let herself into her flat which, thanks to the bonus she'd had from the gig at the Union, was looking vastly improved – almost clean and welcoming. Several bright rugs covered up the worst of the carpet, there were a couple of table lamps with stylish shades which made the lighting much softer and she'd also managed to find some made-to-measure curtains that she both liked and could afford. It was almost pleasant, she thought, as she kicked off her shoes and padded into the kitchen to make tea and toast.

Five minutes later she carried her mug and plate through to her bedroom – or sitting room, depending on what time of day it was – and got her guitar out. Half an hour after that the butter on her toast had congealed and her tea was stone cold but she had the beginnings of another song down on paper. She strummed it through to herself again, trying to hear it from a stranger's point of view. Did the harmonies work, were the chords right? Tcht, she wished she could tell.

She put her guitar down and gulped her cold tea and ate her toast. Her stomach rumbled in appreciation. Trouble was, she was still hungry. She returned to the kitchen and checked her cupboards, more in hope than expectation that there might be some overlooked treat hidden there. As she'd feared, all she had was the heel of a loaf and a couple of tins of beans. She really needed to shop but she had the rent to pay. It was four days till she got paid again but the rent was due in two. Hmm, roof or food? Tough choice. Perhaps she shouldn't have splashed out on the luxuries for her flat. Too late now to regret that extravagance; she could hardly take the lamps and rugs back after this amount of time. Beans on toast it was again then, she thought glumly as she pulled a tin off the shelf. She wondered what Freya was having. Something a whole lot more tasty, she was sure. And more filling.

Freya arrived on the dot of eight and swept into Millie's flat as soon as the door was opened.

'Hey, Mil.' She looked around. 'It's almost stopped looking like a slum.'

'Thanks, Freya. You really know how to raise morale.'

'I am never going to say anything to encourage you to stay in this dump. The sooner you move out, the happier I'll be.'

'Then you're going to be miserable for the foreseeable future. I'm staying put. I can afford the rent.' Millie wasn't going to mention her recent decision between nice food or the rent. 'And, besides which, I've made it my home.'

'Well, at least it's *your* home now and you don't seem to be sharing it with cockroaches and other vermin.'

'I never did.'

'No?' Freya lifted a perfectly plucked eyebrow. 'Come on. Let's rescue Tim before he gets mugged.'

She and Millie skipped down the noisome stairs and over to Tim's car – which, Millie noticed, was just as new and almost as flash as Freya's. She got into the back and sank into the soft leather seats, luxuriating in the air-con and the comfort.

'Where are we going?'

'The Fisherman. It'll be nice by the canal on an evening like this. Besides which, the food is good.'

'Oh, I've eaten,' said Millie quickly.

'Not properly, I bet. What was it? Beans on toast?'

Millie lapsed into silence. She wondered how she was going to be able to get out of an expensive meal. She simply couldn't let Freya pick up the bill. Maybe the cost of a steak and chips was only small change to her but Millie couldn't, *wouldn't*, live off her generosity.

The journey continued in silence until Tim swung the car into the car park. It was already crowded and they had to hunt for a space.

'You two go and bag a table. I'll get the drinks in. What'll you have, Millie?'

'Oh, just a mineral water for me. Could you ask for some ice and lemon as well?'

'Tim doesn't buy water. Thinks it's pathetic.'

'No it isn't,' said Millie defiantly. 'Besides, I'm thirsty.'

'Millie'll have some fizz. And so will I, Tim darling, so best you get a bottle. And get some decent stuff.'

'That's more like it,' said Tim, immediately heading for the bar.

'But—'

'No buts,' said Freya. 'Besides, Tim wants to butter you up about something so just drink it up and think of England. Or maybe that should be France as it's champagne. Anyway, enjoy it.'

'But champagne!'

'You know you like it.'

Millie sighed; she knew when she was beaten. She really didn't want to seem churlish but it was sometimes very difficult being so constantly strapped for cash when your best friend was as rich as Croesus.

'Listen,' said Freya, 'Tim wants a big favour off you. You know there's no such thing as a free lunch – or in this case a free dinner – so don't get all righteous on me and start offering to pay. I said I'd only persuade you to come out tonight if he made a big fuss of you and wined and dined you.'

Millie knew she was beaten – again. This was getting habit-forming. She followed Freya to a table near the canal and admired the swans and ducks gliding about on water while she waited for her drink and luxuriated in the warm sun of a beautiful early summer evening.

'So how are things between you and Tim?' she said to fill the lazy silence.

'Tim's fab. Wonderful. I even took him home a couple of weeks ago. Mum adores him too.'

'And your dad?' Freya's dad was hugely wary of Freya's friends, always worrying they only liked her because of the family fortune.

'He was cool too. I think it's because Tim is "old money". His dad owns a big place in Oxfordshire. I've been there. It makes the palace look poky but at least his dad heats their home and has heard of indoor lavs.'

Millie smiled. As usual Freya was exaggerating. She wondered just how big the Oxfordshire house was, but if Tim's family was rich it explained his car and the fact that Tim hadn't worried about the cost of the drinks – and possibly why he and Freya had initially been attracted to each other. Millie immediately dismissed that last thought as being cynical and unfair.

Tim returned after a while, complaining about the queue

but clasping a bottle of chilled Bollinger, two glasses, a pint of bitter and the menu. He gave the fizz to Freya to open ('She does it so much more expertly than me'), handed the menu to Millie ('The steaks are wonderful here') and took a long slurp from his pint.

'So what is it that you want from me, Tim?' asked Millie, watching Freya pour the foaming liquid faultlessly into the two flutes.

'Blimey, you're about as subtle as a boot in the balls, aren't you?'

'God, I'm sorry.' Millie blushed with embarrassment. 'That sounded so rude.'

'No worries,' said Tim, grinning. 'So Freya has told you I want a favour.'

Millie took a sip of her chilled champagne. Bliss. 'Yes and I'm dying to know what it is. With all this,' she waved a hand at the champagne bottle and the menu, 'I'm wondering what it is that you think you have to schmooze me quite so much. I'm assuming it's legal,' she added as a joke.

Freya leaned across the table. 'Millie is a very proper lady. Her dad is in the Church. She has standards and morals, unlike most of the corrupt individuals you mix with.'

Tim shook his head with a sigh. 'It's all very proper, I promise. I'm helping my dad organise a charity ball to take place at the end of the summer. I need some live music and I'd like to book you.'

'Oh my goodness,' said Millie, almost choking on her champagne.

'There'll be other bands, about half a doz, I hope, all playing different types of music so there'll be something for everyone. It'll be for every age group so we have to have everything from dance bands to hip hop.'

'Blimey. It's a really big bash then.'

'Huge,' chipped in Freya. 'And he's got a load of A-list celebs who have already said they'll come. It'll be monster. It'll be in all the press and mags. And you, Millie, are going to be the star of the show.'

Millie felt as though she'd suddenly entered some sort of parallel universe. A couple of hours before she had been wondering how she was going to eat properly till her pay cheque went into her bank and now she'd been promised a gig that might showcase her in front of people who might make all the difference to her career.

'But A-list celebs? I mean . . .' Millie's jaw hung a little slackly as she contemplated the hows and whys of a university student having that sort of clout.

'Actually, they're my dad's contacts,' said Tim. 'He's organising the ball really. It's for one of his good causes. I'm just doing the donkey work like booking the marquees and getting caterers and florists. But if I tell him how good you are he'll give you a platform. He trusts my judgement.'

Millie took a sip of her champagne while her head tried to catch up with the information. She wondered just who his dad was. 'Old money' was how Freya had described him, but obviously this was 'old money' that had clout and contacts. Millie thought about asking exactly who Tim's dad was but it seemed rather rude. She had a feeling she might be intimidated by the information if she knew.

'What's the cause?' she asked, to fill the gap.

'Fuck knows – some charity my dad is involved with. He thinks me helping him organise the ball will give me something to do over the long vac; stop me getting into trouble.'

Millie didn't really care what the cause was. It was a

fantastic opportunity for her, that was all that mattered for the moment. 'And when's the event exactly?'

'Mid-September, so a few weeks from now. You will do it, won't you?'

'But A-listers will expect proper bands.' Millie hesitated. She didn't want to appear ungrateful but she had always been a realist. 'I mean, no one has ever heard of me. Don't these guys expect the likes of Eric Clapton or Elton John to provide the cabaret?'

'They'll be getting enough names to keep them happy. Trust me.'

Beside him Freya nodded in agreement. 'Honest, Tim and his dad have already got several really big acts on board.'

Millie slumped back in her chair. This was just mad. Stuff like this didn't happen to people like her. She took a swig of champagne and tried to make sense of it all.

'Look, if you don't want to do it, we don't want to pressure you,' said Freya as Tim leant across and topped up her glass. 'We just thought it would be a bit of an opportunity for you.'

'A bit of an opportunity? Are you kidding! It's just . . . Look, it's one thing playing in a bar in France or at the Student Union, but what you're offering . . . Well, I'm not sure I'm ready for it.'

Freya shook her head. 'Yes you are. We wouldn't ask if we didn't think you were.'

'Besides which, you are just fantastic at judging what the audience likes. You seem to know instinctively what they want to hear. It's a real talent.'

'Thanks,' said Millie shyly.

'There is one other thing,' said Tim.

'What?' said Millie faintly.

'The cover versions you sing are fab. You are brilliant at choosing the right stuff for your audience, getting the mood right, appealing to their taste, but I'd really like you to do some more of your own songs. Everyone loved what you did at the Union. And this is such an ideal opportunity for you to push your song-writing career you really ought to take advantage of it. Could you do that?'

'How many?'

'As many as you can.'

Millie let out a long breath. 'I've done a few more. It's just, I really don't know if they are any good. I'm too close to them. I can't tell.'

'Play them to us,' said Tim. 'We'll tell you if they're OK.'

'Tim knows about music.' Freya detected a hint of doubt in Millie's face. 'He does, honest.'

Millie didn't want to sound patronising, but Freya had told her he was an IT student. Just because he was in charge of entertainment at the Union bar didn't make him Pete Waterman.

'OK,' said Millie slowly, not convinced.

'Tell her about your dad, Tim.'

'Tell me what?'

'My dad,' said Tim, 'is Lord Crendon.'

The mad parallel universe that Millie had found herself in had suddenly got a whole lot more mad. 'Lor-lor-lord Crendon? The founder of the Peer Group record label?'

'Yup,' said Tim.

Perhaps that did make him Pete Waterman, thought Millie, swallowing nervously. She had been right – knowing about Tim's dad was intimidating. No, more than that, really scary! 'So that's how you have some contacts.' She was hoping she sounded casual because, inside, her vital organs were doing weird things and she didn't feel as though she was in complete charge of even basic stuff any more; basic stuff like breathing.

'That's right.'

'And can get the headline bands.'

Tim nodded again.

'But I still don't understand why me?'

'Because, Millie, you're fucking good,' said Tim. 'Now will you just put that in your pipe and smoke it and hurry up and choose something to eat before we all die of starvation.'

15

It had been a few years since Luke had last been on a
university campus but things didn't seem to have
changed much. There was still the same mix of the swotty
and the laid back; the trendy and the radical. He mooched
through the grounds, observing the students lounging on
the grass in the summer sun, pretending to revise for exams
but in reality just soaking up the rays; he watched the ones
strolling along the gravel paths in no hurry to get anywhere
or do anything, he noticed those leaning against trees or
loafing on benches, having given up all pretence that they
had anything they ought to be getting on with and were just
reading or chatting to pass the time. Lucky bastards, he
thought to himself. He remembered how idle and idyllic the
majority of his university days had been, with few worries
and less work. Real life would come up and bite them on the
bum soon enough. But good luck to them till it did.

He was looking for the Student Union. He ambled on,
anonymous, invisible, one person amongst hundreds of
others, most of whom were strangers to each other anyway.
It took him about quarter of an hour of aimless wandering
before he stumbled on the place. He'd hoped it would have
had an obvious sign like 'Student Union'; the name 'Soosoo'
hadn't registered on his brain to start with. He was walking

past the sign for the second time when the penny dropped. S-U-S-U – Saltford University Student Union – Soosoo. Oh, the wit and wisdom of the student fraternity, he thought, forgetting that he had been one of the fraternity once, with the same level of wit and wisdom.

Luke pushed open the door and found himself in a typical Union bar: lino floor, pool table, stained deal tables and bench seats around the walls, huge serving counter and an all-pervading smell of stale beer and cigarettes. A young man behind the bar was bottling up ready for the lunchtime rush.

'Sorry, mate, we're not open,' he said, barely looking round.

'I'm not after a drink. I was wondering if you could help me.'

'And I've no jobs going.'

'Wasn't after a job either.'

The bloke stopped what he was doing and turned round. 'So what do you want?'

'I'm trying to find someone.'

'Well, that should be easy. We only have about two thousand students here at any one time. Should be a doddle.'

'She's called Freya Fairbrother.'

'And I've just told you . . . Hang about.' The man called over his shoulder to a girl Luke hadn't previously noticed who was taking glasses out of the washer at the far end.

'Oi, Jeannie. What's the name of Tim Mayhew's bird?'

'What, that rich blonde?' she said in a thick Glaswegian accent.

Luke's pulse rate hiked up a notch. Result.

'That's the one.'

'I'm nay sure. Frances?'

'Freya?' suggested the barman.

'Aye, that's it.'

The man returned his attention to Luke. 'I don't know where you'll find her but her fella organises all the bookings here.'

'Is he around much?'

'He'll probably be in tonight. He's got some band from Leeds booked to perform. I'll say one thing for the guy, he gets some good people here.' The barman reeled off a list of the acts that had performed since Tim had been in charge of entertainment. Even Luke was impressed as he'd actually heard of most of them.

'So do you want me to tell Tim you're looking for Freya?' asked the barman.

'No, it's OK. I'll try and catch up with them sometime.'

'Or I can take a message. Give it to Tim if I don't see Freya.'

'Honest, I don't want to put you to any trouble.'

The barman gave Luke a curious look. 'They're not in any trouble, are they? I mean, you're not the police or anything.'

'No, nothing like that. It's just personal. But thanks for the offer of help.'

Luke left the bar before he could be quizzed further, his shoes sticking slightly to the beery flooring. Well, he'd achieved his aim but what was he going to say to Freya when he met her? 'Hi, my name is Luke and I think I pissed off your friend so much she ran away from her place of work rather than talk to me ever again'? Hardly. However, he had the rest of the day to kill before he pitched up at the Union bar for the evening's entertainment; plenty of time to work out an opening gambit.

He decided to walk into the town and check out some stuff via the internet in the local library. For one thing, he was curious as to who the man in Freya Fairbrother's life was. He seemed to have some clout in the pop world or, at any rate, more clout than most student Union entertainment reps. The line-up of acts at the Union wasn't stellar but it was pretty bloody good for a middle-of-the-road small-town university. Besides, anyone dated by a pretty blonde with as much money as Freya Fairbrother had, had to be worth finding out about. Freya Fairbrother wasn't quite in Paris Hilton's league but her picture (copies of which Luke had studied so he would recognise her) had appeared in several of the glossy gossip mags when she'd shown her face at various parties and events over the last couple of years. And now she had a boyfriend. So there was more than likely an angle for the column – if he looked hard enough. It could be worth a hunt on the internet.

Luke forgot about lunch, he forgot what the time was, hell, he even forgot his main aim in this whole exercise was to find Millie.

'Well, I never,' he said under his breath as he read the numerous Google entries for Tim Mayhew and his rather more illustrious father. That would explain why Saltford University got such class acts to perform at their Union. He left the library and flipped open his mobile.

'Hugo?'

'Hi, Luke. How's the day off going? Obviously the answer is "shit" if you feel you have to ring in to work.'

'Shut up, Hugo, and listen.' Luke swiftly passed the gen on to his editor. 'And with any luck I shall be running into Tim and his bird tonight. There might be quite a lot of mileage in this. Do I detect the sweet sound of society wedding bells? And what a wedding it would be with her dad's money and his dad's connections. Just think of the guest list.'

'You may be a bit premature in this, but who cares? Two beautiful people, both rich, both clever . . . Yeah, sounds like a story to me even if they're not officially linked yet. Great. Go for it. But I don't know why you're telling me this. You don't usually ask my permission before you follow up a lead.'

'I need a favour, that's all.'

'What sort of favour?' asked Hugo warily.

'I want to pretend to be you. I think Freya Fairbrother may have heard my name from a friend and I don't want her to twig who I really am. It would complicate things.'

'So what did you do? Lamp her old man? Knock up her sister?'

'No and no – she's an only child, by the way. I met this friend of hers on holiday . . .'

'And you knocked *her* up.'

'No! I haven't knocked *anyone* up. But I think I upset the friend. And if I did, Freya isn't likely to want to talk to me. Quite the reverse in fact – you know what women are like. And let's face it, Luke Hastings isn't the commonest name on the planet. Once Freya hears it she'll probably refuse to have anything to do with me. All that female solidarity bollocks.'

'But if you're Hugo Bullingdon . . .'

'Exactly.'

'But I can't see why you don't just make a name up. Why does it have to be mine?'

'I want to ask questions. And as it's what hacks do, they

won't smell a rat – at least I hope not. But they might just decide to check me – you – out.'

'OK. It's fine by me. Just don't make my name mud as well. No besmirching the family escutcheon, got it?'

Bong Tree was belting out the song that had first brought them to the notice of most of the British youth and the Union bar was throbbing with the sound. Freya was sitting at a corner table, nursing a vodka and tonic and wondering if the music was really to her taste or not. Tim had raved about them, his dad (according to Tim) thought they were going to be 'bigger than mega' but Freya wasn't sure. OK, the beat was good and the lead singer could actually sing – always an advantage, in Freya's experience – but it wasn't floating her boat. Frankly, she thought, they lacked originality. With her eyes shut they could have been one of half a dozen groups around at present. Still, good luck to them, she thought. If Tim's dad thought they had potential then no doubt they would do well. And while she was thinking about Lord Crendon, she offered up a little prayer that he would have the same opinion of Millie. God, that kid so deserved a break. Still with her eyes shut, she drifted away from the mayhem of the gig at the Union bar to a wonderful world where Millie was headlining Glastonbury and was the darling of the record industry.

The table wobbled. Freya opened her eyes and saw a bloke leaning over it towards her. From his body language he seemed to want something. She looked up to his face, guiltily wondering how long he'd been trying to get her attention, and locked eyes with an absolute hunk. Wow! Dark curly hair, huge brown eyes, nice mouth, a hint of a tan, good skin – she had it all clocked in a nano-second.

182

'Hi,' he yelled over the noise.

'Hi,' Freya yelled back. Who was he? Blimey, why hadn't she noticed him before? Then she decided he looked a bit old to be a student. A visiting professor, perhaps? Well, he could tutor her any time! Hell's bells, he was gorgeous. Out of habit she bestowed her very best smile in return – the one she didn't waste on just anyone.

The god gestured to the vacant chair. Freya nodded. Well, it was just a common courtesy. The chair was unused, why shouldn't Adonis have it? The bloke turned his attention to the band and gave Freya the opportunity to study him covertly from under her eyelashes. Not that she was interested. Lord, no! Of course she wasn't. She had Tim.

The band came to the end of their set and after the applause died down there was relative quiet in the bar.

'Can I get you a drink?' asked Adonis.

'Shouldn't we introduce ourselves first?' said Freya.

'Or we could live life dangerously.'

Freya couldn't help smile. All this and charm. 'In which case I'll have a vodka and slimline, please.' The Union bar didn't run to champagne.

Adonis disappeared into the crush at the bar. She stared after him. He was exactly the sort of bloke Millie needed in her life. Well, assuming he was decently behaved, had good manners and was single. Millie had had enough scumbags so far – first Alex-the-arsehole and then Luke. Freya wondered how she could possibly engineer a blind date between this man and Millie. She got out her mobile.

'Get taxi 2 union. I want u 2 meet a guy,' she texted to Millie. She pressed send. A message popped up and told her that it hadn't gone. With a grimace of annoyance, Freya checked the signal. Ziltch. Bugger!

If Adonis hadn't been buying her a drink she'd have slipped outside and tried again but she couldn't risk pissing him off by being absent when he returned. How rude would that be? She'd just have to wait and tell him she had to go to the ladies and try from somewhere else in a few minutes.

Adonis returned with the vodka and a pint for himself a couple of minutes later and sat down.

'I'm Hugo,' said Luke.

'Cheers, Hugo,' said Freya, sipping her drink. 'I'm Freya.' She put her glass down and looked up at him, widening her eyes deliberately to give him the full impact of her very blue gaze. She didn't want him wandering off until she'd managed to get Millie on the scene. If she had to act the part of the stalking horse to keep him interested, then so be it. Not, she admitted to herself, that it was much of a hardship. 'I've not seen you around before.'

'That makes it mutual then, doesn't it?'

'What do you think of the band?'

'Not really my thing, to be honest.'

'What is your thing then?' Please don't be a geek and say Mendelssohn or, worse, some God-awful band like Girls Aloud, thought Freya.

To Freya's relief Hugo didn't let himself down and reeled off a list of perfectly acceptable names, a couple of which Freya noticed were single female acts. Better and better. When he discovered that Millie could sing and play the guitar, he would just love her. He'd love her anyway, thought Freya. What wasn't there to love about Millie?

'My boyfriend rates this lot really highly,' she said. She wanted to get it into the conversation really early that she wasn't available. He could flirt with her and she would flirt back but she wasn't going to pretend that she was entirely single. It wouldn't be fair on Tim or Hugo – or honest. And Freya was always scrupulously honest about everything. She just hoped that, by being honest, she wouldn't drive him away instantly. To her relief, Hugo didn't look the least surprised, or disappointed, that she was already attached. Well, relief tinged with just a hint of concern. Was she losing her 'femme fatale' touch? Why wasn't this man frustrated that she was already spoken for? But that wasn't the point, Freya told herself crossly. The important person was Millie and Freya had to be sure he was going to save himself for Millie, not her. So what did it matter? She returned her attention to the conversation. Hugo was looking at her slightly puzzled.

'He knows about music, does he?' he repeated.

Freya, still just a tiny bit nettled that Hugo hadn't thrown himself off the nearest cliff on discovering she had a boyfriend, replied that he knew 'a bit'.

She couldn't see what was so funny in what she'd just said that made Hugo smile.

'Is he studying it?'

'No, IT. But he books the acts here.'

'So a man of taste and discernment. Oh, and chutzpah because he must have all of that to get past first base with the acts' agents.' Hugo's eyes were twinkling, as if he was trying to stop himself from laughing.

'Bags of chutzpah,' agreed Freya, although she wasn't completely sure what the word meant.

Freya didn't know why but she had the strangest feeling that Hugo was playing some sort of game with her. But why would he? They didn't know each other from Adam. Perhaps she was imagining it. A tad disconcerted even so, she put her drink down and excused herself to the loo. Stuff her misunderstanding of Hugo's body language, she had to get Millie to meet this guy. And if she left it much later Millie would refuse to come out as she would plead an early start for the supermarket by way of excuse. Freya almost ran into the ladies to re-send her text. Then having waited for all of five seconds for a reply from Millie, she gave up and hit the key for her number.

Freya nearly screamed in frustration. The silly girl had her phone switched off. Arrgghh.

She returned to the table. At least Hugo was still there. It would have been awful if he'd escaped without her getting his number. If nothing else, she would make sure she could keep contact with him. For Millie – obviously.

The band was returning to the stage, ready to carry on. Freya was not filled with happiness at the thought. The music was doing nothing for her and she was much more interested in trying to set up something between Hugo and Millie.

'I'm just going to find Tim. Don't go away, I'll be back in a tick.'

Freya fought her way through the press of students to the back room where she knew she'd find Tim.

'Hiya, honey,' she said, giving him a quick peck on the lips. 'How's it going?'

'Yeah, great,' said Tim, not really looking up. He was counting the gate money. He finished with a pile of tenners and snapped a rubber band round them. 'What do you think of Bong Tree? Good, eh?'

Freya must have hesitated a second or two too long.

'Not your thing, then, babe.'

'Not if I'm honest. But judging by the reaction out there, I'm in the minority.'

'But you're not enjoying it?'

'Not really.'

'They've only got one more set. We'll go as soon as I've given them their fee.'

'Would you mind if I bugged out early?' A crash of music reverberated around the room. The band had started again. Freya raised her voice to be heard over the racket. 'I've met this bloke. He'd be fantastic for Millie. She needs a bit of romance in her life.' Tim raised an eyebrow. 'She does. She's so lonely in that slum she lives in. She needs some love interest to give her something else to focus on apart from that crap job.'

'And the ball.'

'Yes, obviously.'

'And her music.'

'Yeah, and her music.' Freya was on a mission to get Millie a man and didn't want to be sidetracked by any of Tim's diversionary tactics. 'Anyway, about this bloke.' She gave Tim a stare – daring him to try and interrupt. He didn't. 'The band isn't doing it for him either. Suppose I took him to the Monkey Puzzle for a quiet drink so I can tell him all about the marvellous Millie and then you meet us there after.'

Tim shook his head in mock disbelief. 'I don't know why you're asking me, sweetie. You've got this all planned.' He grinned at her. 'Go on. I'll be there in about half an hour. As, I suspect, will Millie. I mean I assume you've already told her to get her arse over to the pub.'

'I haven't – couldn't.' Freya's voice was almost shrill with frustration. 'The useless girl has her phone switched off. I'll get his details and set something up. We must be able to get the pair of them together without either of them smelling a rat.'

'I'm sure you'll manage it. Now bugger off and let me cash up.'

Freya skipped out of the room, happy that her plan was coming together. She returned to Hugo.

'Come on,' she yelled into his ear. 'Let's go somewhere quieter.'

'What about your boyfriend?'

'He's meeting us there. He's got to wait till Bong Tree have finished so he can pay them. Come on.' Freya grabbed her handbag from the back of her chair and led the way to the door.

'Where are we going?' Luke opened it for her.

Freya noticed the display of good manners. So far so good, she thought as she answered his question. 'The pub just across the road. Not far.' Her ears were still ringing from the band's amps but the cool evening air was wonderful after the sweaty, humid atmosphere in the bar. She breathed in the fresh air greedily. The sound of the band faded behind them as they walked companionably along the gravel walkways to the exit from the campus.

'So what are you studying, Freya?'

'History.'

'Enjoying it?'

Freya shrugged. 'I love the uni. Not sure about the work.'

Luke laughed. 'Spoken like a true student.'

'What about you?'

'Oh, I've not been a student for some years now.'

'So what do you do for a living?'

'I'm a journalist.'

'Really? Here?'

'London.'

'Blimey.'

'Don't be impressed. I don't rate my own by-line yet.'

'So what are you doing here, if it isn't a rude question?'

'A cousin of mine is thinking of coming here,' lied Luke smoothly. 'I'm covering a story in the area and said I'd mosey along and see what I thought. It seems pretty good.'

But Freya cared nothing for the cousin. She was impressed with the idea of finding a grown-up with a proper job for Millie. She let her thoughts run away with her; if he had his own pad, Millie could move in with him and escape from the flat. Then she remembered that Hugo and Millie hadn't even met yet. Still . . .

Freya led the way across the road and into the pub – almost empty tonight as it often was on nights when there was a gig on at the Union. 'What's your poison, Hugo?'

'No, the drinks are on me. After all, I'm the one with the job while you're a penniless student.' Luke hoped that it would be easy to get Freya to talk about herself and her best friend over a drink or two. Talking about yourself was what the majority of people enjoyed doing most, especially if you were a good listener – which Luke was.

16

In the shabby and rather chilly sitting room, with the sound on the TV turned down very low so as not to disturb her husband, Hannah was enjoying the last episode of a six-part drama series. Over the action on the box she heard her husband put down his pen, slam a filing cabinet drawer shut and stack the papers on his desk in the study. Oh dear, she thought, it sounded like he had finished his work for the night. She was rather hoping he would carry on for a while longer yet. She glanced at her watch. Almost ten o'clock. He would want a cup of tea and the evening news.

'Hannah.'

She got off the sofa and went to the door of the sitting room. 'What is it, dear?'

'I'd like some tea – and there's the article for the *Church Times* on my desk for you to type in the morning.'

'Yes, dear.'

He took the remote control out of her hands as he passed her in the doorway and changed channels on the TV. Hannah gave a little sigh as she scuttled into the kitchen. Never mind, she would catch the end of the series she'd been watching when it got repeated. But she couldn't help feeling a little twinge of annoyance that she was missing the last half hour of something she'd been watching for weeks.

She told herself that it was only a TV programme; it was much more important that Malcolm keep up to date with world affairs. She conveniently glossed over the fact that he had watched the news at midday and at six as well, just as he had for all the years that Hannah had known him.

In his youth, back in the early seventies, when they had first met, he'd been interested in global affairs because he thought that he was going to change the world. Sadly, though, no one at the time had been interested in the slightly off the wall ideas of a young vicar (apart from Hannah who had been a bit of a student activist herself and who fell in love with his enthusiasm, energy, vision and determination) and the authorities and the press ignored him. Disillusioned and increasingly bitter at the lack of attention he was getting, his ideas had become progressively more radical, his outlook more pompous and his views more trenchant. All his zeal became focused on becoming louder and more forceful, spending hours firing off articles and letters to endless publications and papers. The man Hannah had married was no longer the man she shared her life with, but she'd made her vows and her bed and, as a Christian, she was stuck with lying in it.

Hannah had long since given up apologising for him and spent her energies on trying to make life bearable for those unfortunate enough to come into regular contact with him – the cathedral staff, the diocesan priests and their wives, his congregation, the volunteers, the choir, the organists. The list went on and on. She'd heard it said that he'd been given the bishopric in an attempt to shut him up and rein him in. Whoever had thought that would work obviously hadn't known Malcolm Braythorpe at all well.

Hannah made the tea and carried the tray into the sitting

room. She passed her husband his cup and sat down with hers, clasping her hands round the cup for warmth.

'Before you get comfortable,' said Malcolm, 'would you cast your eyes over that article?'

'Yes, dear,' said Hannah meekly. Taking her cup of tea with her, she made her way along the draughty uncarpeted corridor to her husband's study. In there it was even colder and bleaker than the sitting room. Malcolm wasn't one for creature comforts. Sometimes she wondered if he wouldn't have been better off if he'd been a monk. Austerity suited him – he'd have been completely at home in a cell.

She sat down behind his desk and drew the neat stack of paper towards her. Not for the first time she wondered why on earth her husband didn't haul himself into the twenty-first century and invest in a word processor. She didn't mind typing up his articles, letters and sermons – heavens, she was a good, accurate typist so it was no trouble – but there were all the advantages that computers brought. She knew from visits to acquaintances in Westhampton how useful email and the internet were. And you could do all sorts of other clever things on them. How handy it would be to be able to just add names and addresses to the flower and brass cleaning rotas instead of having to retype them completely every time there was an alteration, to say nothing of being able to print off as many copies as you needed – no need for layers of messy carbon paper. Sometimes Hannah thought she was probably the only person in Westhampton who still used carbons judging by the difficulty she had in buying the blasted things. But Malcolm wasn't going to change his ways now so there was no point in even thinking about it.

Hannah quickly scanned through the article, a diatribe against unecological waste and profligacy, checking it for spelling and punctuation mistakes. She made a few pencilled alterations and put the papers back on the desk ready for her husband's final approval of her suggestions before she typed it up. As she prepared to leave his desk, a stiff, gold-edged, engraved card, paperclipped to a letter, caught her eye in the in-tray. It was from a charity, 'Crisis International', inviting both Malcolm and her to a fund-raising ball in September. Hannah's heart gave a little skip. A ball! It was years – twenty? twenty-five? – since she'd been to anything like that. What fun.

Then reality kicked in. What were the chances of Malcolm accepting? Hannah's heart sank just as fast as it had been lifted. She suddenly knew exactly how Cinderella must have felt. The difference was, Hannah had no fairy godmother – nor would any such creature ever dare to step over the threshold. Malcolm would have such a manifestation of the paranormal exorcised as the work of Satan himself before you could say 'transformation scene'.

Hannah picked up the card and read the letter it was clipped to. She studied it carefully, reading each word, as if, by being familiar with every keystroke, she might improve her chances of going. She even read the small print under the letterhead at the top. As she did, her heart began to lift again. There, under the list of patrons, after the usual roll-call of titled personages, was first her husband's name and then that of Jim Fairbrother. Hannah, who wasn't usually one to scheme, she was far too disingenuous for anything like that, began to form a plan.

Freya pushed Tim's leg off her thigh and rolled over in bed. She groaned as she looked at her watch. Who the hell thought it was a good idea to ring at this hour? It was only just daylight, for God's sake. Actually, Freya knew that was a complete exaggeration but, hell, she hadn't got to bed till the small hours and then Tim . . . God, he was good in bed.

She dismissed the memory as the phone continued to warble a recent pop hit incessantly and irritatingly. The tune had seemed like a good idea when she'd downloaded it; now, suffering from lack of sleep and with the beginnings of a slight hangover, Freya wasn't so sure. She picked it up and squinted at the display. Millie – at last.

'Hi, Mil.'

'Just got your message. Sorry, I was writing a song and it was going well so I switched my phone off. Didn't want to lose the thread.'

'I'm sure Bob Dylan felt the same way about interruptions.'

Millie ignored the comment. 'So who was this bloke that got you so fired up last night that you wanted me to drop everything and come across town to meet him?'

At least Millie sounded intrigued, thought Freya. 'A veritable Greek god. Divine to look at, has a job, seems to be single . . .'

'Seems?'

'Look, Mil, I didn't get the thumbscrews on him but there was no wedding ring and he seemed to be in the market. He was dead interested when I told him about you. Terribly sympathetic about what happened to your job.'

'You told him about that?'

'Only the bones.'

The grunt from Millie down the line didn't sound as though she was much appeased so Freya tried distracting her. 'And he is fab to look at.'

'You already said.'

'Did I? That's because it bears repeating.'

'How good-looking?'

'Wonderful dark brown hair and eyes. And a dark brown voice to match.'

Millie didn't reply. That was exactly what she'd thought about Luke when she'd first met him.

'Mil? Mil? You still there?'

'Yeah. I was just trying to visualise him.'

'Think Orlando Bloom.'

'In *Lord of the Rings* as Legolas? With the long blond tresses?'

'As himself. Orlando's not a natural blond.'

'OK. So he's got nice eyes then.' But were they as nice as Luke's? Not that it mattered as Luke had been a shit and she didn't want to think about him ever again. So why couldn't she get him out of her head?

'He's got wonderful eyes. All warm and deep, like a golden retriever's.' Hmm, thought Freya, she might have used the wrong analogy there. Not everyone had a thing about dogs. 'You'll love him.'

'You said he has a job. Doing what?'

'He's a reporter. Works for a paper. Which makes it even more important that you meet him. Just think, if he gave you a decent write-up, it might lead to all sorts of things.'

'He probably doesn't do gigs in the sticks.'

'Reporters do everything, if there's a story.'

'Yeah, "singer writes song". That would be a scoop.'

'Don't be so negative.'

'Anyway, he probably wouldn't like my sort of music.'

'But he does. I asked him.' Freya repeated the list of Hugo's favourite singers and groups.

'OK, I agree he might be useful, especially in the unlikely event that he'll give me a review. But who says I want a boyfriend? The last couple have hardly been resounding successes. Maybe I want a break from all that sort of stuff for a bit.'

'Just agree to meet him, Mil. Please.'

'You've obviously already made your mind up this is going to happen. Just exactly what have you got planned?'

Freya cheered inwardly. She'd broken down the defences. It was only a matter of time before surrender was all hers.

'Tim and I thought we could arrange a bit of a house party at his dad's place. We need to get you to play to his old man and, besides, it'd do you good to get away from that dump you call home and get some lovely country air in your lungs and some decent food inside you.'

'Not sure,' said Millie. She sounded quite spooked at the suggestion.

Well, thought Freya, the idea of meeting Quentin Crendon would be a bit daunting if you were hoping to make a living out of music. He hadn't frightened Freya one bit, in fact she'd thought he was an absolute pussycat but then her future wasn't dependent on what he thought of her.

'It can't be for a while as his dad is off to Barbados for a month but when he gets back we'll get something organised – end of July, early August. You'll be able to get away from the supermarket for a weekend then, won't you?'

'Probably.'

'And talking about people going away, you will be OK, won't you, when I'm away with Tim?'

'I'll be fine. Got a flat, got a job and what's more I've got a whole load of songs to write. I'm not going to have much spare time to worry about anything, let alone how you and

Tim are surviving in some scabby five-star hotel on some grotty island in the Indian Ocean.'

'Glad to hear it.'

'What? That I'm going to be writing songs or not worrying about you?'

'Both. But you know if you need anything, Mum will be there for you.'

'Yeah. But it should be my mum being there for me, shouldn't it?' said Millie quietly.

Freya didn't know quite what to say. Millie had a point, of course, but she also knew that if Millie just met her own mother halfway there might be some sort of reconciliation. She didn't want to be disloyal to her best friend but if she could just get Millie to pick up the phone and ring her mum . . .

'I know, babe. She'll come round. In the meantime, you've got me. And Tim and I will make sure you have the best-est time when we get you over to his dad's. That's something to look forward to.'

'Fine,' said Millie without enthusiasm.

'It'll be a riot. Trust me, you'll have a ball.'

Freya wasn't the only one thinking about having a ball. Hannah had something similar very much on her mind and was determined to have one too. Quite why she was so desperate to go to the Crisis International ball she had no idea. She just knew that life, since Millie had run away, had been harder and harder. She missed Millie terribly and was constantly fighting against guilt and worry about her only daughter turned out into the world, unprotected and friendless. On top of this, everything was dull and dreary. If she didn't put a little light back in her existence she really

couldn't see the point in carrying on with the daily grind.

Life at the palace had been pretty humourless and bleak before Millie had disappeared but now it was utterly devoid of any sort of life or energy. There were days when Hannah sometimes thought about packing her bags and taking her chances in the outside world too. The trouble was, she still loved Malcolm, after a fashion. And underneath that was the abject fear of abandoning the safety of the stipend and the house and trying to make her own way in the world. She hadn't earned her own living for over thirty years and the prospect of returning to work and fending for herself terrified her. She had nowhere to go and no skills to offer beyond a good typing speed but who wanted a typist these days? It was all computers and word processors so how on earth would she survive? And apart from all other considerations she couldn't find it in her heart to break her wedding vows. She meant every word of them when she'd made them. She couldn't break them now.

But since she had seen that invitation she had had a deep longing to go to something that promised to be, well, fun and frivolous. Earlier in the year she'd surreptitiously watched a programme about a big celebrity ball in aid of some kid's charity and had tried to imagine what it would be like to wear a lovely dress, eat delicious food, drink fine wine and just enjoy oneself. Now there was the chance that she might actually be able to experience it for herself, not just imagine it, and she was determined not to let the opportunity slip through her fingers. It wasn't as if she and Malcolm *never* went out, but the suppers and functions they went to weren't glamorous, never smart and rarely fun. When was the last time she'd worn a pretty dress and danced till dawn? University, she supposed. And since?

Duty supper parties, saying the right thing to the right people, eating the same combinations of tomato soup or chicken liver pate followed by lasagne or boeuf bourguignon and finishing off with a stodgy nursery pudding. A glass, possibly two, of wine to wash it down with, and then back to the palace well before midnight and things became even more drab and rundown. She sighed. Well, this time, Cinders *was* going to go to the ball! Furthermore, she had an idea how to achieve her ambition but she needed some information first.

Patiently she waited until Malcolm had checked and double-checked her corrections to his article and given her the go-ahead to type it up. Then she had to hang on until he'd made phone calls and written some letters before he finally left for a meeting with one of his vicars across the other side of the diocese. She was almost beside herself with impatience when his car finally pulled away from the palace. Instantly the sound of the engine faded she abandoned her typing on the kitchen table and nipped into Malcolm's study.

With slightly trembling hands, and with an ear cocked for the sudden return of the car (it would be just her luck for Malcolm to have forgotten something and return to catch her red-handed), she opened the filing cabinet in his study. Hannah wasn't sure what she was looking for but she was certain that somewhere her husband would have a list of the significant donors to the cathedral maintenance fund. Jim Fairbrother, she knew for a fact, came under that heading, and Hannah wanted his address. Unsurprisingly, the Fairbrothers weren't in the phone book because Hannah had already tried to find out the information there.

Millie had visited Fairbrother Towers, as she had

jokingly called her friend's house, on numerous occasions but as her mother neither drove nor had access to a car, she'd always gone on the bus. Hannah knew the house was somewhere out to the east of Westhampton but she had no idea quite where as she'd never visited it. And she didn't want to ask Malcolm for the details because he'd want to know the reason for her inquiry.

Deftly she flipped through the files in the cabinet. She found what she was looking for in the second drawer. Quickly she jotted the address and telephone number down on the memo pad on the desk and then returned everything to its proper place. Giving the study a last look round to make sure there was no evidence of her visit, she took her piece of paper and left the room.

In the kitchen Hannah picked up the telephone and carefully dialled the number she had found.

'Hello,' said a bright voice. 'Judy Fairbrother speaking.'

'Hello, Mrs Fairbrother. I'm sorry to disturb you. I'm Millie's mother.'

'Oh my goodness. How lovely to talk to you after all this time. It's Hannah, isn't it? Please call me Judy.'

'Oh, OK. Thank you.'

'And how is Millie? What is she up to these days? Did she get the job in the south of France?'

Hannah felt completely at sea. How could she admit she didn't have a clue what her daughter was doing? That she didn't even know where she was living? And what was this about a job in the south of France? Luke had told her he had met her in a ski resort.

'The last I heard she was fine,' she prevaricated.

'That is good news. Your Millie is such a lovely girl. That other business was so unfortunate.'

'Yes, well . . .' Hannah really didn't want to hark back to that dreadful time. 'I was wondering if I could come and see you. There's something I really want to talk to you about and . . . Well, it's complicated.'

'Please come over. I would so love to meet you. When would be convenient?'

'This morning?'

There was the slightest of pauses then Judy said, 'Of course. This morning would be fine. I'll see you in ten minutes?'

'Could we make it an hour?' Judging by the address, it was six or seven miles to the village where the Fairbrothers lived. And then she had to find the house. It was going to take Hannah quite a while to get there with only her pushbike for transport.

When she had hung up, Hannah went round to the garage and wheeled her old sit-up-and-beg bike out and checked the tyres. Satisfied that it should get her to her destination without a problem, she fetched her handbag, locked up the house and pedalled off.

It was only when she was halfway there she remembered she hadn't finished the typing.

Luke was sitting at his desk going through pictures that one of the snappers had got of a Hollywood starlet being poured out of the Zoomzoom Club. Her dress (frankly, he'd seen wider belts) revealed both her boobs and her crotch and she looked like Lady Macbeth after an especially trying night on the ramparts.

'What a dog,' said Archie, leaning over Luke's shoulder. 'That shot won't do her reputation much good.'

'She shouldn't have got off her face then, should she?'

Luke selected the pic that did the girl the least favours and clicked his mouse button to insert it into his column.

'So how was the day off?'

'Productive.'

Archie hitched himself onto the corner of Luke's desk, sending a pile of glossy mags cascading sideways. Luke liked to see what the other hacks in the same game wrote about the celebs currently being limelighted. 'Put me out of my misery – you found Millie.'

'Not quite, but I found Freya Fairbrother.'

'Really?'

'She's studying history at Saltford and is currently dating Tim Mayhew.'

'And who's he when he's at home?'

'Quentin Crendon's son.'

Archie let out a whistle. 'Blimey. Lucky old Millie having a mate with those sort of connections.'

'Crendon won't be interested in someone who just does cover versions, no matter how good her voice is.'

'Point taken. Still, it can't do her any harm. When have you fixed up to see Millie then?'

'I haven't. But I found out why she's so pissed off with me. She thinks I lost her her job.'

'What job? Not the one in the chalet?'

'That and the one she hoped to get with the same tour company for the summer season in the south of France.'

'That would make anyone sore. So what did you do?'

'Nothing. Honest.' Luke recounted the details of the lift pass scam to an astounded Archie. 'And then head office found out and sacked everyone. But I swear it was nothing to do with me. I didn't tell anyone.'

'Hell, you didn't even tell me.' Archie sounded annoyed.

202

'I couldn't. A secret isn't a secret once you tell someone. I promised Millie I'd keep the info to myself so I did.'

Archie didn't look convinced about the reason why his best friend had excluded him from such a juicy bit of information. 'But she thinks you went to the company bosses,' he said after a pause.

'You remember the night she lost her temper with Pat?' Archie nodded, a smile playing across his lips as he recalled the old bag's comeuppance. 'Millie'd just heard the news that the directors had flown out to France to talk to the reps about the scam. She knew the writing was on the wall.'

'And she blamed you.'

'Yes.' Luke sighed. 'But there were a dozen or more reps there. Any one of them could have mentioned it to someone who blew the whistle.'

'How do you plan to clear your name? Until you do she's not going to have anything to do with you.'

'Fuck knows. Got any ideas?'

'I'll think about it. Anything to stop you being a complete wet weekend.'

17

Hannah found it impossible to cycle over the deep gravel that made up the surface of the drive at Melton Hall so she got off and walked. As she scrunched along it, she admired the avenue of trees that lined the route and wondered how many gardeners it took to keep the verges so immaculately tended. Ahead was the startling Victorian gothic edifice that was the home of the Fairbrother family.

Hannah felt quite nervous when she finally reached the bottom of the flight of steps that led to the heavy double oak doors. She flicked the stand of her bike down, took her handbag out of the basket and slowly climbed the shallow steps up to the bell pull. Deep inside the house she heard it ring and a few seconds later a young woman in an overall answered the door.

'Mrs Fairbrother?'

'Goodness, no. I'm Nina the housekeeper,' said the woman with a trace of a foreign accent. 'Mrs Fairbrother is in the kitchen.'

The door was opened wide to allow Hannah to enter. Before stepping into the cavernous hall she glanced at her bike and wondered briefly if it was OK to leave such a downmarket method of transport outside such an opulent place that also boasted 'staff'.

'Follow me,' said Nina.

Hannah pattered after Nina past the massive staircase and along a corridor that led towards the back of the house. Nina opened the door and suddenly the Victorian stone and panelling disappeared and Hannah found herself in a bright, light, shiny, ultra-modern and *vast* kitchen. A slim woman with curly blonde hair was sitting at an enormous pine table leafing through a pile of correspondence, a phone at her side and a laptop glowing in front of her. She jumped to her feet as Hannah entered.

'Hannah, how lovely to meet you at long last.'

Hannah was slightly taken aback by the warmth of the greeting and even more shocked when Judy took two paces towards her and hugged her.

'And, er, lovely to meet you too.'

'I sort of feel I know you through Millie. She was always such a welcome visitor here. A lovely girl. A real credit to you.'

'Thank you.' Hannah realised that Freya had hardly ever visited the palace, except on a couple of rare occasions when she'd waited in their kitchen for her dad's driver to pick her up after some after-school activity or other. Millie, on the other hand, had often gone to visit her friend. 'Freya was always welcome to come to us but I don't think we had much to offer in comparison to her home life. No computers, no horses . . .'

'Freya is a very lucky girl to have been so spoilt by her father. Now, tea, coffee?'

'Coffee please.'

Across the kitchen Nina began to put real grounds into a complicated coffee maker and get out cups and plates from a cupboard.

'Now, tell me, what can I do for you? Is it about Millie?'

Hannah felt a lump form in her throat. She shook her head.

'But Millie is OK?'

'She was when I last heard about her.' It was as close as Hannah could get to admitting that Millie hadn't been in touch for months, although she suspected that Judy knew this from Freya.

'She's still at odds with her father?'

Hannah nodded. 'I can't tell you how grateful I am for what you did to help her. I should have been there for her but . . . well, Malcolm has very strong views.'

Judy shrugged. 'I know. It was mostly Freya's doing. If I'm honest, Jim was against us getting involved, what with him being such a friend of the Bishop's, but Freya can be very persuasive. In fact she threatened that she'd leave home and take Millie with her if Jim didn't let her stay here.'

Hannah was touched by such fierce loyalty.

'And she'd have done it too,' added Judy. 'Jim wouldn't admit it but Freya has him wrapped around her little finger.'

Nina put a plate of homemade biscuits on the table and the conversation paused while the two women helped themselves and nibbled at the delicious shortbread. A minute or so later she brought over the coffees and then left the kitchen discreetly.

'You know Freya is still very much in touch with Millie.'

Hannah looked up.

'She tells me odd snippets about what Millie is getting up to. She's back in the country. Did you know that?'

Hannah shook her head.

'Things still difficult at home then?'

'Malcolm can't come to terms with what she did.'

'Getting pregnant isn't a crime,' said Judy gently. 'She didn't do it on purpose.'

'No. Well . . .'

'Look, I imagine you know my feelings about religion.' Hannah did. Jim might have been a born-again Christian but despite Malcolm's invitations and exhortations to Judy to come to the cathedral, she'd consistently refused to see the light. 'But I thought forgiveness was all part of it.'

'I know. But she disappointed him so badly.' Hannah stared at Judy, willing her to get just an inkling of what it was like to live with a man like Malcolm, a man who saw everything in terms of right and wrong, black and white, and who would never dream of meeting anyone halfway. Did she see a glimmer of understanding? She wanted to tell Judy that she'd had to take Malcolm's side or she might have been homeless too, that his rages terrified her, that she had been sure Freya would stand by Millie, whereas she, Hannah, would have been alone. But that would have been disloyal to her husband so she kept silent.

'The reason I came to see you seems so trivial in comparison.'

'Tell me what I can do for you. If I can help, I will. That's what friends are for.' Judy looked at her with sympathy and concern.

Hannah realised with a shock that Judy understood and really wanted to be a friend. It was a wonderful feeling. She had acquaintances through the cathedral but no one she felt she could confide in. Until now.

Hannah guiltily told her about the ball and how much she wanted to go.

'So you want me to persuade the Bishop to take you, is that it?'

'Not quite. You see, I thought that, as your husband is a patron of the charity too, you might be going.'

Judy lifted her shoulders and shook her head. 'I don't know. We get invitations to so many things. Of course we only get invited because they expect Jim to drop a fat cheque into their coffers in return. I can't think they invite us for the pleasure of our company.'

Hannah's heart fell. This had seemed such a good plan. It hadn't crossed her mind that someone else with an invitation simply might not want to go to the ball. Her disappointment must have shown on her face.

'Tell you what, I'll go and see if there's an invite in Jim's study.' Judy got up from the table with an exhortation to Hannah to help herself to more biscuits. She returned a couple of minutes later with a card that Hannah instantly recognised. Her heart lifted again.

'As you can see, we've been invited. I checked in Jim's diary while I was there and we're free that weekend so there's no reason why we shouldn't go. I just need to persuade Jim that it would be a good idea.'

'Oh.' Hannah hardly dared ask the next question. 'Do you think you'll be able to?'

Judy laughed. 'Look, if I tell him it's the thing I want to do most in the world, going to a ball with my new best friend, he'll agree. Don't you worry.'

But Hannah hardly heard the bit about Judy's persuasive powers with her husband. The words 'my new best friend' filled her with a happiness she hadn't known for many months.

'And,' Judy continued, 'I'll tell him that we need to make up a table with you and Malcolm and a load of our other chums. It'll be such fun.'

Hannah allowed herself to dare to believe that it would be.

'I'm sure that'll do the trick,' she said. 'I know Malcolm thinks very highly of Jim.'

'Only because he's loaded and gives the cathedral oodles of cash when it's strapped,' said Judy with refreshing honesty. 'Bishop Malcolm can't possibly approve of his business activities. All that non-environmentally friendly construction work, and his ecologically unsound collection of cars, to say nothing of his trappings of wealth – the horses and the computers.'

'He doesn't seem to mind. He's never mentioned it to me.'

'Isn't that convenient?' said Judy with a smile.

Hannah suddenly found herself laughing. Judy joined in.

'Now, we don't want the men to think that you and I plotted all this. I'll tell Jim that you and I met at some charitable coffee morning and hit it off. No need for him to know the real truth.'

Hannah clasped her hands together. 'That would be wonderful. I feel dreadfully guilty about wanting this but we never seem to do anything fun and I would so love to go.'

Judy smiled at her. 'And why shouldn't you? I'm sure Christianity allows for fun, doesn't it? What are you going to wear?'

Hannah's face fell. 'I haven't thought. I'll get my old patterns out. I expect I'll be able to run up something that would do.'

'No,' said Judy. 'You can't go to a ball in "something that would do". You need to look like a million dollars. You won't enjoy it if you don't feel comfortable and, no disrespect to your dressmaking skills, but if you're in a homemade frock I think you'll feel out of place.'

'But I can't afford to buy anything. The housekeeping would never stretch to it.'

Judy leant back in her chair and eyed Hannah's figure. 'What size are you? A ten?'

Hannah nodded.

'Come with me.'

Meekly Hannah followed her hostess out of the kitchen and up the massive oak staircase. She couldn't imagine why someone with all this money would choose to live in such a dark and old-fashioned house. If she had any say in where she and Malcolm lived it would be in a modern house with proper heating, double glazing and a hot water system that really worked. Of course, with Jim Fairbrother's money this house probably had all of those things. The kitchen was certainly a showpiece and Hannah thought she might manage to like her own house if she had a kitchen like that.

'Don't you just hate this house?' said Judy as if she had plugged into Hannah's thoughts. 'Jim adores it. Loves all this grandeur but I think it's like living in a museum.'

'The kitchen is wonderful,' said Hannah tactfully and truthfully, thinking about her own dreary space, with dated units, chipped paint and cracked tiles.

'The kitchen was designed by me,' said Judy. 'The old one was hideous.' She shuddered. Hannah thought it had probably been very like her own one.

'Here we are.' She opened the door to an enormous bedroom. Hannah couldn't believe the luxury of the thick carpet, the beautiful and *huge* bed and the elegant curtains framing the window. Judy walked the width of the room and then opened another door. The room was lined with glass doors. Hannah, already reeling at the sight of so much opulence, was staggered to notice that behind the door were rack upon rack of clothes. This wasn't a room, it was a giant wardrobe.

Judy's clothes were arranged by colour and type. There was a long row of skirts, another of trousers, one of blouses and a further one for suits. And then there were the shoes: flip-flops, sandals, stilettos, loafers, courts, mules, in suede, leather, satin, canvas – it was like a shop. Hannah thought of her own little wardrobe in her bedroom with her two half-decent suits, a selection of skirts and a couple of blouses, most of which had come from charity shops or jumble sales or she had made herself, and her three pairs of sensible shoes.

'Here we are,' said Judy, pulling open one of the glass doors. There, behind it, were a dozen or so fabulous long dresses all swathed in protective plastic. She flicked through the hangers and picked out a dark green one. Hannah thought the fabric might be wild silk. Judy held it against her.

'Hmm,' she said as she considered the effect.

'But I can't wear this. It's far too lovely,' protested Hannah.

'Why can't you wear it just because it's lovely? I don't understand. The fact that it's lovely is precisely why you *should* wear it.'

'But, but . . .'

'Look, I'll probably never wear it again. It's just going to waste sitting here in this cupboard. Try it on.'

Before Hannah could think of a reason why not, Judy left the walk-in wardrobe with instructions to call her when she needed zipping up. Hannah slipped out of her saggy, baggy tweed skirt and blouse and folded them up carefully. Then, almost reverently, she unzipped the plastic cover and felt the rich material of the dress. It was heavy and luscious and Hannah wondered what it would feel like on. With excitement that she had never felt before regarding a dress she undid the fastenings and stepped into it. Carefully she pulled the cool fabric up her body and slipped the straps over her shoulders. Then she looked in the mirror. She was stunned. She had a real figure that went in and out. The dark green made her skin look pale and creamy instead of wan. Gone was the drab, washed-out middle-aged woman and instead she saw a slim, elegant lady. She couldn't believe the transformation. She understood how Cinderella must have felt. She looked . . . pretty.

'Are you ready for me to zip you up?' called Judy.

Hannah opened the door.

'Wow,' said Judy. 'Fab. Turn round.' Hannah did. 'There. Now look in the mirror. No – wait.' Judy dived past Hannah and returned a minute or so later with a pair of impossibly high, strappy, and altogether beautiful sandals. 'Put these on first. They're probably too big but no matter. It's just for the effect.'

Hannah slipped her feet into the shoes and turned to the mirror. She had to hold the hem up slightly to be able to see the shoes beneath it. Now the dress was done up and fitted properly and she had suitable shoes to go with it, the image in the mirror was even better. Judy moved behind her and pushed Hannah's hair up off her face and caught it on the top of her head.

'I can see where Millie gets her good looks from,' said Judy. 'When I've finished with you you're going to be the belle of the ball.'

18

Archie stared out of the window at London wilting and shimmering in the heat wave and for once in his life he was experiencing a feeling of altruism. He had formed an idea as to how to help Luke prove that he hadn't blown the whistle on the lift pass business and was now waiting for Brenda Chivers, the consumer affairs editor, to return to her desk. From where the *Inquirer*'s offices in London's docklands were situated he could see as far as the Eye and beyond, despite the dusty heat haze and the thin layer of smog that veiled and blurred the view. Below him was the molten silver snake of the Thames as it wound its way through the capital to the sea. It sparkled and glimmered as the ripples caught the blinding rays of the midday sun. If it was this hot in July, what was it going to be like in August? Archie thought he might take a few days' holiday; he'd see if he could get some cheap, last-minute deal. He heard movement near him and turned to face Ms Chivers.

'Greater love hath no man,' he muttered to himself as Brenda, the 'consumers' friend', approached. But not a friend of anyone on the paper. Known almost universally by the non-politically correct brigade as Batty Brenda, she had a reputation for BO and man-hunting in equal measure.

Under normal circumstances one of these characteristics would have been enough to keep Archie as far away from such a woman as possible and both would have guaranteed it; however, in the interests of his best friend, Archie was about to offer himself as a sacrifice. He took a deep breath and squared his shoulders.

Brenda, spotting Archie waiting by her desk to talk to her, exuded zeal, enthusiasm and body odour in almost equal quantities. She boomed a greeting to him. In return Archie offered her the barest hint of a false smile. He was terrified of encouraging her in case she thought he was interested in her. Other men on the paper had been pursued by her and Archie had no intention of offering Brenda any sort of encouragement regarding friendship whatsoever. There was something 'jolly hockey sticks' about her, mixed with the steely desperation of a woman who was facing the prospect of being left on the shelf with no hint of ever being taken down and dusted again.

'I might have an idea for a story for you,' began Archie, feeling unusually nervous in the presence of a woman.

She looked at him expectantly and licked her lips. On most women this might have been attractive, even seductive, but Archie was reminded of a python, just before it got its coils round a victim.

'Fire away then,' said Brenda, pulling out a chair. She sat down, grabbed a notebook and clicked her biro expectantly.

Archie told her about the lift pass scam. Brenda looked less than impressed. 'Archie, my love,' Archie shuddered at the term of endearment, 'it's high summer. This is not the time to run a story about ski holidays. Wait till November.'

But Archie couldn't wait to see winter return. Luke

needed help now. 'Yeah, but I bet stuff like this goes on all year round. Reps are paid bugger all, we know that. They're bound to find ways to supplement their income. If you were to include this in a piece about holiday rip-offs in general, wouldn't it make it more rounded? It's not just the chicken and chips brigade in Marbella getting stung but the posh set in their snobby ski chalets too.'

Brenda considered what Archie had said. 'Maybe. But why are you taking an interest?'

Archie launched into his pre-prepared lie about how he had been blamed for the reps getting the sack and how he wanted to clear his name. 'So I thought if you were to run such a story it would give you a legit excuse to question the company about how they found out.'

'Why can't you?'

Shit, why couldn't he? 'Because I was on a holiday with them when the whistle was blown. They may think that I want some sort of recompense,' he bluffed.

'And why would they tell me?'

Blimey, what was this, the Spanish Inquisition? He hadn't expected Brenda to question him in this sort of detail. More bluster required. 'Because they reacted by the book. They found out the problem, disciplined the miscreants, dealt with it in a way that will make sure their reps never try anything like it again. They should come out of it smelling of roses and I would have thought they'd be quite glad to show themselves as decisive and honest.' He smiled at her, pleased with his performance.

'Maybe,' said Brenda, tapping her pen on her notebook thoughtfully. 'What was the company?'

Archie told her. 'And all I want to know is who blew the whistle. I'm happy for you to run the story as yours.'

Brenda snapped shut her notebook. 'There might be some legs to this story. I've heard of a number of other dodgy practices on package holidays that the reps get up to – overcharging for trips, taking backhanders from bars they recommend, stuff like that. It's a feature I've thought about doing for a while but the lift pass scam is a new one on me. And you're right about it making the whole feature more rounded. "Rip-off Reps." Yeah, I like it. I'll go to the head office of the lot you fingered first. It's at Crystal Palace. Let's see what they have to say. Want to come?'

Archie couldn't think of anything worse than being cooped up in a car with Batty Brenda for half a day. 'I'd probably just cramp your style. But let me know how you get on. Besides, I've got a killer deadline myself.'

He glanced over at Luke who was working at his desk, his back to the rest of the office. Casually Archie returned to his own desk on the other side of the building, hoping to God Luke didn't go ballistic when he discovered what he had just done.

Millie was in the staffroom of the supermarket sipping a cup of tea and flicking through the pages of that day's *Inquirer*. She still had half an hour left of her lunch hour but she was vaguely considering going back to the shop floor early, out of sheer boredom. She had no spare cash with which to go shopping, she had no book as she hadn't had time to get to the library for days and, as she'd forgotten to bring her notebook to work, she couldn't carry on with some ideas for another song. The other shelf-stackers and cashiers, also on the same lunch break as her, had gone to Saltford's weekly market to look for clothes but Millie had excused herself as she was so skint she didn't even have the cash for a couple of pairs of socks, let alone anything more exciting. They'd tried hard to persuade her to join them but she'd been adamant. And now she was regretting it. Mooching round the stalls in the sunshine with a bunch of mates would have been vastly preferable to her solitary spell in the canteen but it was too late now. By the time she got to the market she'd only have time to turn round and come back.

She finished the main bit of the paper and chucked it across the canteen table. It flopped open and the travel supplement fell out. Millie sighed as she looked at the colour shot on the front picturing some idyllic beach hideaway. Lucky old Freya was away somewhere similarly exotic with Tim. And Tim's dad was off on a trip to the West Indies. And where was she? Stuck in a grotty supermarket in Saltford. Still, she thought, when she was rich and famous she would be able to jet off on wonderful holidays and stay in the penthouse suite in luxury hotels. She'd seen *Pretty Woman* and knew how the super rich got treated in such swanky places. Wouldn't it be lovely . . .

Millie flicked open the front page. 'RIP-OFF REPS' shrieked the headline above two pictures. One snap was of somewhere hot, sunny and sandy but the other – Millie could barely believe it – the other was the main street of the ski resort she'd worked in all winter. Drawn like a rabbit to a snake, she began to read the story in the paper. Quickly she scanned through the first few paragraphs detailing things that had gone on in Magaluf and Ayia Napa till she got to the bit she was dreading. There in black and white were all the details of the scam she'd been involved with. She noticed, with relief, that no names of any reps were mentioned. At least, she thought, no one would know that she'd been mixed up in it.

She'd heard, often enough, that you couldn't believe half of what you read in the papers, that the facts were invariably wrong, but she couldn't fault this story. Every detail was completely recognisable, even down to the amount the reps were due to pay themselves at the end of the season. It was all correct, that is, apart from the fact that the reporter had written that it had been employees of the tour company who had blown the whistle. Huh, thought Millie. Well, they'd got that wrong. It had been that shit Luke Hastings, who was a client. But water under the bridge, and all that. The story couldn't do her any harm now.

She pulled the main bit of the paper towards her and began to tidy the pages up automatically. She supposed it was because she was thinking about Luke in a vague sort of way that the name 'Archie Green', above a story about a fire in the Midlands, caught her eye. Millie stared at the name for thirty seconds or so, wondering if it was just coincidence. Or perhaps her memory was playing tricks; she remembered Luke's friend had been called Archie, but was his surname Green? Anyway, he said he had a desk job. Yeah, but what sort of desk job? Just because she'd thought he was some sort of accountant or City type didn't mean he was. Perhaps she was just getting paranoid now. Or was she?

She needed to talk to Freya about this. Quickly she got her mobile out of her locker and sent a text to Freya. 'Need 2 tlk ring me.' Then she remembered that Freya was still on her hols. Millie sighed and wondered how long she'd have to wait to get a reply.

Luke strode over to Archie and threw the travel section onto his desk, his face like thunder.

'And just how the fuck is this going to help me? And don't deny you didn't have anything to do with this. Brenda didn't fall over this story without your help. Go on, admit it.'

Archie leaned back in his chair, out of hitting distance. 'Well, you weren't getting anywhere.'

'So you thought you'd make sure I never did. Is that it?'

'No. Absolutely not.' Shit, Archie wished that Brenda had warned him that she'd finished her feature and was going to run it. To be honest, it had been a while since he'd gone to her with the idea and he'd pushed it to the back of his mind.

'Then your explanation had better be bloody good.'

Archie swallowed. His friendship with Luke was going to be on very stony ground if Batty Brenda hadn't come up with the name of the employee who had blown the whistle about the lift passes.

'Look, you need to give me a while. Honest.' He looked pleadingly at Luke, willing him to believe and trust him. 'I'll have an answer that I think you'll like in just a little while.' He silently prayed to God that he would have. But fuck! He'd have to go and see BB again and wheedle the info out of her.

Archie wandered over to Batty Brenda's desk and waited patiently for her to finish on the phone. She, meantime, beamed a big, welcoming smile that displayed her rather large yellow teeth, and gestured that he should sit down. Archie ignored the offer. He wanted nothing to impede a swift getaway once he'd finished his business with her.

The phone was replaced on its rest and Brenda turned the full spotlight of her attention onto her visitor. Archie thought he knew how rabbits felt in the glare of fast approaching headlights. Scared and impotent. Actually,

Brenda would probably have rendered even Casanova impotent.

'Nice article on the reps, Bren.'

'Thanks. Glad you liked it.'

'I was just wondering . . .'

'Yes?' Brenda sat forward on her chair expectantly.

Archie took a step back. 'I was just wondering if you found out the name of the person who blew the whistle on the ski lift passes.'

'Oh.' Brenda sagged back in her seat again.

Obviously he hadn't said what she'd wanted to hear. She wanted a pound of flesh – or, dreadful thought, lunch.

He was wondering if he might get away with just a drink when Brenda added, 'Well, I don't see why I should tell you who my sources are.'

Boy, did she sound sulky. She needed schmoozing, that much was evident. He steeled himself. He hoped Luke would one day appreciate what he was about to do. Shit, lunch invite it was then.

'Tell you what, why don't we go to the Grapes at lunchtime?'

'The Grapes?' Her eyes gleamed. 'I haven't been there for ages.'

No, thought Archie, because when people from the office go there, the last person who gets invited to join them is you.

'That would be very nice.'

Only for Brenda, Archie thought.

She glanced at her desk diary. 'Only I can't do today. It'll have to be tomorrow. What time?' she asked.

'I'll meet you in the lobby at about one-ish.' Then he'd tell her that he had to be back at his desk by two. He could cut the encounter down to about forty minutes if he spent time ordering drinks at the bar and going to the loo. Perhaps less, he thought hopefully.

'See you tomorrow then, Archie.' She smiled coquettishly. Archie felt bile rise in his throat.

19

'Ring u 18r,' read the message from Freya on Millie's phone.

'Gr8,' she texted back.

She returned to fronting up the salad dressing shelves in the supermarket. The job was mindless – making sure all the bottles and jars were in neat lines with the labels showing – which allowed her time to let her mind wander to other more pressing subjects. Like was she being paranoid about the newspaper story and was Archie Green the bloke who had stayed in her chalet?

She had barely pressed the 'send' button when her phone rang. So much for '18r'. Millie checked up and down the aisles before she answered it.

'Freya. I'm working.' Then she remembered. 'Sorry. How was your holiday?'

'Fab. Flew in a few hours ago. I'm at home. Just got your message.'

'Look, I really shouldn't talk now.'

'Take a break. Surely you're allowed one.'

'Not yet. There are rotas.'

'So what's the hot goss you have to pass on so fast?'

Millie checked the coast was clear once again. Swiftly and succinctly she told Freya about the previous day's newspaper story and Archie Green's by-line.

'Probably just a coincidence,' said Freya reassuringly, after a pause while she considered all the implications.

'Oh yeah?'

'You're just getting paranoid. Anyway, what does it matter to you? You're out of it, it's all over.'

Millie saw the manager appear round the end of the aisle. 'Got to go. Ring you later. We'll chat properly then.' She shoved her mobile into her pocket and carried on working. She was still pretty confident that taking personal calls wouldn't earn her the sack but there was no point in antagonising the manager unnecessarily.

Freya, sitting on her bed, her suitcase open with clothes spilling out and across her carpet, flicked through the electronic phone book on her mobile till she came to Hugo's entry. She stared at it. Millie needed cheering up. Maybe now was the time to get Millie over to the Crendon place and get her to showcase her music to Tim's dad. And she'd promised Millie that if she did that she'd invite Hugo along so she could meet him. She glanced at her watch. Midday – probably as good a time as any to ring a reporter. Not that she knew for certain one way or the other. Freya wasn't in the habit of ringing reporters. She pressed the button to call him.

'Hi, Freya,' he said. 'Good to hear from you.'

'Hi. How's things?'

'Fine, but busy.'

'Sorry, is this a bad time to call?'

'No, no, it's fine, honest.'

At least this Hugo bloke seemed pleased to hear from her. 'Sorry I haven't been in touch since we met in Saltford.

I was away. I was wondering . . .' she paused. 'Me and my boyfriend are planning a bit of a party. I was wondering if you'd like to come along?' Nothing. No response. 'It'll be fun,' she added. Still nothing. 'Hugo? Hugo?' She looked at her phone. The battery symbol was empty. Bugger. She'd try later. She found her charger in her case, plugged it in, connected her phone and wandered down to the kitchen. She thought she could detect the smell of something yummy being baked. She wondered what delights Nina was knocking up today.

Her mother was sitting at the big pine table, answering letters, emailing and paying bills. Her mother had a perfectly good study but she never used it. In fact her mother only seemed to use the kitchen and her bedroom suite. She hardly ever made use of any of the other twenty-odd rooms in the house.

'Morning, darling,' her mother said. 'Sleep well? Recovered from your flight?'

'Yeah, slept like a log, thanks. And the flight wasn't that bad. Club Class is pretty comfy.' Freya smiled at Nina. 'But I'd kill for a cup of coffee, please.'

'Of course. Would you like me to make you some breakfast too?'

'No. Coffee's fine. My body clock is all arse about face. I'm not sure whether I wouldn't rather eat dinner.' She slumped into a chair next to her mother. 'Don't suppose we have a copy of yesterday's *Inquirer* in the house, do we?'

'God knows. Why?'

'Because there's a story about Millie.'

'Millie?'

'Well, not her exactly.' Nina put a coffee on the table in

front of Freya who grabbed it gratefully. 'That business with
the lift passes – I told you about it.'

'Did you, darling?'

Really, Freya thought, her mother could be so vague
sometimes.

'You know, the rep who bought them didn't pass the
discount on to the punters but split it between the other
reps,' she explained patiently.

'I do remember something now. Isn't that why Millie had
to come back here?'

'Yes.' Freya rolled her eyes in mock frustration and
slurped her coffee. 'But it doesn't answer my question. Do
we have yesterday's *Inquirer*?'

'Nina?'

'I don't know, Mrs Fairbrother. I may have used it for
rubbish.'

'Oh. Damn,' said Freya. She shrugged. 'Oh, well. I don't
suppose it really matters.'

'If I didn't use it for rubbish,' said Nina, 'it will be in the
cupboard under the stairs for cycling.'

'Recycling,' chorused Freya and her mother together.

Nina shook her head. English was so tricky. Russian was
so much easier.

'I'll finish my coffee and go and look in a min.'

'I saw Millie's mother a few days ago,' said Judy.

'Poor old Hannah? What was she up to? Running a
jumble sale?'

'She came here.'

Freya spluttered into her coffee. 'Here?'

'She came to see me about a ball she wants to go to.'

Freya put down her coffee. She was now in serious
danger of spilling it everywhere. 'No! A ball? Don't believe

it. The beastly Bish would never agree.'

'Which was why she came to see me. She wants your dad
to twist his arm. You know how he and the Bishop are
buddies.'

'Blimey.' Freya contemplated the news. 'So what's the big
event?'

'To be honest, darling, I'm not entirely sure. Some cause
or other your father is involved with.'

'And the Bishop too if he's been invited. Must be a
church do then.' Freya grinned and rolled her eyes. 'Sounds
like it'll be a right rave. Has it got a theme? Vicars and tarts?'

Judy giggled. 'Certainly not. And for God's sake don't say
stuff like that to your father. You know how it gets his goat.'

'Aw. Spoilsport. Anyway, it doesn't sound half as fun as
the ball Tim's involved with. That one is going to be a blast.
Loads of A-listers, some fantastic bands. You want to ditch
that lame dance you're going to and come along to this one.'

'I can't. I've promised Hannah we'll make up a party with
her and the Bishop. The poor woman just wants to have a
bit of fun. Besides, I've been to dozens of balls. One more
or less won't make any difference to me. And maybe
Quentin will organise another do and I can go to that.'

'But this church hop will be the highlight of Hannah's
life.' Freya wrinkled her nose. 'I suppose she deserves a
night out. Fun doesn't seem to be a feature of the
Braythorpe home. God, the palace was a dreary place. I
always had to make excuses when Millie invited me over.'

'I remember,' said Judy drily. 'You said after your first
visit that the place gave you the creeps and you never
wanted to go there again.'

'It was gross. Even on a warm day it was perishing. The
place was like something out of Dickens. When I went into

the kitchen I expected to see some poor little scullery maid sitting in the cinders surrounded by rats and cockroaches.'

'Don't exaggerate.'

'You've never been there.'

'But I shall be going soon. I'm meeting Hannah there to take her shopping for shoes.'

This time Freya did splurt her coffee. She wiped up the splatters on the table with her sleeve. 'What?' she shrieked. 'I just don't believe it. Wait till I tell Millie. She won't believe it either.'

'I'm lending Hannah a dress. We're much the same size.'

'Except she's scrawny and you're slim.'

'You're wrong there, miss. Hannah has a very nice figure and with a bit of make-up and a decent hairdo, she'd be very pretty.'

Freya shook her head. 'Nope. Don't see that.'

'Where do you think Millie gets her looks from? Not her father, that's for sure.'

'Point taken.'

'But we have different size feet so I can't help her out with shoes too. Somehow I've managed to persuade her that loafers and lace-ups aren't going to go with the dress.'

'I shall want a full report on the expedition. And I want you to tell me what you think of that mausoleum they live in. Now,' Freya stood up, 'I need to find that paper.'

Luke put down his mobile. Maybe things were looking more hopeful on the Millie front although, as he'd heard nothing of what Freya had had to say past 'I was wondering', he had no idea of the reason for her call. He wondered what she was wondering about. He hit the reply button to call her back and got the automatic voicemail message. He cleared the call and left no message. Freya's phone was either out of signal or switched off. She'd try again – he hoped.

He returned to the story he was writing. As he sat down he saw Archie go over to Brenda's desk. He watched Brenda give Archie a coy smile and twiddle her hair round a finger. Archie and Brenda? Luke rubbed his eyes. He knew Archie was a bit of a ladies' man and would go for anything in a skirt, but Brenda?

'Right then,' said Archie with false cheer. 'Ready?'

'Ooh, yes,' she replied with a faux shy glance from under lowered eyelashes – the sort of look Princess Di had perfected and which had looked fine on her. But on Brenda? Archie suppressed a shudder.

'Jolly good. Let's go.' He led the way out of the office, into the lift and down through the large atrium. The pair crossed the busy road, unaware that they were being watched by a bewildered but amused Luke from ten storeys above them, and turned down a side street. Instantly the ultra-modern buildings were left behind and now the road was flanked by old Georgian terraced houses, a rare example of the original architecture of the place in an area that had been fairly comprehensively flattened, first in the Blitz and then by property developers. Halfway along the road was the paper's local. Archie held open the door to the saloon bar for Brenda who squeezed past, brushing against his thigh. Archie looked at the width of the doorway in amazement. A Teletubbie could have got past without making physical contact.

Inside, there were several dozen people all talking nineteen to the dozen and crowded around the bar. For most of the staffers on the paper, lunch was taken in liquid form – not necessarily alcoholic but liquid all the same.

'You bag a table and I'll get the drinks. What would you like?'

Brenda ordered a glass of white wine and Archie pushed his way through to the bar.

'Blimey, Archie,' said one of the sports reporters. 'You and Brenda?'

'Don't ask,' said Archie grimly. 'And it's not what you think.' He got the drinks and made his way across the room to Brenda who had installed herself at a cosy little table for two in the corner. Archie gave her the wine and a copy of the bar menu before he sat down. He pushed his chair back from the table, ostensibly so he could stretch his legs but actually he was trying to put as much space between him and her as possible.

After they'd chosen and ordered their food, Archie launched straight into the business of extracting what he needed to know.

'Right, tell me all about this holiday company.'

Brenda leaned forward. Archie did likewise. He could see the hairs on her top lip. 'I spoke to a woman in their customer relations department. She was really helpful. She told me that it was part of an ongoing operation following a rumour they'd heard about the customers being diddled by the reps. She and her partner flew out to the Alps during the Easter break to snoop around for themselves.'

'And they dug the stuff up?'

'Indeed they did. Although Deirdre—'

'Deirdre?' Archie almost fell off his stool. 'You sure that was her name?'

'Yes. I mean it's not terribly common. Quite old-fashioned, I thought. But not half as weird as her partner's name – Cuthbert.'

Archie threw a twenty pound note on the table and leapt to his feet. 'Sorry, Brenda, but I've got to dash. Pay for the food out of that. And you can have my sandwich too.'

He fled from the bar before Brenda had time to draw breath. He knew this move was rash and he'd pay later, but hell, this was an emergency.

Archie ran all the way back to the atrium of the office block, pressed every call button for the bank of lifts and elbowed his way into the first to arrive, almost before the startled occupants had time to get out. He raced across the open-plan office and collapsed panting into the chair by Luke's desk.

Luke raised an eyebrow. 'Christ, I know Brenda's not the ideal lunch companion but she's not that scary, is she?'

Archie was too full of the news he had to impart to notice that Luke had spotted his lunch date. 'It was Cuthbert and Deedee.'

'It was Cuthbert and Deedee what?'

'Who blew the whistle. They both work for Surf and Snow. They were sent out by the company because their head office had already heard a rumour,' panted Archie.

Luke flopped back in his chair, a look of relief on his face. 'So I really am in the clear?'

'Of course you are. You always were, you knew you hadn't done it. But now we know who did.'

Luke leaned forward and clasped Archie warmly by the hand. 'My God, mate, you did all this for me. You are such a pal.'

'You'd better believe it,' said Archie, wondering how he was going to get rid of Brenda now she thought he was interested in her and also explain his precipitate departure from the pub.

Luke picked up his mobile and began pressing keys. Now he knew the truth, it was time to come clean to Freya and to get the news to Millie. It rang. Thank God. She answered. More thanks. 'Freya, we've got to meet. It's really urgent.'

Millie stood outside Oxford Station and shivered slightly. The summer heat wave had gone, to be replaced by light rain and a chilly breeze so it already felt like autumn despite the fact that it was only August. She wished Freya would hurry up and get here. The rain might have been only light but it was penetrating and Millie was feeling distinctly damp. She jiggled from foot to foot to keep her circulation going. Arctic it was not, but after weeks of fantastically hot weather her blood had thinned and now she felt freezing.

Suddenly a little convertible zoomed round the corner by the traffic lights and Millie felt her spirits lift automatically. Freya always had that effect on her. She slung her backpack over her shoulder, picked up her guitar case and waved with her free hand. Freya screeched to a stop and leaned across to open the passenger door. Millie stowed her luggage before hopping in herself. Freya leaned over the gear stick to give her mate a big hug.

'Mil! It's been ages,' she squealed, her excitement at seeing her friend again obvious in her voice.

'Too long, Frey.'

'I know, I know.' Freya flicked on the indicator, slipped the car into gear and pulled away from the kerb. 'My fault for going away. Then Mum wanted me home for a bit. She's sure I'm kept in chains and on bread and water at uni. As if.' Freya rolled her eyes. 'But you know what Mum's like.'

'Yes,' agreed Millie, wishing her mother was the same – or even that she just cared a bit.

'And it didn't help that that scuzzy shop you work in wouldn't give you a whole weekend off till now. I mean, really. Aren't there rules about how many hours you can work or something?'

'Dunno,' said Millie. 'I'm just grateful for the money.'

Freya took her hand off the wheel and squeezed Millie's arm. 'I wish—'

'Yeah, I know what you're going to say, but don't bother. I mean, I am grateful. But . . .'

Freya sighed and shook her head. 'God, you're fucking stubborn, Millie Braythorpe. If I didn't love you quite so much I'd slap you.'

'Ah, but you do love me. Now, tell me all about your holiday and the rest of the goss.'

Millie snuggled down in the bucket seat of Freya's little car and listened to her friend's news. She felt no jealousy at the descriptions of the wonderful tropical island Freya had spent several weeks on but just enjoyed the experience vicariously.

'Hey, and you'll never guess,' Freya suddenly said, destroying Millie's daydream about white sand, and palm trees and warm waves lapping at her feet.

'What?'

'Your mum wants to go to a ball.'

Millie sat bolt upright and nearly banged her head on the low roof of the car.

'What!'

'I know. My mum was a bit shocked too.'

'Hang on,' said Millie. 'I'm losing the plot here. Can we take this story from the top?'

Freya related the details she knew about Hannah's visit to her mother.

'So how was my mum?' asked Millie quietly.

'My mum said she looked pretty desperate. She didn't seem to have much life about her. She's really missing you, Mil. Honest.'

Millie stared out of the window. Part of her thought that it served her mum right to be miserable but a bigger part felt really sorry for her. She'd escaped from her dad's tyranny. What chance did her mum have to get away? She didn't have a pal like Freya on her side. A small pang of conscience inserted itself into Millie's thoughts. Yes, her mother had betrayed her but she had abandoned her mum. Maybe there was fault on both sides.

She was aware of Freya staring at her with a concerned look. Millie pushed her thoughts away. Freya had gone to a lot of trouble to make this a nice weekend away for her, it wouldn't be fair to be all mopey.

Brightly she said. 'So what's this ball in aid of?'

'God knows, some sort of church fundraiser. Mum didn't seem to know either but you know how vague she is about some stuff.'

Millie nodded. That was one of the things she loved about Freya's mum, the way she sometimes drifted about in a little world of her own.

'Can you imagine Dad at this do?' said Millie with a wry smile. 'He's going to hate it,' she added gleefully. 'Almost worth being there with them to see it.'

Freya grinned too at the thought. She drove expertly along the country roads, chatting about this and that and occasionally pointing out things of interest for Millie. Ahead, to the east, Millie could see a line of hills which Freya told her were the Chilterns. They passed through a couple of pretty villages with greens and ponds and idyllic looking pubs festooned with hanging baskets. Then Freya swung the car into a narrow lane.

'Almost there.'

Long grass and fronds from overgrown hedges brushed the side of the car. Then the lane suddenly widened as the hedges were replaced by tidy post and rail fences and the verges became almost manicured. Freya slowed the car to negotiate a cattle grid and then there in front of Millie was a huge grey mansion with mullioned windows, sweeping lawns graced by a couple of majestic and stately cedar trees, and a lake with a fountain. She half expected to see ladies in crinolines promenading – or whatever ladies in crinolines did – along the gravel paths.

'Blimey,' muttered Millie.

'Not bad, is it?'

Millie didn't think that 'not bad' was quite the mot juste but hell, when you lived in a house like Freya's, sodding big came as standard, she supposed.

'Lovely,' she agreed.

Freya drove the car round to the back of the house and parked up next to a row of several other vehicles – all new, all shiny, all expensive.

'Come on,' she said, throwing open her door. 'Grab your guitar. I'll get your bag.' She opened the boot and hauled out Millie's bag. 'Sorry we're using the tradesman's entrance but everyone does.'

Millie followed her friend through a courtyard and then through a door into a cavernous kitchen.

'Hi, Mrs Mo,' called Freya. 'We're here.'

A dumpy woman wearing a floral apron bustled out of a door on the far side of the kitchen.

'Welcome,' she said, wiping her hands on her apron. 'You must be Miss Millie.'

Millie extended her hand, wondering who the hell she was meeting exactly. 'Pleased to meet you,' she said.

'Millie, this is Mrs Mollington. But everyone calls her Mrs Mo. Mrs Mo is the housekeeper here. Oh, and the most wonderful cook. She spoils me rotten.' Freya gave Mrs Mo a big kiss on the cheek. 'Don't you?'

'You only get what you deserve, Miss Freya.' But Millie could see she just loved the compliment. 'Do you know when your other friend is arriving, Miss Freya?'

'Oh, goodness no.'

'Who's that,' asked Millie. 'Anyone I know?'

'Absolutely not,' said Freya quickly. 'Someone Tim has invited. I'll tell you about the arrangements later, Mrs Mo.'

Millie thought she caught Freya shooting a warning look to Mrs Mo but when she looked at her friend properly she was just her normal smiley, friendly self.

'Right then,' said Mrs Mo. 'Now, Miss Millie, I expect you want to see your room.'

'Do I? Oh, yes, of course.'

Mrs Mo led them through the enormous kitchen and then through a heavy swing door at the far end. They emerged into a vast, light hall, dominated by a huge refectory table in the middle with a bowl of beautiful flowers in the centre. The floor was made of oak and polished to a mirror shine. At one end was a huge window with tiny leaded panes that all seemed to be slightly different shades of 'clear'. The little bits of glass, judging by the flaws and flecks, must have been as old as the house – and how old was that? Millie wondered. She wasn't hot on architecture but thought it might have been Jacobean. At the other end a flight of stairs led upwards and then divided to lead to galleries that led along each side of the hall. Millie imagined the generations of women who had descended them, their long dresses sweeping the treads. Around the walls were the portraits of such ladies and their husbands.

Freya gestured to them. 'Tim's relies,' she said. 'If you ask him he can give you chapter and verse on each one. Some are even quite colourful. One was a bit of a lad and had four wives – one or two of them simultaneously.'

'Really. Which one?'

Freya peered round at the pictures. 'Can't remember. They all look a bit alike to me.'

She had a point, thought Millie. There was a definite similarity amongst a lot of the facial features. And she could see Tim was part of the gene pool.

Mrs Mo led the way up the stairs and along a corridor that branched off from one of the galleries. Millie wondered if she would be able to find her way back to the kitchen – or anywhere for that matter. Sat nav might be useful, she thought.

'Here you are,' said Mrs Mo, throwing open a heavy oak door. Millie entered the room. It was vast. Quite as big as Freya's mum's room back at Melton Hall, which was the most stunning bedroom she had ever seen – till now. In the middle of one wall was a huge double bed, big enough for a whole family to sleep in, and opposite was a curved bay window with a padded window seat that ran around the wall underneath it. The ceiling was patterned with intricate plaster work and the fireplace was in a huge alcove that was supported by a couple of slender pillars. In front of the fire was a large flower arrangement of pale cream and yellow roses that filled the room with a delicate perfume. The walls were panelled with wood and painted the palest shade of yellow and the carpet was cream. The room was light, bright and beautiful. Millie gasped.

'Nice, isn't it?' said Freya.

'Nice doesn't even get close,' said Millie.

'And your bathroom is here,' said Mrs Mo, opening a door hidden in the panelling. Millie peered through it. The bathroom was down a couple of steps and seemed to have been built into the thickness of the walls. The floor was stone, as were two of the walls. The other two, behind the shower, loo and basin were conventionally tiled. Despite the fact that it was slightly cave-like, it was warm and cosy – probably courtesy of a huge, floor to ceiling, heated towel rail, over which were hung a couple of big bath sheets. A luxurious bathrobe was on a hook beside it. Mrs Mo opened a cupboard, filled with yet more fluffy towels

'There's plenty more towels in here. You just help yourself to whatever you need.'

Millie nodded. How many could a girl possibly need for one weekend?

'I'll leave you to unpack. If you need anything, you just let me know,' said Mrs Mo as she left.

'Blimey, Frey, is this the life or what!' said Millie, bouncing up and down on the bed.

'And the lovely Mrs Mo – couldn't you get used to being looked after by her?'

Millie wasn't sure. For Freya it wasn't such a culture shock, but for her . . .

'Get unpacked, and then come downstairs. I think Tim is in the billiard room.'

'Billiard room? Frey, you're having a laugh. What is this, the Cluedo House? Tim in the billiard room with the lead piping?'

'I'll tell him.'

'So where's the billiard room?'

'Back down the bottom of the stairs, turn right and head to the end of the corridor. You'll find it.'

Freya went, leaving Millie to hang up her few clothes in the cavernous wardrobe and to explore the facilities of her room: TV, stereo, DVD, books, magazines . . . Heaven on earth, she thought. She knew it was shallow and she knew there was more to life than possessions but being rich really did have advantages. This room was living proof.

Millie found the billiard room quite easily. First she followed Freya's directions and then she followed the music. The billiard room turned out to be more of a games room with a huge full-sized snooker table in the middle and a selection of old-fashioned one-armed bandits and jukeboxes around the walls. Freya was busy feeding tokens into one of the fruit machines and jumping up and down with delight when they spewed out a handful of winnings. A fifties jukebox was playing an old Elvis hit.

Tim greeted her like a long lost friend.

'And Dad is really looking forward to meeting you when he gets back tonight. He says he can't wait to hear you play.'

'Oh, good,' said Millie, feeling a surge of nerves pulse through her system. For a few minutes she had forgotten that this was the raison d'être for her visit. She ought to be grateful. Most budding musicians would give their left arm to be heard by Quentin Crendon, but Millie was just plain scared. Supposing Tim had got it all wrong? Just because his dad had a nose for a star turn didn't mean he did too. And what did uni students know about music? They may not have booed her off the stage at the Union but it didn't mean she was any good. Millie, in her fear, casually ignored the fact that most people her age knew exactly what they liked or didn't like and had pretty sophisticated tastes.

'So, until Dad whisks you off to his lair to see what you can do, just enjoy yourself.'

Millie gulped. The prospect of having Quentin Crendon 'see what she could do' was worse than exams. At least with them, if you cocked up you couldn't see the look of exasperation on the examiner's face that anyone could be so useless. Well, it was too late to escape now.

'What would you like to do?' asked Tim, patiently.

Millie hadn't a clue, but run away and get a train back to Saltford seemed like a good option. However, Tim needed an answer that didn't seem churlish or ungrateful. She shrugged, hoping that it implied that she was happy to tag along with anything anyone else wanted to do.

'Fancy a swim?' asked Freya, coming to her rescue.

'Love one but I haven't got a cozzie with me.'

'Oh, there'll be some in the pool house,' said Tim casually. 'There's bound to be one that fits. Tell you what, why don't we all have a dip before lunch and then we can think of something to do this afternoon.'

The rest of the day seemed to pass in a blur of swimming, fun, hedonism and delicious food. Until the dinner gong sounded and Millie was told by Freya that Quentin had just arrived, Millie almost managed to relax and enjoy herself.

21

Quentin Crendon pitched up just in time for dinner. He was quite a surprise to Millie. She wasn't sure what she expected from her first encounter with the landed gentry but Quentin wasn't it. She hadn't thought he would be wearing ermine and a coronet but a bright blue and orange Hawaiian shirt, purple Bermuda shorts, a ponytail and pierced ears did come as a bit of a shock.

'Millie,' he boomed as he strode into the den where Tim and his house guests were enjoying a pre-dinner drink. 'I thought I was never going to meet you.'

He extended his hand which Millie took tentatively.

'Glad to meet you, sir,' she said. Was 'sir' all right or should she call him your lordship?

Quentin guffawed. 'For fuck's sake, Millie, didn't Tim tell you I loathe all that sort of flim-flammery. Call me Quen.' And he threw his other arm round her shoulder and gave her a big squeeze that nearly left her breathless. 'And I am really looking forward to hearing you play. Now let's eat.'

Dinner turned out to be a four-course extravaganza produced by the wonderful Mrs Mo and served by a couple of girls from the village. It transpired that, for the local population, Lord Crendon was the main employer. What with a posse of gardeners and groundsmen outside, supervised by head gardener and chauffeur Mr Mo, and all Mrs Mo's assistants inside, there wasn't much in the way of unemployment for several miles round about.

The food that Millie managed to force down was delicious, but every time she looked up she saw Quen and remembered that in a short while her future would be decided. She tried eating slowly to delay the inevitable but finally the last of the plates were cleared, her coffee cup was empty and Quen was pushing his chair back. Millie swallowed nervously. This was it.

'Come on then, Millie. Why don't you fetch your guitar and then we'll go along to my studio?'

Millie nodded and did as she was bid. Even dragging her feet and taking time to have a nervous pee before she returned downstairs didn't use up more than a few minutes.

Quen led her along a labyrinth of corridors to the far end of one of the wings. He threw open a door and in front of Millie was a proper recording studio.

'Wow!' she said.

'Great, isn't it? I love gadgets and toys and this is my pride and joy.' Quen settled himself in a big leather office chair at the mixing desk and gestured to a stool for Millie. 'Is that stool OK for you? I don't know whether you'd rather sit or stand when you play.'

'A stool is fine. Thanks.'

'We're not going to bother with any of this magic now.' Quen waved a hand at the computerised gizmos beside him. 'I just want to hear you as you are. So make yourself at home, get your guitar sorted out and then in your own time . . .'

Millie fiddled with her guitar, getting the tuning just right, and then hitched herself onto the stool so she was comfortable. She looked up and hoped she appeared a lot more confident than she felt. Her heart was thundering away behind her ribs and she wasn't entirely sure that her hands were completely steady. She'd always suffered from a few butterflies before she performed. Even at Georges' bar in France she'd been a bit nervous but she'd never experienced a blue funk like this before. She wondered if it would affect her voice.

'Ready?' asked Quen.

'Ready,' said Millie. She launched into 'Cracklin' Rosie' and when she got to the end of that she played one of Dido's hits as a contrast. Quen nodded but didn't say anything about her performance. Millie felt another burst of panic. Was it so crap that he didn't know how to let her down without being brutal? She sat there, wondering when the ordeal would be over. Perhaps he would dismiss her now. She hoped he would.

Instead Quen said, 'Tim tells me you've written some of your own stuff.'

Millie nodded.

'So, could I hear something of yours?' he prompted gently.

Still feeling sick and scared, Millie played the song she'd played at the Union. She was aware of Quen staring at her as she played. Obviously he'd never come across someone so freakily awful before. The last chord died away. Her mouth was dry and she swallowed to try and get some saliva circulating again.

'Thank you, Millie,' said Quen. 'The one thing that is absolutely obvious to me is that I need to get you some professional singing lessons as soon as possible.'

Millie's heart sank out of her ribcage and plunged past her

knees. She'd always thought her voice was quite good. Now she knew the truth: she couldn't hold a tune in a bucket.

'Right,' she said, willing her voice not to betray her disappointment. She'd told herself nothing was going to come of this audition. She'd been certain that Tim had been wasting his and his father's time, but despite everything, despite all her sensible, sound advice to herself, a little bud of hope had been at the back of her mind saying 'maybe . . .' and 'perhaps . . .' Now a chill blast of reality had frozen that bud to death. Millie felt devastated.

'Well, thank you for taking the time to listen to me,' she stammered as she got off the stool. She grabbed her guitar case and clutched it to her as she prepared to make her escape.

'No, the pleasure is all mine,' said Quen.

Yeah, right, thought Millie. Still, she imagined she'd given him a good laugh and he had a funny story to tell his record industry mates. 'Have you heard about the girl who thought she could sing?'

She didn't bother to put her guitar away, she just wanted out of the place. She stumbled out of the studio and tried to remember the way back to the main entrance hall and then the sanctuary of her own room. She turned down several corridors but nothing looked familiar. She was lost. For a second she panicked. Then, despite her crushing sense of disappointment which had been paralysing her thought processes, she reasoned that this wasn't the Amazon jungle but a country house and either she would find her way to the entrance or she'd come across something familiar or she'd run into a member of staff. All she had to do was keep going and she was bound to achieve one of the three objectives.

In the near silence of the empty passageways Millie became aware of the sound of voices. Clutching her guitar and its case, she headed towards the noise. She was sure one of them was Freya's. Was the other Tim's? She stopped padding along the thick carpets to listen.

Not Tim's but familiar. For a second or two she couldn't place it, then recognition crashed into her head. Luke! What the hell was he doing here? was the first thought that struck her. The second was that Freya must have invited him. Why on earth would she do that?

Drawn like filings to a magnet, Millie stole along the corridor towards the voices.

'And Millie doesn't know I'm here?' said Luke.

'No. I'll break the news to her in the morning.'

'She's going to be mad.'

'I know. And I agree, she won't like it one bit, but—'

A door shut. The voices disappeared.

Too fucking right I won't like it, thought Millie, rage replacing all her other feelings. Bastard Luke had somehow inveigled his way into Freya's life and now they expected her to spend a weekend in his company? Well, they could think again.

Millie leant against the corridor wall. A while back she'd wondered who the third person would be to betray her – and now she knew. Her mother had let her down first, then Luke had shafted her and got her the sack, and now Freya was conniving with that bastard. Millie didn't stop to think about Freya's motivation for such a move, she just knew it had to be true.

Stifling a sob that threatened to choke her, Millie made a decision. She wasn't going to stay in this place a minute longer. What was the point? Quen thought her music was the pits and her best friend – no, her *ex*-best friend – was busy selling her soul to the devil. Well, fuck 'em. Anger, disappointment and misery jostled for pole position in Millie's emotions. Tears threatened to spill down her face but she blinked them back. She wasn't going to waste energy crying over this lot of Judases.

She stamped along the corridor to the door that Luke and Freya had gone through and found that it opened into the main hall. Thankfully it was empty. She assumed the others were in a conspiratorial huddle, planning their next move, somewhere they reckoned she wouldn't find them. As if she was going to waste time looking. She would rather fry her own eyes than see any of them again.

In five minutes Millie had cleared her room, got her guitar stowed and was back by the front door. She paused. And where was she going to go exactly? She was in a massive house, miles from anywhere, certainly miles from the nearest station, and she was planning to do what?

With a surge of defiance and anger she wrenched open the front door and stormed off down the drive. Who cared? She certainly didn't. She didn't care if she had nowhere to go. She didn't care if it was late. She was leaving and that was that.

It took her half an hour to walk as far as one of the pretty villages they had driven through on the way to the Crendons' place. By the time Millie reached it, her shoulders were aching and her feet were sore. She had comfy shoes back in Saltford but she hadn't brought any for the weekend. Yomping across Oxfordshire hadn't been something she'd expected to do. Lights from the pub streamed across the village green and a hubbub of voices wafted on the still evening air towards her. She needed a rest and the thought of spending a few minutes in a friendly pub seemed a whole lot more enticing than hiking on. Anyway, she'd be able to find out about taxis or buses. Now her rage had subsided she knew she wasn't going to be able to walk to Oxford – not in the shoes she had on.

Millie opened the door and pushed her way into the crowded bar. The place was packed. It wasn't going to be a good idea to try to force her way through to the bar with a backpack on and a guitar case under her arm. Millie took them both off and stowed them near the door. Then, using her elbows selectively, she managed to squeeze through the press of people to the counter.

'Yes, miss,' said a jovial bearded man.

'A glass of lime and lemonade and a bit of information please.'

'Yes, dear.' The bloke began to pour the drink. 'And what information do you want?'

'Can I get a taxi from round here?'

The man stopped pouring and looked at her. 'Have you ordered one?'

'No.'

'Not at this time then, my dear. Isn't that right, Clive?'

Another man standing near Millie concurred. 'No, they don't come out this way at this time of night.'

'Well, is there a bus then?'

There was a burst of laughter. Millie took that to mean no. Now what? She was tired, she was miserable, she was almost broke and now she was stranded. The weekend that had started out with so much promise was now just dust and ashes.

Without warning, tears began to roll down her cheeks. The barman looked at her dumbfounded. Obviously most of his customers didn't walk in and break down.

'Sorry, love,' he mumbled, handing her her drink. 'You're not from round here, are you?'

Millie shook her head and began to fumble in her purse for some money.

'Put your money away. Have this on the house,' the barman said kindly. His kindness just made Millie cry even harder.

A woman bustled up beside her. 'Eee, Brian, you daft git. What have you done?'

'Nothing. Honest.' Brian looked justifiably aggrieved.

'Come with me, lass.' She took Millie's arm.

'My stuff,' Millie managed to blurt out between snotty sobs. She pointed to her pile of kit by the door and quickly wiped the worst of the tears off her face with her sleeve.

'I'll get that in a minute. Don't you worry.' The woman led Millie behind the bar, up a flight of stairs and into a cosy sitting room. She made Millie sit down in one of the armchairs and disappeared, only to reappear hauling Millie's pack and guitar.

'You carried this lot far, my dear?' she asked, dumping the items with a sigh of relief.

'Not very,' said Millie, blowing her nose vigorously on a tissue she found in a pocket.

'But there's nowhere much hereabouts.' She looked at Millie curiously but said no more. 'Now, I'm going to make you a nice cup of tea and then I want you to tell me what happened to you to make you so upset.'

Millie's sobs had subsided to the convulsive juddering stage when the pub landlady returned with a steaming mug of sweet tea.

'Thanks,' mumbled Millie. She took a sip and smiled weakly.

'Now, young lady, suppose you tell me what the matter is? Has someone attacked you? Are you hurt?'

'No, nothing like that. I'm just being pathetic.'

'Then what was it, dearie? Is there something I can do to help? And let's start by introducing ourselves. I'm Betty.'

Millie swallowed a sob and gave her name in return. She paused before telling Betty the details of the mess she was in. She didn't think anyone was going to be able to help her with the complete dog's breakfast her entire life was turning out to be. What was it about her that each time things seemed to be getting better they got even worse? So what was the point of giving Betty chapter and verse about Luke and Freya and her embarrassing audition with Quen. She improvised with, 'I had a row with a friend I was staying with.' Which wasn't anywhere near the truth but it would do. And it was probably believable.

'And you just lit out?'

'Mmm.'

'Must have been a humdinger of a row.'

'It was.' Millie sipped some more of her tea. She didn't want to think about the past couple of hours. It was all too raw.

'So what do you plan to do now?'

'I don't know,' said Millie in a small voice. Tears threatened again. She'd been impetuous and stupid but she couldn't have stayed at the house. And now, with nowhere to spend the night and no transport, she was up shit creek and no mistake. She blew her nose again on a now disgustingly soggy tissue.

'Would you like to stay here for the night?'

Millie glanced up. 'Oh no. I mean, I couldn't put you to any trouble. Besides, I could be anyone. I could be a mad psychopath.'

The landlady contemplated her, her arms crossed under her ample bosom. 'Do you know, when I first saw you come into the pub I said to myself, there's an escapee from Broadmoor or my name isn't Betty Dunn.'

Millie smiled wanly. 'There you go then. You've got me bang to rights.'

'I thought as much. But I like to live on the edge so I'll take the risk if you will. What do you say?'

'It's too much to ask.'

'No it's not. The spare bed is all made up and if you feel you have to offer me something in return I am sure we can come to some arrangement in the morning. Maybe you could help with bottling up or give a hand with cleaning the bar.'

'Anything, honest. That's really kind of you.'

'Good, that's settled then. Follow me.'

Millie dutifully did, clutching her guitar and her half-drunk mug of tea. Betty led the way with the backpack along a narrow corridor to a tiny little box room. There was just space for a chest of drawers and a single bed – quite the opposite of the opulent luxury room Millie had so nearly occupied, but it looked cosy and comfortable and, being at the back of the pub, the noise from the bar was reduced to a barely audible hum.

'This is lovely. Thank you so much.'

'The bathroom is next door. There's lashings of hot water. But, if you want my opinion,' Millie knew she was going to get it even if she said she didn't, 'you need to get straight to bed and have a good night's sleep. Things won't seem so bad in the morning, you mark my words.'

Betty left her to sort herself out and bid her goodnight. Millie looked at the bed and a wave of utter exhaustion swept through her. She yawned widely and flipped open the top flap of her rucksack. She'd just clean her teeth tonight and have a proper wash in the morning. Two minutes later she was back in the bedroom and in her nightie, ready for bed. Wearily she climbed into the bed – sheets, blankets and an eiderdown, no modern duvets for Betty Dunn – and snuggled down. Worn out by the traumas of the last few hours, Millie was asleep in seconds.

22

'Here you are pet, I thought you'd like a nice cuppa to start the day.'

Millie opened her eyes. Where the hell was she? Then she saw Betty and remembered all the hideous events of the previous evening. And Betty's kindness.

'Did you sleep all right?'

Millie yawned and stretched. 'Yes, thank you, Betty.'

'Now, there's no hurry so you have a bath or a shower or whatever you want and then come down to the kitchen and I'll make you a nice plate of bacon and eggs.'

'Toast would be fine, honest,' protested Millie.

'We'll see about that,' said Betty, shutting the door behind her.

Millie showered, dressed and made her way downstairs as directed. The smell of frying bacon wafted towards her from the kitchen and suddenly the idea that toast would make an adequate breakfast seemed pretty lame.

'Morning,' she said to her hosts as she entered the warm bright kitchen. Sun streamed through the kitchen windows and a powder-blue sky promised this was going to be a beautiful day. Despite the awfulness of the previous day's events, Millie felt her spirits lift.

Brian looked up from his paper. 'Well, you look happier today and no mistake.'

Millie nodded. 'Sorry I was such a wet blanket yesterday.'

'Never you mind about that now. You tuck into this.' Betty opened the Aga door and pulled out a plate piled with egg, bacon, mushrooms, tomatoes and fried bread.

'Goodness,' said Millie.

'And things will look even brighter when you've had a decent breakfast. Tea? Coffee?'

'Tea please,' said Millie through a mouthful of bacon and egg. Breakfast was delicious and despite the daunting quantity that had been placed before her she had no problems in polishing it off. Brian and Betty watched her as she mopped up the last smear of egg yolk with the final corner of fried bread.

Millie cleared her mouth and then cleared her throat. 'I can't thank you enough for rescuing me. I don't know what I'd have done without your kindness. I must pay you for my bed and board.'

'We won't hear of it, will we, Brian?' said Betty firmly.

'But last night you said—'

'Last night I had to say something to make sure you weren't going to hightail if off in the blue again. Anyone with half an eye could see you were in a bad way. In that state you might have done anything.'

Millie felt the colour rise in her face at the shame of her idiocy. She'd been such a fool last night, running off like that, with no money, no plan and no transport. She'd been so lucky that these wonderful people had taken her in. Goodness only knew what might have become of her without their kindness. But they must still think of her as a complete flake. How embarrassing.

'Then let me do something else to help out. You said I could do some work.'

'All done for today, lass,' said Brian. 'So there's an end to it.'

'Oh.' Millie didn't know what to say.

'So where are you going to go from here?'

'I thought maybe there's a bus to Oxford. Or a taxi? Would one come out this far in daylight.'

'It would cost you a pretty penny. And the bus went at nine. There won't be another till three,' said Betty. 'You're very welcome to stay here till then if you'd like.'

'Thank you.' What Millie really wanted was to put as much space as she could between her and Lord Crendon's mansion. Sadly that didn't seem to be an option. Her disappointment must have shown on her face.

'Tell you what,' said Brian. 'I'll see if there's anyone in the village planning on going into Oxford. Maybe we can arrange you a lift.'

'Please don't go to any trouble. You've been kindness itself as it is. I can wait till three – if you don't mind, that is.'

But Brian had already reached across to the dresser and pulled the phone towards him. With studied care he dialled a number.

'Come on, lass,' said Betty, clattering a couple of plates together and picking up the teapot. 'You can help me with the dishes while he gets on with that.'

Betty handed Millie a tray then went across to the sink and ran the hot water. Millie stacked the plates and carried them over. Between them they cleared away all traces of breakfast while Brian made several calls. Finally he put the phone own and turned to them.

'Jacob says he's got an errand to do in town. He'll be

round in about ten minutes. Can you be packed and ready for him in that time?'

Millie nodded. 'I didn't unpack.' She went to fetch her stuff and then returned and stood awkwardly by her possessions.

'I wish I could thank you properly.'

'Get away, lass,' said Brian. 'It was nothing.'

'It was a great deal,' Millie corrected him.

Betty came forward and clasped Millie to her large bust. 'You just take care of yourself. No more running out into the night, young lady. I'm sure no situation is so bad it can't wait till daylight breaks to get it sorted.'

'No, you're right. I was stupid,' agreed Millie. Everything had seemed terrible last night and today, with the sun shining, it still wasn't good but perhaps not worth risking life and limb over. The fact that Quen thought she had a rubbish voice didn't mean she'd never get work again – she probably would; there were plenty of pubs in Saltford that might let her sing for a few quid. And the students seemed to love her at the Union. Yes, his low opinion was a blow but not the end of the world. More upsetting was what Freya had done. Freya – what had possessed her? Millie shoved that thought into a deep cupboard in her mind and slammed the door. She was not going to think about that. Not now and maybe not for a while. It was too upsetting.

A horn hooted out the front of the bar.

'That'll be Jacob,' said Betty. 'Now off you go and you take care.' She planted a fat wet kiss on Millie's cheek and pushed her towards the door of the kitchen. 'Brian will let you out the front.'

Millie followed Brian to the door of the saloon bar and waited while he unlocked it.

'Jacob is sound. He'll see you get to where you want. Have a safe journey.'

Millie was tempted to give him a hug but her guitar and her rucksack would have got in the way. Besides, she thought it might embarrass him.

'Goodbye, Brian. And thanks.'

She walked out of the dimness of the bar into bright sunshine and for a few seconds she was blinded.

'There you are!'

Millie blinked to try and see what the hell was going on. Her eyes adjusted and there, getting out of the car right in front of her, was Quen.

'No,' she said. 'No! What's going on?' She turned to Brian for some sort of explanation. He'd promised her a lift with some bloke called Jacob, not Quen.

Brian shrugged his shoulders. 'Sorry, your lordship,' he said. 'Sorry, Millie.' Obviously he wasn't sure what the hell was going on either. 'I *was* expecting Jacob,' he said to Millie as if to underline the worth of his apology. 'Jacob Mollington. I didn't know you had anything to do with the big house.'

Quen took a couple of steps towards Millie. 'Mr Mo told me about the call as soon as he got it. We've been worried sick about this lady all night. She just disappeared without a word. If Mr Mo hadn't put two and two together this morning and come to me I'd have had the police out searching by now. Under the circumstances I thought I'd better come and fetch her myself.'

'But I don't want to be fetched,' said Millie, thrusting her chin out and finding courage she didn't know she had. 'Don't you get it? I want to get away.'

Quen looked as though he had been slapped. 'But why?' he stammered.

'Because you think my singing is shit.' Even Millie was shocked by how rude she sounded. 'And because of what Freya has done,' she added rather lamely.

Quen looked even more lost. 'But where on earth have you got this idea from that I don't like your voice?'

'I got it from you. You said I needed lessons.'

'Fuck,' said Quen. 'I did. And you do.'

'There, you see!' yelled Millie in triumph, her point proved.

'Because if you're going to sing professionally for the rest of your life in places the size of Wembley Arena, as I really think you will, you need to have your voice trained properly. You have a wonderful instrument there and you must take care of it. It would be a sin to damage it. Lessons will prevent that.'

'I don't understand.'

'Obviously.' Quen rolled his eyes. 'Millie, I wish you'd said something at the time. I thought you realised I thought you were sensational. I don't offer to arrange lessons for anyone. But you're special, Millie. Tim was right. Christ, if I hadn't liked your performance I would have stopped you after a couple of verses. Didn't the fact that I let you sing three numbers tell you anything?'

'No. I've not really done an audition before.' Millie slowly put down her guitar and her backpack. Things were getting surreal again. 'So you liked my stuff then?'

'Yes. It's fantastic. And I want to hear more of it. I couldn't believe it when Freya said you'd left. I rang all the taxi companies but no one had given you a ride. I was beside myself. We all were. Freya is in bits.'

'Huh,' said Millie ungraciously. Serve her right. In bits, was she? Millie knew about being in bits and she didn't think Freya was anywhere close to the level of disintegration she'd gone through yesterday. She might have got the wrong end of the stick with Quen but there was no excuse for Freya to be conniving with Luke.

'Come on back to the house, Millie,' said Quen. 'Apart from anything else, you and I have a lot to discuss. And I want to hear more of your own work. Tim tells me you've been working hard on some material.'

Millie shook her head. 'I can't.'

Quen rolled his eyes again. 'Look, I'm not sure what is going on with you and Freya but I think you've got the wrong end of the stick there too. If it's got anything to do with this bloke Luke then you certainly have.'

'No, you don't understand.'

'I think I do.' Quen held his hand up to silence Millie. 'Tell you what, if you come back with me, and if Freya can't convince you that she really does have your best interests at heart, then I'll drive you to anywhere you want to go straight away. No questions asked, no delay. Deal?'

Millie still wasn't sure. Maybe Freya did think she was doing right but that bastard Luke was a whole other issue. He'd probably pulled the wool over Freya's eyes, like he had hers.

'You got it wrong about what I thought of you,' wheedled Quen. 'You could be wrong about Freya too.'

Millie scuffed at the gritty surface of the pub car park with the toe of her shoe.

'Go on, Millie,' said Brian. 'His lordship is a proper gent, he'll honour his promise. What have you got to lose?'

'For God's sake, Brian, how many times have I told you to call me Quen?'

'His lordship,' continued Brian as if Quen hadn't said a

word, 'is as straight as a die, so if he says he'll do something, he will.'

Millie wasn't sure she entirely trusted Quen but Brian was another matter.

Betty emerged from the door of the bar. 'Goodness, you still here? Oh! Your lordship. I didn't see you there.'

'It's Quen,' said Quen with a heavy sigh.

'Yes, so you say, your lordship. I though Jacob was fetching Millie.'

Quen explained the situation a second time.

'So what's keeping you, lovey?' said Betty. 'His lordship will get you to the station later if that's what you really want and maybe, in the meantime, you can sort things out with your friend.'

Millie couldn't pit herself against three people relentlessly determined to make her kiss and make up with Freya. Millie could not see the point of an encounter with her ex-friend but if she went back with Quen, she would prove him wrong about Freya's good intentions. Conniving cow! Quite where that would leave her relationship with Quen, though, she wasn't sure.

Heaving a defeated sigh, Millie agreed. Before she could change her mind she found Quen and Brian had bundled her kit in the boot and got her belted up in the front seat.

Just a few minutes later Quen had the car parked at the back of the house where they were met by a relieved Mrs Mo.

'What did you go and do a thing like that for?' she grumbled at Millie. 'Worried us all silly.'

'Sorry,' mumbled Millie.

'I should think so too. Now you come in and I'll make you a nice cup of tea.'

Mrs Mo bustled off just as Freya emerged from the kitchen door. Millie felt a surge of renewed anger. She turned away and retrieved her backpack and her guitar from the boot.

'Millie, I know what it looks like,' began Freya.

'Huh!'

'But you're wrong. Luke isn't what you think.'

'What? Not a bastard? Not a prize sneak?' she said over her shoulder, dragging her rucksack out of the car.

'No, not really.'

Millie turned back to her erstwhile friend. 'Maybe he's convinced you, but I know what he did to me. So save your breath, Freya.' She barged past her and into the house and cannoned straight into Luke.

'Shit,' she exclaimed as she realised who it was. She began to turn to flee but Luke caught her by her arm.

'Oh no you don't. Not till you've heard my side.' Millie struggled but Luke held her tight. 'And you're not getting away from me again, young lady. It's taken me months to track you down.'

'Stalker,' she snarled. Then, 'Let go, you bully.'

Quen, followed by Tim, strode into the kitchen. 'Children, children, enough!'

Millie, shaking with rage, stopped trying to yank her arm free and Luke relaxed his grip so his fingers weren't actually hurting her any more.

'We're all going to sit round this table and discuss exactly what the problems are over a nice cup of tea,' said Quen, with a steely note in his voice. Even Millie, in her state of righteous indignation, found she didn't feel like contradicting him.

Right on cue Mrs Mo plonked a huge brown china teapot

in the middle of the table and then reached for five mugs off the shelf on the dresser. Millie sat sulkily on the chair Quen had pulled out for her, refusing to look at Luke who sat opposite, or Freya who sat beside her.

Mrs Mo poured tea and milk into the mugs and passed the sugar bowl and a plate of shortbread around. Millie, sulking, refused both and fiddled with the handle of her mug desultorily.

'Right, Luke. You go first,' said Quen.

Millie harrumphed and muttered, 'This should be interesting,' but everyone ignored her.

Luke explained that although Millie had confided in him about the lift passes, he'd said nothing, not even to Archie, and couldn't understand why Millie just disappeared. He'd searched the resort high and low till the end of his holiday but couldn't find her and, in the end, he'd had to give up and fly home.

'I wasted a whole day's skiing,' he said to underline his dedication. 'I wouldn't have minded that so much but I knew I'd already paid over the odds for the sodding pass.' The others laughed at his attempt at humour but Millie just glowered. He then told them how he'd tracked Freya down but he'd used a false name so she wouldn't blank him instantly. 'I had to find out what the fuck I'd done to upset you, Millie. I knew Freya would know. When she told me, I couldn't believe it. I knew I was the innocent party in this. Anyway, I told Archie, who came up with a plan to find out who had blown the whistle. Trouble was, he involved the consumer desk on the paper we both work on, hence the story about the reps. But the upshot is that I now know who did blow the whistle – and it wasn't me.' Millie narrowed her eyes but remained silent. Luke paused and took a deep breath. 'Millie, if I told you that the head of customer relations at the company you worked for is called Deirdre, would that make any sense to you.'

Slowly Millie's eyes widened. 'Deedee?'

'One and the same.'

'Deedee?'

Luke nodded again. 'She went out there with a mission and that was to find out what the reps were really getting up to. As soon as she was asked for a deposit on her lift pass, she smelt a rat. It didn't take her long to work the rest out. She was there to snoop and snoop she did.'

'I caught her and Cuthbert rummaging around the chalet one morning,' said Millie thoughtfully. 'They said they wanted to find where I kept the coffee, but I knew I'd told everyone. But at the time I didn't think anything of it.'

'They were searching for evidence of wrongdoing amongst the reps.'

'To think I even mended her jacket for her. What a cow!' Millie's anger transferred itself from Luke to Deedee in an instant. 'The double-dealing bitch.'

Then another thought struck her. 'And I blamed you for it all. And I thought Freya had betrayed me too.' Her face crumpled for the umpteenth time in less than a day. 'You must think . . .' She stopped She couldn't even begin to imagine how badly they thought of her. She buried her face in her hands and bawled.

Freya got up and put her arms round Millie. 'Millie, of course we don't think badly of you. God knows, you've had enough shit happen in your life recently for you to get a bit paranoid.' Millie snuffled noisily. She'd been such an idiot. She'd got Quen wrong, she'd got Luke wrong, she'd got Freya wrong. No wonder her life was a complete mess. If she couldn't even suss out the intentions of people who cared about her, no wonder everything was so fucked up.

Millie looked over Freya's shoulder at Luke. How on earth could he have any feelings for her at all after the shabby way she'd treated him? But it seemed he did. He was smiling at her, just as gorgeous as she'd remembered him in her dreams during all those lonely nights. He must have really cared for her too, to have gone to so much trouble to prove his innocence. Wanly Millie smiled back at him. Slowly both their smiles faded as the impact of their true feelings for each other became clear and the gaze they exchanged was long and meaningful.

Quen disappeared from the table and reappeared a minute or two later with a magnum of champagne.

'You may not think this is appropriate but I do. I want to celebrate finding a wonderful new talent, and to having that talent restored to me when I thought it had been lost. I also think we ought to drink to friendship. Mrs Mo, if you could find me some glasses please.'

23

By the time the five of them had emptied the big bottle of champagne, Quen had persuaded Millie to leave her job and move into Crendon House, despite her initial protests.

'I'll have to work out my notice.'

'Oh no you don't. I want you to start serious voice training right now. The last thing I want to do is to risk you damaging your vocal chords. I'll get Mr Mo to drive you to Saltford to clear your flat and tell the supermarket you won't be coming back.'

'But I'll have to pay the landlord three months' rent in lieu of notice,' said Millie, worrying where on earth she was going to find that sort of cash. She had twenty pounds in her handbag and about another twenty in her bank and that was that.

'I shall take care of that.'

'But the expense!'

'Millie, my dear, have you any idea of the sort of money you're going to be worth when I start to promote you?'

'N-n-o,' stammered Millie.

'Let's just say that the rent on a flat in Saltford is going to seem like small change soon.' Quen stood up. 'If my paying your rent for you is going to give you sleepless nights, you can write me an IOU, but frankly, my dear, I don't give a damn. Now I am going to ring some people to get things in motion for your future and I suggest you four finish building bridges.'

Strangely, about five minutes after Quen left, Freya and Tim found they had an urgent errand to run regarding arrangements for the ball, and Mrs Mo had also left the kitchen. Luke and Millie were alone.

'So,' said Luke, taking Millie's hands in his across the table, 'what does a guy have to do to get an apology around here?'

Millie blushed to her roots. 'Oh Luke, I can't believe I got things so wrong.'

'If only you had confronted me at the time, told me that you blamed me for it all, it would have saved so much hassle.'

'I know what I'm like. Once I get an idea in my head, that's that. I wouldn't have believed you. You would have denied it and I would have called you a liar.'

'Perhaps I should have levelled with you from the start and told you I was a hack, then you wouldn't have confided in me and none of this would have happened.'

'Why didn't you?'

'I just get fed up with people thinking that because I work for the press I am their magic key to being a celebrity.'

'I wouldn't have thought of using you like that.'

'Lord, I know *you* wouldn't have done. But Chelsea and Venice? They're the sort of girls who would apply to go on *Big Brother*, thinking that all that exposure would make them rich and happy.'

Luke got up and came round the table to where Millie was sitting. She got to her feet. Millie found herself standing so close to Luke she could see his chest rise and fall with each breath he took. She looked into his eyes and with a whoosh remembered just how devastating she'd found them that first evening in the chalet, the evening she'd nearly dropped vin chaud all over the floor. Quickly she lowered her eyes and looked at the floor. It was all wrong. Everything was going too quickly. Less than a couple of hours ago she would have cheerfully buried him alive and now all she wanted to do was bury her face against his chest.

'Come on, Millie, you and I have a lot of catching up to do. Let's go somewhere we can be sure of not getting disturbed.' The spell was broken again and Millie put thoughts about what actually hugging Luke would be like out of her mind. He led the way out of the house and across the courtyard.

The day was perfect. The sky was speedwell blue with a flock of tiny puffy clouds scattered across it. The temperature was pleasantly warm and the air was still and filled with the warblings and twitterings of numerous birds. They walked away from the house and through the kitchen garden.

'Freya tells me there is a river down here somewhere. Let's see if we can find it.'

They wandered along a gravel path and down the steps that led over a ha-ha. Across the flower-filled meadow was a line of willows. They headed towards them and then flopped down in the shade of the trailing fronds by the slowly flowing stream. Millie lay on her back looking up towards the crown of the tree while Luke propped himself up on his elbow and stared at her.

'Freya told me about you. Why you left home.'

Millie lowered her eyes and bit her lip. 'She shouldn't have done.'

'She wanted me to understand what a rough year you've had.' Luke reached out and pushed a strand of hair off Millie's forehead. She felt a little stab of electricity at his touch. 'She needed me to understand quite why it mattered so much to you that you thought I'd done the dirty on you. Why didn't you tell me about the reason for your row with your dad?'

'Because I was so ashamed. I should have had more sense than to get pregnant.'

'Freya said it was because you were so naïve and innocent. And that your boyfriend really pressurised you.'

'It doesn't alter the fact I slept with him and behaved like a slut.'

Luke shook his head at that statement. 'Is that what your father said?'

Millie glanced up sharply. 'Amongst other things.'

'I don't think your mother thinks that.'

'How the hell do you know that?'

'Because I went to see her.'

'You what?' Millie sat bolt upright and was obviously about to let fly when Luke stopped her.

'She didn't know it was me.' He explained about the fake parcel. 'And she was worried sick about you. I'd never met her before but it was obvious that she was fraught. When she rang me she was desperate for news.'

'She let Dad throw me out,' mumbled Millie. A lump began to form in her throat at the memory. 'He went ape and she hid in the kitchen. I wanted her to help me stand up to him but she left me to fend for myself.' A tear rolled down her cheek. 'I thought she loved me but she abandoned me. And when I said I had to leave, she just let me go.'

Luke, watching her, could see the pain reliving the past was causing her and sat up too. He pulled her against him and cradled her while she cried silently. He didn't know what to say. Julie had cried buckets over all sorts of things – bad performances, bad auditions, bad hair days – but Luke had always found her rants and tantrums fake and somewhat laughable. This outpouring of utter grief was a new experience to him

Luke hugged her close. If he could have absorbed her pain by osmosis he'd have willingly done it but, as it was, all he could do was just be there for her. He stroked her back and made soothing noises as Millie wept. He let go of her for a second and pulled a hanky from his pocket which she took and used to blow her nose.

'I'm sorry,' she stammered.

'Shhh,' said Luke. He rubbed her back some more. 'What's to be sorry about?'

'Being so wet.'

Luke pulled back from her so he could look at her face. 'You are a bit soggy, I'll give you that.'

Millie snuffled and smiled wanly. She blew her nose again. 'I must look hideous.'

'Millie, you could never look hideous,' he said softly. He kissed her forehead and pushed some stray tendrils of hair off her face. Then he took the hanky from her and wiped away her tears. He handed it back. 'Blow,' he instructed.

Millie blew.

'Better?'

She nodded. 'A bit.'

And then Luke kissed her on her lips. It wasn't what she was expecting but it felt so right. Millie gave herself up to the sensation of the softness of his skin against hers and closed her eyes to allow all her other senses to savour the moment too. She could smell aftershave and the clean, crisp scent of freshly laundered clothes. She slid her hands up and touched the skin on his cheeks, warm with just the faintest hint of roughness from stubble, and then pushed them on up into his hair. It was thick and curly and wrapped itself around her fingers as if it wanted to draw her hands into itself. Involuntarily her lips parted slightly and Luke's tongue fluttered against them. She could taste him, clean with a hint of champagne, and she could feel his warm breath on her cheek as he exhaled. She breathed in to capture even more of the scent, the essence of him. Luke withdrew his lips from hers. She felt the cool air from the shade of the willow wash over her face again. She opened her eyes and gazed into his deep brown ones as a little sigh of disappointment escaped.

'Don't stop,' she whispered.

Millie lay back on the grass and Luke lay beside her, propped up on one elbow so he could look at her and traced the outline of her mouth with his forefinger. Then he leant forward and began to plant kisses on her eyes, her forehead, her cheeks and then finally her mouth. This time Millie parted her lips and allowed his tongue to explore it. She felt him nibble on her lower lip, she could taste the saltiness of him, she felt herself washed away with abandon, feeling a thrill like nothing she had known before.

'Wow,' she whispered.

'Wow, indeed,' said Luke. He kissed her again and folded his arms around her, holding her tight. He kissed the top of her head. Millie relaxed against him, feeling happy, fulfilled and, for the first time in an age, loved.

24

The next couple of weeks passed in a blur. Millie moved out of her flat. It took only half a morning for her and Mr Mo to get all her worldly goods into the back of a horsebox borrowed from the estate. As soon as her lamps and bright rugs were removed, the bedsit reverted once more to the dingy dump it had always been. Millie shuddered. How could she ever have thought that this place could be homely? No wonder Freya had tried to drag her away from it. Well, she was away from it now. Although, quite what would happen if things didn't pan out the way Quen was predicting, Millie wasn't sure. It was scary to look beyond the next few weeks. She felt as if she was standing on the edge of a cliff and when she stepped off she was either going to fly or plummet. But which was it going to be?

Once the kit was stowed in the back of the horsebox they drove to the supermarket where Millie handed in her notice. The manager was sorry to see her go but admitted that he'd known this moment would happen.

'I knew I wasn't going to keep you. You were always too good for this place,' he said. 'I've employed a lot of shop girls in my time but never one quite like you. What are you going to do now?'

Millie couldn't bring herself to brag about the opportunity that had come her way so she just said she'd got a job at a stately home.

'Much more your style,' said the manager kindly. 'You've got too much class for an outfit like this. But me and the rest of the team will really miss you, Millie.' He wished her well and Millie was surprised to feel almost sorry she was going. He'd been a good boss and had offered her a degree of security and a bit of a lifeline when her life had been in a complete mess for a second time in just over a year.

When she got back to Crendon House and had unloaded her stuff – most of it straight into the cellar for storage – she discovered that she hadn't been the only one having a busy morning. Quen had been hitting the phones putting a team together to help Millie attain her potential. Once she had finished unpacking, he dragged her off to his studio and outlined how she would be spending the next few weeks.

'And I expect you to work your socks off,' he said with mock severity.

Her mornings were to be spent in the studio being taught how to sing properly, how to warm her vocal chords up, exercise her diaphragm and voice projection techniques. He'd got a musician friend to help her with her compositions. He'd made arrangements with a stylist to sort out her clothes and hair and hired a personal trainer to get her fit.

'I sit on a stool with a guitar,' she'd argued. 'I'm not Madonna. I shan't be bouncing around a stage doing dancing.'

'I wouldn't bank on it,' said Quen. 'You're young and pretty, your fans may well expect you to bounce around a bit. Besides, tours are exhausting. You'll need stamina.'

Millie found the whole idea of fans being able to dictate what she did rather bizarre but she didn't argue. If Quen had wanted her to learn to walk on hot coals, she'd have given it her best shot.

After the first couple of days at Crendon House, Quen left her to the ministrations of 'the team' and jetted off to do whatever he did in the States.

'Deals, make money, talent-spot,' he'd said when Millie asked. Once he'd gone, she felt rather abandoned.

She was so busy she barely had time to notice that she hardly saw anything of Tim and Freya either. Their paths crossed at mealtimes but even then Tim and Freya were so engrossed in making plans for the ball they couldn't focus on anything else. As far as Millie could see, it was like organising a military operation, it was so complex. What with marquees and caterers, florists and security, car parking arrangements and portable loos, the list of jobs to be done seemed neverending.

'Blimey,' said Millie over breakfast one morning, 'I thought this was a Crisis International bash. You seem to be doing everything.'

'They're doing plenty. Plus they're doing all the PR. The division of labour is pretty fair. Because the ball is being held here and we know the lay of the land, it makes more sense for us to talk to the companies who will be pitching up with generators and portaloos and want to know where to put them.'

'If you say so.' Millie wasn't convinced things were entirely equal. 'How many guests are coming?'

'About four hundred. We've got a guest list of three hundred and Crisis International have about a hundred coming. Their lot are the great and the good and ours are the rich and the famous. But either way they're all paying through the nose for tickets. But then that's what people do at fundraisers, that and buy weird stuff at the auction.'

'Auction?'

'Yes,' said Freya. 'We've asked the A-listers to donate stuff – tickets for stage shows, signed gold discs, dresses, that sort of stuff.'

'Wow, that should raise a mint.'

'That's the idea. We should get even more if we ply them all with loads of drink. You know what people are like when they've had a few.'

Things quietened down over the weekend. The contractors shut their offices and Quen allowed Millie a couple of days off her training regime as long as she promised to do an hour of singing exercises and a run round the estate each day. Luke escaped from the city and raced down the motorway to see them all. He arrived as they were enjoying breakfast on the terrace.

When Millie saw him appear round the corner of the house she felt such a surge of happiness shoot through her, she thought the emotion would fizz out of her extremities. Luke wandered over the flagstones and dropped a kiss on Millie's forehead.

'Hi, folks. Not intruding, I hope.'

'You could never intrude,' said Freya. 'However, Tim and I have got things to attend to, so we'll have to abandon you to Millie's loving care.'

'What things?' said Tim.

'Things!' said Freya, grabbing his hand and pulling him out of his chair.

Millie and Luke watched them go. 'Not subtle but

effective,' said Luke. He pulled a chair close to Millie's and sat down so his knees were almost touching hers. 'How has the week been?'

'The same as I told you on the phone last night, and the night before.'

'But I want to hear about it again.'

'Then let's walk. I'm supposed to be doing my fitness training.'

'I didn't think walking was what your trainer prescribed.'

'No, but we might be able to think of something more energetic to do en route.'

Luke smiled wolfishly. 'Now that sounds more like it.'

Millie was awoken twice on Monday morning before her alarm was due to go off. Firstly by Luke slipping from under the covers and trying to get dressed silently in the dark.

'I'm awake,' she said sleepily when her brain had finally cottoned on to what was going on.

'Back to sleep,' whispered Luke. 'Not your fault I have to get back to London. I didn't want to disturb you. You need your sleep.'

'That's not what you said last night,' said Millie with a giggle.

'That was then, this is now.' He leaned over her to give her a farewell kiss. Millie clasped her arms about his neck and pulled him back onto the bed, pressing her cheek against his and inhaling the smell of his skin and his hair. Then she turned her face to give him a chaste peck on the lips.

'You'd better go or I'll get carried away.'

'Again?' Even in the dark, Millie could see the twinkle in his eyes. 'For a bishop's daughter you are very good at sins of the body and carnal knowledge.'

'Only because I have had such expert tuition. I haven't always had this level of expertise.'

'Glad to hear it.'

Luke gave her another kiss and slipped out of her room to hit the road before the traffic got too bad.

Millie snuggled under the duvet and thought back to the night that had just passed. Her body ached deliciously from where Luke had kissed and nibbled her skin. Just remembering what he had done caused her muscles to tighten with desire. She had no idea that sex could be so absolutely fulfilling and wonderful – and abandoned.

Millie fell into a contented sleep and dreamed of Luke until the throb and roar of a lorry engine in the garden outside her room propelled her back to reality.

Rubbing the sleep from her eyes, she staggered out of bed and tottered across to the big bay window. She knelt on the window seat and pulled back the curtain. A huge truck with its own mechanical grab was unloading mountainous bundles of canvas and poles. The marquees for the ball had arrived. Tim and Freya were out on the lawn giving directions as to where the grab was to dump the loads, while a posse of hefty-looking blokes was starting to make preparations to get the big tents pitched.

Obviously, with this sort of racket going on, there was no chance of further sleep. A glance at her alarm clock told Millie that it was almost time for her to be getting up and heading for the gym anyway. She slipped into her tracksuit and made her way to the back of the house. By the time she had worked out and showered, the truck had departed, leaving behind mountains of canvas and metal. It didn't look to Millie as though much progress had been made but then what did she know about marquees? Besides, they had till Saturday to get it all sorted. Surely that was heaps of time.

After breakfast and before her singing lesson, Millie wandered out to see what was going on at close quarters. Some of the canvas was now spread out on the ground and blokes with power tools were beavering away making Meccano-like constructions with shiny steel girders and huge nuts and bolts.

A blonde in a hard hat and incredibly tight jeans was issuing instructions.

'Oi, you,' she yelled over the noise. 'Yeah, you, shit-for-brains.' A man twenty yards away looked up. 'If I catch you taking short cuts again, I'll have you off this site so fast you won't have time to say P45. Now do the job properly or sling your 'ook.' The bloke muttered and returned to his job. Millie hid a smile. She didn't know who the woman was but she obviously ran this operation with a rod of iron. She turned to go back to the house and almost cannoned into another blonde.

For a second the two women stood staring at each other.

'Fuckin' 'ell,' said the blonde. 'It's Mil.'

'Chelsea,' exclaimed Millie.

'Venice. That's Chel.'

The two girls hugged each other amid exclamations of 'What are you doing here?' and 'Well I never!' Venice yelled over to Chelsea to come and see who she'd found and the process was repeated a second time with even louder yelps and squeals.

'So, come on,' said Venice. 'How come a chalet girl winds up at a pad like this?'

'It's a long story,' said Millie. 'I'm a friend of a friend.'

'Cor, we wouldn't mind having friends like that. How

fucking good would that be? It'd beat putting up sodding tents for a living.'

Millie laughed. 'When you said your dads made tents, I thought of camping holidays. I never imagined you meant dirty great things like this.'

'Yeah, well, we play it down. You'd be amazed at how many people expect you to offer one for free, or at a knock-down price, if you tell them you're in the marquee business,' said Chelsea.

'It doesn't surprise me one bit.'

'I mean, if we did, how would we be able to afford to go skiing again? And talking of skiing, what happened to you at the end? We never got to say goodbye and thank you for being so great, or anything.'

Millie explained about everything.

'What a bummer,' said Chelsea. 'I never did like Deedee. Prissy cow. Still, water under the bridge.' She changed the subject. 'You involved with organising this ball then?'

Millie shook her head. 'I'm just a friend of the people who are. When they told me about it I had no idea what would be involved. And it's costing a fortune.'

'I can believe,' said Venice. 'Mind you, our dads are doing this lot at a discount. They got rung up by this charity. Said they could have an invite if they did the tents.'

'Fair do,' said Millie.

'So we'll be here on Saturday an' all. You coming?'

'Sort of.' Millie explained she'd be performing.

'Fuckin' hell. And all that time in France you never said.'

'No, well. Luke and Archie knew.'

Chelsea and Venice's faces broke into smiles. 'We liked them, didn't we, Chel? Specially Archie.'

'He had a soft spot for you, Ven. You could have been in there. Shame we lost contact.'

'Well, your luck may be in at the weekend. He and Luke are going to be here too.'

'Nah! Get away!' Both girls looked thrilled at the prospect.

'You make sure you don't let him get away this time, Ven,' said Chelsea.

Millie smiled. With a load of friends other than Freya and Tim, the ball looked as though it was going to be a whole heap more fun than she had ever hoped.

Activity around Crendon house got more and more frantic as the week wore on. By Wednesday the complex of marquees was up and finished. There was one huge tent for dining and dancing and next to it were two smaller tents for the caterers and waiting staff. There were also two 'corridor' tents. One led to the house and the other to the complex of portaloos. Everything had been boarded out and then carpeted so the ladies' high heels and long dresses would be safe from the ravages of gravel or grass. The marquees themselves had all been lined with swags of pale yellow and white, and the effect was stunning.

Chelsea and Venice had made Tim and Freya wait until they were completely finished before they allowed them a preview.

'Like it?' asked Chel.

'Wonderful,' was Freya's response.

'You wait till the chandeliers are up and the pillars are hidden by flowers,' said Tim, also impressed. 'It'll be magical by the time we've finished.'

'Right, we'll be back on Saturday,' said the cousins, 'so

we'll have a look then. Meantime, best we leave you with this.' Venice handed over a brown envelope. 'That's the bill.'

Tim opened it. 'That can't be right,' he stammered. He passed the bill to Freya. She looked down at it in trepidation. The bills they'd had so far had been horrendous – pretty much what they'd been expecting but horrendous all the same – and they were both terrified that they wouldn't be able to bring the event in on budget. A bigger bill than expected for the tentage might really throw a spanner in the works.

'Zero?' said Freya. 'But . . .'

'We had a word with our dads,' said Chelsea. 'We twisted their arms and said it'd be a bigger gesture if they let the charity have the tents for free. They might even get some PR out of it. And they said sod it, all right, so there you go. Just you make sure the charity gets the difference.'

'We certainly will,' said Freya and Tim in unison.

'Right, see you Friday.' The two girls were just about to leave when Venice came running back. 'Frey, you will make sure Mil looks the biz at the ball, won't you? Only you know what she's like about clothes.'

'Don't worry,' said Freya. 'I'm taking her shopping this afternoon.'

With the tents ready, it was the turn of the florists and the electricians to move in. After checking briefly that they knew what they were doing and that the two teams understood the importance of liaising over where power points for the fairy lights were going and how the cables were to be concealed by greenery and ribbons, Tim and Freya left them to it. They both had more than enough other jobs to be getting on with and Freya wanted to be sure of clearing her afternoon to get Millie kitted out for the big day.

Freya met Millie coming out of the gym.

'Get yourself showered and changed,' she said without preamble. 'We're going into Oxford.'

'Why?'

'To get you something for the ball.'

'Why?'

'Because, Millie, I'm fresh out of magic wands, so we've got to buy something instead.'

'No, I mean why do I need something for the ball?'

Freya grabbed Millie's arm and dragged her along the corridor as she spoke. 'You are going to be performing. Therefore, people will be looking at you, therefore you need to look good. You may think jeans and a grungy top are what a rock chick ought to wear but I don't. Oh, and neither does Quen. He's given me a fat cheque to spend on you and spend it I'm going to.'

Millie might have been inclined to argue with Freya but Quen . . . She whizzed in and out of her shower and hauled on the clothes that Freya passed into the bathroom.

'A skirt and sandals?' she protested.

'Easier to slip in and out of than jeans when you're trying stuff on.'

Millie grumbled and got dressed.

'Now get back in there and shove some make-up on. We can't tell how good the dress is if you turn up looking like a dog.'

'Thanks a bunch!'

'Actually, you could never look like a dog but you need to give these outfits your best shot. I do shopping, you don't, so trust me on this.'

Half an hour later Freya had locked her car in the main car park in Oxford and was dragging Millie off into the city centre.

'What about here?' asked Millie as they passed a big department store.

'Last resort. There's a couple of boutiques I want to try out first. We need to find you something simple and elegant which will show off your fabulous hair and which won't look ridiculous with a guitar strapped over the top.'

'Jeans and a T-shirt?'

'Wash your mouth out, Millie Braythorpe.' Freya skidded to a halt. 'Here we are.' She pushed open the door of a shop and hauled Millie in behind her. The carpet was deep, the shop was tiny and it reeked of opulence. Around the walls were racks of clothes made from fabulous fabrics, feathers and beads and in every conceivable colour in the spectrum. Millie gulped. Anything here was going to cost a fortune.

A shop assistant in a simple black dress and her glossy hair smoothed into an elegant chignon appeared from behind a curtain.

'Miss Freya,' she said with a broad smile. 'And this must be your friend you told me about.'

'Yes, this is Millie. Millie, this is Madame Wozniak. She's a genius.'

Millie stepped forward and shook the shop assistant's hand.

'You are right, she's lovely,' said Madam Wozniak. She walked around Millie, looking her up and down. 'That skin and that hair! I think we may have something that would do. Size eight?'

Millie nodded, embarrassed by the attention and the praise.

Freya guessed what was going on in her friend's head. 'Get used to it, Mil. When the public get a load of you, everyone will want to comment on you.'

Madame Wozniak showed Millie into a massive changing room with mirrors all around, an armchair and a table with fashion magazines on it. Millie didn't have a lot of experience of the retail industry having mostly frequented jumble sales and charity shops but even she knew that this was unusual. A few minutes later Madame Wozniak bustled into the room with an armful of sumptuous dresses and hung them up on the rail by the door.

'See what you think of these,' she said and left, closing the door behind her.

Freya flew to the dresses and began shuffling through them. She pulled a couple off the rail. 'Get your kit off and try these first.' She held a shimmering olive-green gown out to Millie and a simple black sheath dress with diamanté trim at the collar. 'I think we need to go for simple and understated.'

Millie slipped off her skirt and top and climbed into the green dress. If felt like cool water running over her skin as she pulled it up and slipped the straps over her shoulders.

'Blimey. It doesn't leave much to the imagination,' said Millie, catching sight of her cleavage. 'I can't wear this. I wear more in the bath.'

'Don't exaggerate. It's lovely. And you've got fab tits so flaunt them.' Freya tilted her head and considered it. 'Maybe,' she decided. 'We'll put that on the maybe pile. Now try the black.'

'No, funereal,' was the verdict when that was on.

'Too fussy', 'too drab', 'too last season' and 'ohmigod, no' disposed of the next few dresses.

'Look, the first one was fine,' said Millie. 'Maybe if we stitched up the front a bit it would be better.'

'Stitch up a Paris original?' gasped Freya. 'For God's sake don't let Madame Wozniak hear you say that. She'd have a seizure.'

'It was just an idea,' muttered Millie, getting fed up with the whole process.

'Look, try this. It looks like shit on the hanger but it might be OK on.'

Millie sighed heavily and slid into yet another garment. Freya did up the zip and then stood back. The tawny material was shot silk that shimmered amber and flame and burnt umber and exactly reflected the colours in Millie's hair. The fabric was fine enough to cling to Millie's figure yet heavy enough to move and sway as she moved. The hem flared at the bottom and was cut into a big fishtail at the back, making the dress pool behind her. The plunging neckline was revealing but not excessively so and it made Millie look sexy and smouldering and absolutely beautiful.

'Perfect,' breathed Freya. 'This is the one.'

Millie was staring at herself agog. 'I've never seen such a lovely dress. Can I really have it?'

'You certainly can. You get changed again and I'll deal with the sordid matter of the finances. Then we'll find you some shoes.'

Hannah and Judy were also shoe shopping but with a more limited budget. Hannah had been looking forward to this expedition for days, since Judy had rung her to fix it. Malcolm was away in London for some bishop's convocation so Hannah was completely free for once. Now she had Judy as a friend, life had become rather more fulfilling and this was showing in her face. The dead look had gone from her eyes and her hair had regained some of its bounce and body. She had even been learning some basic computer skills on Judy's laptop in her lovely kitchen, which had given her confidence a much needed boost. But the icing on the cake was going to be shopping for something especially for the ball!

'Try these,' said Judy, pulling a pair of strappy beaded sandals off the rack and handing them to Hannah. Hannah had been hoping to buy something pretty to wear on her feet but these . . .

'But they're so . . .' she searched for the right word. 'Impractical.'

'Yup,' said Judy cheerfully. 'And absolutely delicious.'

'But when would I wear them again?'

'In the summer, with a nice dress.'

Hannah mentally rifled through her dowdy wardrobe. Nice dresses didn't seem to feature in it at all. She had a couple of shabby cotton skirts and a few cheap T-shirts but no nice dresses. Maybe she'd look out for one next time she was in the charity shop.

Judy beckoned to the bored assistant who was more interested in examining her fingernails than helping any customers. 'Could we try these in a size six?'

The assistant sloped off to get the shoes.

'They don't look very comfortable,' said Hannah, eyeing the thin straps and high heels.

'Try them and see what you think. You can always slip them off under the table now and then. I don't suppose you'll be dancing *all* night.'

Neither did Hannah. She couldn't imagine Malcolm dancing at all and she didn't think that, given her age and looks, she was likely to have men queuing up to sweep her off her feet.

The shop assistant came back and held out the shoes. Hannah slipped them on. She teetered a bit, not being used to heels.

'They are gorgeous,' she murmured.

'And they're the right colour to go with the dress,' said Judy encouragingly.

'Are they dreadfully expensive?'

Judy looked at the price label on the display shoe. 'Not too bad at all. Sixty quid.'

'Oh no, that's much too much.' Hannah slipped them off.

'Don't be ridiculous,' said Judy crossly.

'But I haven't saved nearly enough out of the housekeeping for that. I'll look for something in the Oxfam shop.'

'You'll do no such thing.' She gestured to the shop assistant. 'We'll take them.'

Hannah shook her head vehemently. 'No, I can't afford them.'

'Who said anything about you affording them? I'm buying them. Present.'

'Oh no, Judy. You can't do that.'

'I can and I shall. And that's that.'

Hannah knew she ought to resist more strongly, refuse to accept them, except she absolutely longed to own the shoes, even if they were completely impractical. Their impracticality was their appeal. She couldn't remember the last time she'd had something in her wardrobe that was just pretty but useless.

However, she might be able to afford to indulge herself a little more in the near future. Judy and she had been spending quite a lot of time in each other's company lately and Judy had been putting a lot of ideas into Hannah's head. Ideas she was pretty certain her husband wouldn't approve of but, as Judy had pointed out, she was entitled to a life as much as the next person and devoting herself entirely to her husband's needs and wishes had stripped her of her identity and her only child.

It was time, Judy had said, for Hannah to make a stand, even if it was only over a little thing like having a pair of pretty shoes.

25

The day of the ball dawned bright and sunny.

Thank fuck for that, thought Freya as she jumped out of bed. Sloshing about in pouring rain would make the last-minute arrangements really tricky. It would be next to impossible to stop contractors from trailing mud onto the cream carpet in the marquee. She pulled on jeans and a T-shirt and hurtled out to the huge tent. As early as she was, the catering contractors were there ahead of her, along with the florists. She could hear the chink of crockery and cutlery being laid and the tent was filled with the scent of flowers in dozens of buckets. Even though the marquee was a long way from being finished, it still looked breathtaking. The huge round tables were now covered with pale lemon cloths and in the centre of each was a large multi-branched candelabra. Those on the nearest tables already had a surrounding of creamy roses and yellow freesias. The supporting poles had been wrapped in yellow and white ribbons intertwined with tiny fairy lights and 'growing' up each one was a fantastically realistic fake wisteria with huge drooping clusters of cream flowers. The carpeting was cream and the dance floor the palest beech.

Freya looked about her with satisfaction. Perfect. Satisfied that the staff knew what they were doing and were getting on with it efficiently and on schedule, she returned to the house in search of breakfast. Millie was in the kitchen picking at a piece of toast.

'Get her to eat some scrambled egg, Miss Freya,' said Mrs Mo. 'She might take some notice of you.'

'Fat chance,' said Freya. 'Come on, Mil. You need to keep your strength up today of all days.'

'I'll be sick if I eat it.'

'Nervous?'

'You have no idea.'

Freya had to admit that Millie did look rather pale.

'You'll be fine.'

Millie shook her head. 'I just feel . . .' she paused. 'I just feel as if something terrible is waiting to happen.'

'Like?'

'I don't know.'

'It's just nerves. But don't worry, you'll be fine. Quen is thrilled by the progress you've made in the last couple of weeks. You're going to knock 'em dead.'

'Yeah, maybe.'

Millie went to the studio to practise and Freya had a solid breakfast, which placated Mrs Mo, then went to the office to get her checklist.

Tim was there going through the security arrangements with the manager of the company hired to do the job.

'. . . chauffeurs can then come into the house. We've got a room allocated to them on the ground floor with soft drinks, tea, coffee, sandwiches, satellite TV and so on. None of them should stay in the car park. I only want your guys patrolling that.' He turned to Freya. 'I've had the final guest list from Crisis International. The total is four hundred and twelve. They've sent the seating plan with it. All you have to do now is allocate the tables.' He gave a wodge of paper to Freya. She ran her eye over it.

'No problem,' she said as she flicked over a page. She ran her eye down the continuing list of names. One leapt off the page at her. 'Holy shit.'

'What?' Tim sat up straighter. 'Don't tell me we've got some hideous dietary requirement that we can't cope with? Not at this stage.'

'Worse than that,' said Freya grimly. 'Look.' She handed back the sheaf of paper with her finger pointing out a name.

'Fucking hell. The Right Reverend Bishop Malcolm Braythorpe. Oh . . . my . . . God.' He blew his cheeks out and exhaled slowly. 'And he and his wife are coming with your parents.'

'Shit, I should have guessed.'

'Why?'

'Mum said she was going to a ball with Hannah but I never guessed it was ours. I should have checked. Damn and blast and fucking hell.' She let out a cry of rage and frustration. 'What are we going to do?'

The security manager looked bemused. He hunched his shoulders and said, 'So what's the problem with this bishop guy?'

'He's Millie's dad. She's one of the star turns and they don't get on.'

'Oh, is that all?'

Freya couldn't be bothered to explain. 'Are we going to tell her?'

'No. Perhaps we can get your folks to leave early and put Millie on late.'

'What about the programme? The beastly Bishop will see her name on it. We can't alter that. If he knows she's here he might come looking for her. Mightn't it be better if she knew?'

'If we tell her I know what'll happen,' said Tim. 'She'll do a runner.'

'You're probably right.' Freya slapped her hand against her head. 'It's not as if she doesn't have a history of doing just that. We can't risk her doing it again. Not today. Not when this might be her big chance.' Freya considered what options she had for damage limitation at this late stage in proceedings. 'I'll make sure Mum's table is at the back of the marquee, and I'll put the Bishop with his back to the stage. Millie might not spot him. And I'll ring Mum and tell her what's happened. If the Bishop gets in a strop about what Millie is doing, Mum can do her best to stop him making a scene.'

'Is he likely to?'

'You've never met this bloke, have you?'

'I don't see why we have to set out quite this early,' grumbled Jim Fairweather as they drove towards the Bishop's palace.

'I've told you. I've promised Hannah that I'll do her hair for her.'

'I don't see why she can't go to the hairdresser like you do.'

'For God's sake, Jim, you of all people should know what Bishop Malcolm is like. You and he can have a nice chat while I'm upstairs with Hannah and then we can all set off together when I'm done. And don't forget what I told you about Millie. No mention that she's going to be there.'

'I don't like subterfuge.'

'And I don't like the fact that Hannah is dying inside

because of the rift between her and her daughter. Maybe they'll get reconciled tonight.'

'And maybe they won't. I can't see Malcolm changing his mind about her.'

Jim swung the car into the cathedral close and it scrunched to a halt on the gravel forecourt of the palace.

'Don't forget,' warned Judy. 'Because if you do I'll tell Freya and you know what she'll think of you.'

Using Freya was her ultimate threat. Jim would never do anything deliberate to make Freya angry with him – and they both knew it.

Bishop Malcolm opened the door and welcomed them.

'Come in, come in. Let me offer you something to drink. Orange juice or perhaps mineral water?'

Jim had been hoping for something a little stronger despite the fact that he knew about the Bishop's abhorrence of alcohol. He'd hoped that an exception might have been made for guests. Apparently not.

'I'll pass,' said Judy, who had taken the precaution of downing a swift but large gin before they'd left home. 'I'll pop up to Hannah and give her a hand, shall I? Don't worry, I'll find her,' she added, not wishing the Bishop to accompany her and catch a glimpse of Hannah before she was completely ready.

She left the room and headed up the stairs, thankful she'd also taken the precaution of wearing a warm pashmina. Even in September this house was perishing. Freya's observation that the Addams family would have felt at home in it had been spot on.

She found the right bedroom fairly swiftly.

'Can I come in?' she said, poking her head round the door. Hannah was sitting at her dressing table looking terrified. 'Come on, stand up and give me a twirl,' said Judy, hoping that with a bit of encouragement Hannah would gain some confidence in her appearance.

Hannah stood up and did as she had been asked. Then she lifted the hem of the dark green gown to reveal the shoes.

'Aren't they perfect?' she said, a little smile coming to her lips as she contemplated them.

'Perfect,' agreed Judy. 'Now then, sit down again and let me get going with your hair. I don't think we should keep the men waiting too long.' Out of a carrier bag that she had brought with her Judy produced a can of hairspray, some hairpins and a hairband with dark green feathers sweeping off it. She'd actually bought it especially for Hannah but she wasn't going to let on.

'Look what I found in my dressing table,' she lied, showing the fascinator to Hannah. 'This will look wonderful in your hair.'

'If you think so.'

Hannah allowed Judy to style her hair and then touch up her face just a little with a hint of mascara, some powder and a dab of lipstick.

'There,' said Judy, standing back to get the complete effect. 'What do you think?'

But Hannah's shining eyes said it all.

Judy led the way downstairs to the sitting room.

'Ta-dah!' she said as she threw open the door. 'What do you think?'

Hannah entered the room. There was a flicker of amazement on the Bishop's face before he clamped down on it and looked disapproving. Obviously he didn't like the fact that his wife could look this lovely. 'Isn't she sensational?'

Judy interjected quickly. She wasn't going to let bloody Malcolm spoil the moment for Hannah.

'Fantastic,' said Jim. 'Stunning.' Judy could tell he really meant it. He'd often seen Hannah around the cathedral and knew what a frump she usually was. But now . . . Judy shot her husband a look of gratitude as Hannah glowed with pleasure at the compliment.

The Bishop, realising that he was outnumbered, kept silent.

'Well, boys,' said Judy archly, deliberately hoping to irritate Malcolm. God, the man was such a hard bastard. 'We're ready if you are.'

Jim hurriedly put down his orange juice. The sooner they set off, the sooner he would get something proper to drink.

Luke left Archie at the bar that had been set up in the pool room and headed to the house to find Millie. He ran up the stairs two at a time and banged impatiently on the door of her room.

'Mil, Mil, it's me,' he called.

'Wait a sec,' yelled back Millie.

Luke leaned against the door jamb. The seconds ticked by. 'Hurry up.'

'Patience.' There was the sound of scuffling. 'Right, you can come in now.'

Luke threw open the door. He'd been about to say something along the lines that he hoped the wait was going to be worth it but the words died on his lips.

'Oh, Millie!'

'Like it?'

Luke took a step closer. 'Like it? I love it. You look just

stunning. I can't believe how incredibly sophisticated and beautiful you look.'

Millie made a mock curtsey. 'Thank you, kind sir. Freya picked it out.'

'Freya has impeccable taste. How do you feel?'

'Wearing such a fab frock has given me a bit of confidence but I'm still as nervous as hell. Have you seen the guest list?'

'Seen Quen's bit – the A-list part. The paper got sent a copy. In fact I have a brief to report on it so I'm getting paid to be here. It's so tough, I can tell you. Have you seen the guys that Quen has got to come along? There are some top names on it.'

'I've heard, yeah. People who can really sing.'

'People who are going to be running scared about the competition after tonight,' corrected Luke. 'Remember, I've heard you too. And Quen doesn't take on charity cases.' Luke gave her a hug and kissed the top of her head. 'I'd give you a proper kiss but I think I'll get yelled at for messing up your make-up.'

'Too right you would. Once I've done my set you can mess it up all you like.'

Luke grinned at her lasciviously. 'Come on, Archie's with me. He's dying to see you again.'

'Great. I've got a surprise for him too.'

'Will he like it?'

Millie nodded. 'Love it, I should think. And it's not "it", it's them.' She told him about Venice and Chelsea. 'You'd never believe how tough they were on the men they employ. Those two are as hard as nails when it comes to business.'

Luke wasn't terribly surprised. 'They were no fools,

either of them. It was one of the reasons they were so likeable.'

Freya met them as they were going down the stairs. She was looking tense, but considering what a massive event she was largely responsible for, it was hardly surprising.

'Where are you going?' she asked, somewhat brusquely.

'The bar,' said Millie. 'To meet Archie.'

'Oh, that's all right then. Probably not a good idea if you are in the main marquee too much.'

'You make it sound as if you want me to hide away,' joked Millie.

'We don't want to spoil the impact of your entrance,' said Freya glibly.

'I hadn't thought of that. I can lie low if you'd like me to. As long as I get to eat, I don't really mind. I missed out on breakfast, remember, and now hunger is beating the nerves as to which is making me feel the worst.'

'Lie low – that's a brilliant idea. Why don't you stay in the bar for now? Most of the guests have gone straight to their tables and are ordering drinks there.'

Millie shrugged. It was all the same to her and it was Freya's show, after all.

When she and Luke made it to the bar, Archie had already found Venice and Chelsea and was staring unashamedly at their cleavages. Even Millie could understand why, their décolletages were spectacular.

It was a happy scene as the five friends were reunited. Luke bought champagne and they all toasted Millie's debut. Venice and Chelsea admitted to being green with envy over Millie's dress and then wanted to know when the *Inquirer*'s photographer was going to turn up so they could get their picture taken with 'Millie the superstar'.

'Fancy them boys not telling us they worked for the press when we met them,' said Venice. 'Meeting celebs and racing round the country to get stories. What a great way to earn your keep.'

'And talking of keep being earned, I'm going to find a bite to eat and then go and warm up properly. Besides, if I stay here I shall be tempted to drink more champagne and it wouldn't do to go on stage tipsy.'

The other four wished her luck and then went to find their respective tables. They gathered by the gilded easel at the entrance to the marquee to check out the seating plan.

'Oo-er,' said Chelsea. 'There's a couple with the same name as Mil. Fancy that.'

Luke followed her gaze. 'God. What the hell is he doing here?'

'Do you think he knows Mil is here too?' said Archie who had grasped the implications.

'Dunno, but you can bet your bottom dollar Mil doesn't know her dad's here. No wonder Freya didn't want Millie swanning around in the main tent.'

'What's all this about Mil and her dad?' said Venice.

Smoothly Luke told the girls that Millie and her dad had fallen out. 'And as a result, he threw her out.'

'Well I never,' said Chelsea. 'The old git. And poor old Mil. She's such a wonderful kid. Talk about a tough break.'

'Yeah, well, I can't see her dad being thrilled about his daughter becoming a pop star. He's got very decided views on just about anything you care to name that involves people actually enjoying themselves.'

Venice snorted. 'Sounds a right load of laughs. I've a good mind to find this geezer and give him a piece of my mind. If he's so stupid not to be able to see what a diamond daughter he's got then he must be a right tosser.'

Luke couldn't help agreeing with her sentiments. It seemed that everyone whose life had been touched by Millie thought this of her except the one person who was closest.

'Well, I think all we can do now is to make sure that Millie doesn't meet her father and get upset by him until after she's performed. It should be relatively easy at an event on this scale. Besides, I think we can safely say that Millie's dad is the only one who isn't in a penguin suit.' Luke gestured to the far end of the tent where an imposing man in a purple soutane was gazing disapprovingly at the merry-making going on around him. Beside him was a woman in a stunning green dress who bore a remarkable resemblance to Millie. Luke was astonished by the transformation from the mousy woman who had opened the door in Westhampton and this much more confident sophisticate. Someone had worked some magic on her and no mistake.

26

J udy Fairweather was trying to make sure all the guests at
her table were having a good time. It was an uphill task,
however, given the disapproval that radiated from Malcolm
Braythorpe. Hannah, though, was in a haze of wonder and
seemed perfectly content to just gaze at the dresses and
jewels sported by the other women and to drink in the
atmosphere of the event. All around her were faces she
recognised from newspaper pictures and the TV: actors,
politicians, musicians. She was clearly bowled over by the
company she was in. The other guests, once bolstered by a
glass or two of champagne, realised that Bishop Malcolm's
filthy mood had nothing to do with them so they just
ignored him and chatted amongst themselves, leaving him
to glower and mutter on the sidelines.

Jim had relaxed quite a lot now he was on his third glass
of champagne and was happily networking with various
business contacts and their wives who were also sitting at
their table. Judy, having made the introductions between
the other wives and Hannah, and having done enough small
talk to look sociable, was now free to worry about how she
was going to stop the Bishop cottoning on to the fact that his
daughter was part of the entertainment. She'd made sure
that Malcolm was seated with his back to the stage and she

wondered if she would be able to distract him sufficiently so that he'd miss the announcement of his daughter's name when she made her appearance. Judy picked up the programme that had been placed on the table. Well, that would have to go for a start. There was Millie's name in big letters, along with those of the other bands scheduled to perform. Swiftly Judy slipped the programme into her handbag before any of the others realised what she was up to.

The evening got underway. Delicious food was served by dozens of waiting staff, wine flowed, the bands played, couples got up to dance, the noise rose to a level where to be heard you had to shout and it was apparent that the event was an unqualified success. A number of official photographers snapped the laughing guests, most of whom were only too happy to pose. The exception, naturally, was Bishop Malcolm who swatted them away and scowled if he spotted them approaching.

Freya, hovering in the background, began to relax. The nightmare of the Bishop finding out about Millie and vice versa began to recede. He would find out when she began to sing, unless her mother could work a total miracle and make him blind and deaf, but by then it would be too late. Millie would have been launched and a lot of hugely influential people would know of her existence, and whatever her father did was unlikely to have an effect on her future. The one thing Freya was pretty certain about was that even Millie's dad wouldn't make a scene in front of all these people.

She checked her watch. The band playing were due to finish their set in a few minutes and then, as the coffee and brandies were served, it would be time for the charity auction. After that it was Millie's turn to perform. Freya, knowing that she wasn't needed for the next thirty minutes or so, went to find Millie.

She wasn't in the bar which was now empty but for a few diehard old soaks. Freya took a closer look and saw that, propping up the bar, were two cabinet ministers and a newspaper editor. Perhaps they weren't diehard old soaks after all. Or maybe they were. Freya skipped off to the kitchen – Millie might well be there keeping Mrs Mo company – but the kitchen was in darkness and Mrs Mo had retired for the night. She tried Millie's room but that was empty too.

Freya began to panic. Shit, Millie had caught sight of her dad and done a runner again. That was the only explanation. Bugger, bugger, bugger. What was she going to tell Quen? He'd be livid.

Freya charged through the house, her long skirts swishing round her legs, her high heels catching in the carpets. The studio. She'd try there. But that was dark and deserted. Freya had got to the point of almost giving up and going to break the news to Quen that Millie had scarpered when she hear a faint burst of applause from the games room. The chauffeurs were there, she remembered. Maybe one of them had seen Millie. She threw open the door and there was her quarry. Millie was perched on a chair entertaining the drivers – and they were loving it. She was between numbers and several of the men were clamouring for her to play requests.

'Play "American Pie",' called one.

'No, that Bryan Adams one. The Robin Hood song,' called another.

'Do you know—'

But Millie held up her hand. 'I'm going to have to stop in a minute.' A collective murmur of protest ran through the room. 'Sorry, guys, but I'm booked to play for the paying guests. But thanks for letting me practise on you. And for the sarnies. You've been really kind.' She caught sight of Freya. 'Hi,' she said. 'I hadn't forgotten the time. I'll be along in just a tick.'

Freya nodded. Typical of Millie to look after the underdogs. She couldn't imagine any of the other turns doing a quick free concert behind the scenes for the staff. Of course she hadn't exactly encouraged Millie to be front of house so she'd had to find something to do to pass the time before her big moment but she could have chilled out with a DVD on her own.

Millie played a last couple of numbers and then slid off the chair as the chauffeurs applauded and whistled.

'You're very kind,' said Millie. As always she sounded surprised that people liked her playing.

When, thought Freya, would she realise that she had the most stonking talent and learn that people would pay proper money to hear her?

'How are you feeling?' Freya asked her as they walked through the house. 'Still nervous?'

'What do you think?' Millie held her hand out and Freya could see it was trembling.

'You'll be fine. They're going to love you. And you look like a million dollars too. Quen is going to be so proud of you.'

'Do you think so? I owe him so much.'

'I think you'll find he's probably got some deals lined up which means you'll be paying him back in spades.'

Freya led the way to the back of the marquee where they

could peep through the staff entrance to view the proceedings. On the stage and with his back to them was a well-known comedian who was doing his best to get the wealthier members of the audience to bid against each other for a football shirt signed by the entire England team.

'So that's fifteen thousand pounds I'm bid. Elton, it's against you.' There was a pause then, 'Thank you, Elton. Sixteen thousand. Dale? No? All done? Going once, going twice.' Bang. 'Sold.'

Freya pulled a piece of paper out of her bag and studied it. 'According to this there's only about three more lots. Then it's you. The staff will set up your kit and do a sound check. All you have to do is walk out there and knock 'em dead.'

Millie gulped. 'All I have to do . . .' She shook her head. 'What if I fuck up?'

'You won't. You're a total pro and remember, everyone is on your side.' Well, not everyone, thought Freya but no need for Millie to know that. Not till her set was over. And please God, maybe her father might find it in his heart to be proud of her just this once and then forgive her.

The auction closed, the comedian announced that if his maths was correct they'd made nearly two hundred thousand pounds and the room erupted into a storm of self-congratulatory applause. As he left the podium the crew got rid of the lectern and put in place a stool for Millie. Then they plugged in her guitar, did a quick sound test and left. Lights illuminated the little stage and Quen, at the side of the marquee with a radio mic, announced the next act.

Polite rather than loud applause filled the marquee as Millie, a name unknown to all but half a dozen of the audience, stepped into the lights and made herself ready. The applause died away and Millie struck the first chord, ready to start.

At the back of the marquee a commotion made those further forward turn their heads to look. A large man dressed in flowing purple was striding between the tables, pushing people who got in his way aside, followed by a woman who was trying to hold him back.

'No, Malcolm, no,' she was saying, a note of desperation audible in her voice, but the man strode on.

Millie, on stage, froze, her face deathly white, the chord dying away. She'd imagined all sorts of things that might go wrong, any number of scenarios where she'd forgotten the words, played out of tune, the audience had walked out in disgust, but never this. Not her father, not him ruining her big moment, spoiling this chance in a lifetime. How could he? Internally she felt herself crumple. She wanted to curl up and hide but she was on stage and the centre of this scene. She shut her eyes.

Another man stood up. 'Oh no you bloody well don't.'

Millie's eyes flew open at the voice. It was Luke. He stood squarely in the Bishop's path. Millie was sick with apprehension. Now what?

'Get out of the way,' snarled the Bishop.

'Or what?' snarled Luke right back.

'I won't have my daughter make an exhibition of herself.'

'I think you gave up any rights to say what your daughter can or can't do the day you threw her out,' countered Luke.

Around the two warring men the guests were silently agog. Such a public spectacle. Several got their mobile phones out to record the confrontation, and no doubt send them to anyone who might be interested – or possibly pay.

Some people further back from the scene stood up so they could rubberneck properly.

Millie found her voice.

'Dad, don't,' she said into the microphone. 'Please don't.'

Malcolm switched his attention from Luke to his daughter. 'Dressed like a harlot and about to prostitute yourself,' he yelled at her. 'I am disgusted. Flaunting yourself like that. As if anyone wants to hear what you've got to offer. Jezebel.'

There was a shocked intake of breath from the entire audience. Millie hung her head, beaten and humiliated. It was no good. She couldn't fight him, not even with Luke championing her.

Archie stood up next to Luke. 'I've had enough of this. Luke?' Luke nodded. They knew how the other thought. This was a no-brainer as far as they were concerned. They'd heard and seen enough and they were going to put a stop to it. They grabbed the Bishop by his arms and began to manhandle him out of the tent. Malcolm fought them but age and numbers were on the side of his two opponents. As he yelled about 'abominations' and 'retribution', they ejected him. His yells and shouts faded into the night. Hannah, standing in the middle of the tent, looked almost as stricken as her daughter as she stared after him.

There was an embarrassed silence that lasted about five seconds before a hubbub of noise broke out again as everyone began to discuss and comment on the amazing spectacle they had just witnessed. Hannah stood rooted to the spot until Judy came up behind her.

'Come on, Hannah,' she said gently. 'Come and sit down.'

'No. I must see Millie.'

The two women turned to the podium but it was empty. Millie had fled.

*

'I can't do it, Freya,' Millie sobbed noisily. 'I can't go out there again. Not after that.'

Freya ached for her friend. It had been hideous to watch as a bystander but how much worse to have been at the centre of it. It wasn't surprising that Millie was completely devastated. Anyone, even someone with hippo hide for skin, would have been hurt by such vile comments and Millie was fragile.

Quen appeared, mortified for his protégée. 'Millie, if I'd known your father was here I would have done something to prevent that, I swear.'

Millie shook her head and sniffed. 'He sp-sp-spoils everything. How c-c-can he do it?'

Quen, who would have done anything for Tim, couldn't fathom why a father would behave like that to his only child – and in public.

Venice and Chelsea pushed through the staff door.

'Mil, Mil,' they clamoured. 'Mil, how could he do that to you? You've got to show him now. You've got to get out there and prove you're better than him.'

Millie, tears streaming down her face, smiled sadly at them, grateful for the show of support but how could she go out there? She could never show her face in public again.

'I sh-sh-should have guessed the dream was too good,' she sobbed.

'The dream is still there,' said Quen. 'You can still sing, you're still beautiful, everyone who has ever known you adores you.'

'No th-th-they don't. Dad doesn't.'

'Then he is in a minority of one. Trust me, Millie, the crowd out there is totally on your side – even more so after what happened. You know what the British are like about supporting underdogs.'

Millie shook her head. 'But the things he said . . .'

'Were mean and hurtful and untrue.'

The staff door opened yet again. It was Hannah.

'Millie,' she said tentatively.

Millie buried her face in Freya's shoulder. 'Go away,' she sobbed.

Hannah stood there, devastated but determined. 'Millie, I want to apologise. I was so wrong to let him bully me. And you. I should have stood up for you. I didn't think he'd actually make you go.'

'Well he did,' snuffled Millie indistinctly.

'I know. And I know what you've been through.' She put out a hand and touched Millie's shoulder.

Millie shrugged it off and turned on her angrily. 'No you don't. You have no idea because you weren't there.'

Hannah looked stricken. 'I know, I should have been there. Even if you find it in you to forgive me for that, I shan't. But whatever happened, you're still my little girl. I still love you.'

Millie shook her head.

'Millie,' said her mother. 'I know how hurt you are but if you don't get out there and sing, he'll have won. You can't let him do that.'

'Why not? What's the point?'

'Look, I don't know much about things but even I know what a chance this is for you. If you don't take it you'll end up regretting it for the rest of you life. You've got to grab the chances when they come round.'

'She's right,' said Quen.

'Too bloody right she is,' chorused Ven and Chel.

'See,' said Freya.

Millie wasn't convinced but at least her sobs seemed to have subsided.

Hannah handed her a hanky. 'You never have one,' she said with a smile.

Millie took it and smiled shyly back. Maybe not a complete reconciliation but a truce perhaps.

Yet again the staff door opened and Luke and Archie appeared.

'Where's Dad?' asked Millie, more in fear than curiosity.

'When we got him outside we were met by a gang of chauffeurs who were sneaking round the side of the house. They said something about wanting to hear you sing properly and to see you get some recognition. Anyway, when we asked them to take care of the troublemaker they seemed very happy to help. Last we saw, one of them had gone to fetch a tow rope.'

'You're joking,' said Millie, perking up.

'Gospel,' said Archie. 'And the other drivers were bending his ear about how wonderful you are.'

'He won't believe them,' said Millie, morose again.

'Who cares?' said Archie. 'In no time at all you are going to be rich and famous and you can tell him to get knotted.'

'But I don't want to,' said Millie in a quiet voice. 'I want him to be proud of me.'

'Oh Mil,' said Venice. 'Only you could be so nice. Anyone else would get off on rubbin' 'is nose in it.'

In the tent a slow handclap started and began to crescendo.

'The natives are getting restless,' said Quen. 'I'd better get some music organised.'

Millie blew her nose again and squared her shoulders.

'No, you're right. I've got to brace up.' She turned to Freya. 'Do I look a wreck?'

'You still look better than most people do on a good day. It's unfair that you don't go all red and puffy like the rest of us when you cry. There's no justice.' Millie smiled weakly. Then Freya took the hanky out of Millie's hand and wiped away a couple of smudges of mascara. 'There, almost like new. Now go on before you change your mind.'

Quen held out his hand and Millie slipped hers into it. Then he led her through the door before she had a chance to back out. The marquee erupted. Her mother and friends slipped out behind her, not wanting to miss a second of Millie's triumph.

'Fresh from a gritty drama, played out in a marquee near you,' said Quen, standing beside Millie with his hand on her shoulder – just in case she had another attack of nerves, 'I give you the one and only Millie Braythorpe. A kid with more talent in her fingers than many so-called pop stars have in their whole bodies. Ladies and gentlemen, give it up for Millie.'

Millie began playing before the applause had quite finished but the room was soon hushed. She began with the song that had caught Tim's attention at Saltford and given the poignancy of the words, the audience went wild at the end of it. Embarrassed by such a reception, Millie launched into a cover version of an old Buddy Holly favourite. As she played, couples got up to dance. Before she hit the second verse, the dance floor was packed. She swung into another of her own compositions and the floor became even more crowded. When she paused, they roared their appreciation until she played some more. Luke and Archie danced with Venice and Chelsea, Hannah sat in a complete daze of pride and Jim and Judy exhausted themselves by displaying their ballroom skills, whirling and jiving along with kids half their age.

When Millie finally left the stage, she was shaking with excitement.

'They liked me,' she stammered. 'They really liked me.'

'Of course they did,' squeaked Freya. 'I am so proud of you. You are such a star.'

Hannah crept up to them. 'Oh Millie,' she said, tears in her eyes. 'I can't believe you're my daughter. You were wonderful.'

Suddenly Millie had flung her arms round her mother and the pair were hugging and laughing.

'And you look so beautiful,' said Hannah.

'Not like a jezebel?'

'How could he? I am so mad with him. No, I'm beyond mad. In fact I made a decision earlier. I'm going to move out.'

'No?' Millie's hand flew to her mouth. 'But you can't.'

'Why not? Because I'm a bishop's wife? What difference does that make? He's still making my life a misery and as for what he did to you . . .' Hannah snorted at the thought of it. 'I've put up with his bullying for long enough. He's not the man I married. He's changed and become a tyrant and a bully and a power-mad megalomaniac. And I'm not going to put up with it any more.'

'Blimey,' said Freya.

'But where are you going to live?' said Millie. She knew about being homeless and she'd had Freya to look out for her. Her mother didn't have anyone.

'Your mother, Freya, has got me a job working for your father's company. I have very good secretarial skills and she's been showing me how to use a computer. I can manage all sorts of programmes now. With a half-decent wage I can afford to rent somewhere in Westhampton. Frankly, Freya, meeting your mother was the best thing that has happened to me in a long time.'

'Good grief, Mum, you're serious.'

'Yes I am.'

Luke joined them.

'I can't thank you enough for standing up to Dad like that,' said Millie. 'You and Archie were amazing.'

'It was entirely our pleasure. In fact, since I've known how he treated you I've rather been hoping for an opportunity to give him some of his own medicine. Frankly, Millie, I'd do it all again for you.' He leaned forward and kissed her. Millie responded and those around looked on and smiled.

27

Quen insisted Hannah stayed the night and Judy and Jim drove a chastened but livid Malcolm back to Westhampton. He was, Judy reported gleefully to Freya the next morning, so completely unrepentant that even Jim had been shocked. She didn't think that Jim was likely to stay friends with him in the light of his outburst and mean-spirited behaviour. Not very Christian, had been Jim's verdict.

Of course the next morning the tabloids were full of the news about the fracas at the ball which Millie found deeply embarrassing – all over again.

'But they all mention you too, my dear,' said Quen, over a very late breakfast. 'All publicity isn't necessarily good publicity but in light of the reviews your performance got, I don't think this will do you any harm at all.' His mobile phone trilled. He flipped it open and answered the call. He got up from the table and walked over to the window where he watched the contractors dismantle the fairytale tent.

Millie, knackered from the late night and emotional wringer that she'd been through but still buzzing with adrenaline, pushed scrambled eggs around her plate with one hand and flipped through the pages of the Sunday tabloids with the other. The grainy pics of her dad that had been captured from people's phones made her cringe. She thought that, on balance, she could have done without this exposure, but if her dad hadn't been there perhaps it would never have happened. And if her dad hadn't been there she wouldn't have found her mother again. She glanced at her mother who was eating her breakfast and looking more relaxed than she had done in years. There was a bit of Millie that was deeply saddened that her father didn't appreciate her music or her ability but her mother did and that was something to be grateful for. And Luke appreciated her music. And Quen. In fact a whole roomful of people had applauded her and if her father didn't want to take pride in his daughter, well, so what? She wasn't going to let him ruin her life. Not any more. She had the support of people she knew really loved her and that was all she needed.

'Told you so,' said Quen, snapping his phone shut.

'Told me what?'

'That was the producer of the *Morning Show*. They want you on the sofa on Monday.'

Freya squealed. 'You're kidding?'

'The *Morning Show*?' breathed Millie.

'No wind-up,' said Quen. 'Millie, my girl, I think you're on your way.'

Luke cheered and Freya crowed and Hannah looked as if she was going to cry again.

'Now, before we get carried away,' said Quen, 'I need to get Millie sorted out legally. I'm going to sign you up for Peer Group Records.'

'Sign me up. What? A record deal?'

'Dead right. You'll need an agent to make sure I'm not robbing you blind but I was going to offer you a hundred K to start with.'

'A hundred pounds,' said Millie. 'That's very generous.'

Quen slapped his forehead. 'Explain it to her, Tim.'

Tim did and Millie went white. 'I don't believe it!'

'You better had, my girl. And that will be just the start.'

'Millie,' breathed Hannah. 'You're going to be such a star.'

'We'll see,' said Millie.

'There's no "see" about it,' said Quen. 'This is a rock solid, copper-bottomed certainty.'

'It certainly is, Millie Braythorpe,' said Luke. 'And another rock solid, copper-bottomed certainty is that I love you.'

Millie smiled at him wickedly. 'Or do you just love my prospects?'

'I loved you from the moment I clapped eyes on you in France. Let's face it, if I hadn't fallen for you quite so hard I wouldn't have wasted a whole day of my lift pass looking for you.'

'That clinches it. It has to be true love,' said Millie.